ALSO BY ANN BEATTIE

The Doctor's House

a novel

ANN BEATTIE

Scribner

NEW YORK   LONDON   TORONTO   SYDNEY   SINGAPORE

SCRIBNER
1230 Avenue of the Americas
New York, NY 10020

SCRIBNER and design are trademarks of
Macmillan Library Reference USA, Inc., used under license
by Simon & Schuster, the publisher of this work.

For information about special discounts for bulk purchases,
please contact Simon & Schuster Special Sales:
1-800-456-6798 or business@simonandschuster.com

Designed by Kyoko Watanabe
Text set in Garamond 3

Manufactured in the United States of America

1   3   5   7   9   10   8   6   4   2

Library of Congress Cataloging-in-Publication Data is available.

ISBN 0-7432-1264-9

For
Jean Dunbar

*L*ate at night the fairy tiptoed to the window and waited for the ghost. The ghost rode in on the wind and tapped on the glass and made it shake in the window frame. The rattling glass was the ghost's music and its signal she should come out and fly.

The fairy had done this many times before so she was not afraid. Sometimes the ghost squeezed himself through the window and stayed with her in her bed but other times he let her know that they were going flying. She pushed the window up just the tiniest bit so that even if someone knew she was gone they would never guess she had left through the window. Then she held her breath so she could shrink enough to escape.

The ghost helped her exit by poking a ghost finger through the crack. The fairy walked the finger ledge and settled into the hollow between the ghost's neck and shoulder which formed a cradle to nestle in. He liked it best when she curled up because often he was sad and when he was he did not like it if you looked right at him.

Everything became quiet as they flew. They went up very very high where all the noise faded. They couldn't hear mothers and fathers fighting or dogs barking or even a telephone ring and the silence was beautiful.

If people saw the fairy they would have seen her pass by so fast that they would mistake her for something else such as a leaf swept up by the breeze in autumn.

SOME TIME AGO, my brother Andrew began looking up girls from high school. At first I didn't think much about it, because I didn't realize it was going to be girls, plural; I thought it was just going to be Josie Bower. That was the girl he mentioned: Josie, who had survived cancer, but missed much of fifth grade, and whom many of the boys considered a tomboy, and therefore one of their own, before she had the surgery that left her with a limp. I had some curiosity, myself, about how Josie was doing. When he called to tell me he'd found her in Connecticut, I was eager to hear about her. I didn't exactly get it back then; I thought it was nice that he wanted to find out how she was doing after twenty-five years.

But Josie, who taught history at a private school and who was the mother of twin girls, as well as twin kittens, proved to be only a jumping-off point to Alice Manzetti, who had been her best friend in high school. Alice had something of a reputation, though I have no idea whether it was deserved or not. In fact, no girl's reputation was "deserved," because the boys were admired for being aggressive and the girls were blamed if they didn't resist capture. In retrospect, I think that because Alice was dark-haired and a little exotic, she would have had her reputation no matter what she had or hadn't done. Our father called her "a looker." Mrs. Manzetti was her daughter's opposite: shy, self-deprecating, with no fashion sense whatever. Mother and daughter neutralized each other. Mrs. M—as she was known—came to every sports event because Alice was a cheerleader. Some of the meaner boys called Mrs. M "the Witch," but I found her dark, curly hair flecked with gray attractive, and I thought it was noble that in spite of her husband's consistent absence, she came to everything, shy as she was. I was also shy, but I tried to pretend otherwise. I chewed gum (better than cigarettes as a way to avoid talking) and grew long hair to hide behind. I hung out with the vaguely artsy crowd that disdained makeup. To this day, I don't know how to apply it. All our defenses seem so transparent years later—it left me wondering whether Josie might actually have wanted sympathy, though she insisted her surgery never be spoken of, and whether Alice might not have been so outgoing, but just the flip side of her mother.

I'll never know, because my only information was what my brother reported. Then and now I've admired his ability to connect with people, but my life is the opposite of Andrew's. Since my husband's death—he died in his thirties, not long after finishing medical school, in a car crash that was not his fault—I've lived in the carriage house in Cambridge he and I rented, which I managed to buy with the insurance money. I work as a freelance copy editor, editing manuscripts that sometimes come to me so incomplete that at the end of a paragraph by one particularly lame writer I found, in parentheses, "You fill in." *You fill in:* that became my mantra, whenever I felt put upon. Although I have friends, I don't feel the need to see them constantly: a phone call, or even a postcard (ours has been the generation of the ridiculous postcard), suffices. I see my brother often, because he lives nearby. Andrew and I are close; there was never any estrangement, even during the time he was married and living on the West Coast. I don't like planes, and his marriage was so turbulent that time after time he and his wife would cancel visits east because they'd stopped speaking to each other. Even if I had liked flying, it was not exactly pleasant to realize I'd probably be subjecting myself to a tense few days if I went for a visit. Andrew is embarrassed about those years, though he's hardly alone in having made a mistake in marriage.

After their breakup, he plunged into a hectic social life with women before he started looking up girls from high school. He and I would be having coffee, and he would mention that a woman I'd never heard of was so threatened by some female colleague he knew from work that she'd suddenly become clingy (Sue McCamber), or he'd tell me that in the middle of the night he'd realized that the woman he'd been dating had begun infantilizing him (Dana—or was it Dina?). The discussions he and I had about the women reminded me of *Jeopardy!*: some bizarre action described, with some girl's name the inevitable solution. *Who is Sue McCamber?*

Andrew introduced me to Sue McCamber after she had figured in his life for several months. Sue was the divorced mother of a little boy. She was younger than my brother, and slightly New Age flakey (she saw significance in her son's middle name being the same as my brother's). Still, I came to like her. She was pretty—is pretty, though I don't see her anymore, since he doesn't—in an unself-conscious way, and charmingly bumbling in her girlishness. One time she walked out of her clog and hobbled for half a block before she realized what was wrong and started laughing. She didn't mind asking what a word meant if she didn't know, and she was always the first to jump up to help, even if all you were doing was making tea. No one before me had ever made tea for her. All her life, all she'd seen was tea bags. You'd think that with fancy coffee places opening everywhere she would at least have seen freshly brewed tea, but she acted as if she were at a seance, looking into my eyes for a sign when I placed the teapot on the table. The next time she came she brought scones. I had hand-cut marmalade, and even Andrew—who prefers a beer, or strong coffee—really enjoyed the tea party. Several times I took care of her son while she and Andrew went to dinner and a movie. The people in the big house that hides my house from the street have a small boy also. I was quite experienced in looking after children and, frankly, Vincent was so well-behaved and bright that his visits were a pleasure. I don't know why Sue and Andrew broke up; his account to me was garbled and seemed to have something to do with living vicariously. He seemed to assume that he and I were implicated, together— as if my baby-sitting and his long relationship with her were one and the same, and I must not settle for being a nursemaid instead of a mother, just as he could not settle for being a husband, instead of a lover. Why a person couldn't be both I couldn't imagine, but it was none of my business. There was the further complication that he had been seeing another woman when he'd dated Sue: Dana-Dina, whom I never met.

The woman I did know, and liked very much, was Serena Wythe. He went so far as to buy her an engagement ring, though that was the beginning of the end. She came to my house with him in a lull between snowstorms, and helped shovel my walk. Though he tried to make light of their good deed, saying he couldn't stand another minute of being cooped up inside and that they'd made the long trek over so he could introduce me to the woman he'd fallen in love with, I saw in retrospect that he had come, as he sometimes did, because I was a touchstone, and when things got too crazy in his life, he had a tendency to want to retreat to surer, safer territory. That was what I always represented. He didn't usually make such retreats alone, interestingly enough, but rather to bring along the person who had upset him; I once explained this to a friend by saying that it made me feel like those people who demagnetize watches—when on the arm, the watch simply stops. Once my brother clasped my wrist— a habitual gesture, when he was upset—it was as if he assumed that magically the connection would deactivate his anxiety. In any case, this was some time before he began looking up high school girls. That day he was there to shovel snow and to announce his great love for Serena. Also, unbeknownst to her but obvious to me: he was there to ask me, in effect, to make it all—except the snow—go away.

She reminded me of someone. She was unusually pretty, so you'd think that I'd have known at once why she looked familiar—but it took a while before I brought back the face of the nurse who told me in the hallway of intensive care that my husband had died. I had never seen that particular nurse before and only saw her briefly then, yet I found that years later her face had imprinted itself in my mind. At the time, I had been shocked—as had the nurse—that the doctor who was supposed to have told me had not. Considering the extent of Mac's injuries, some part of me had been waiting to hear it, but for a split second I had tried to convince myself that nurses, in the middle of the night, were simply not so strikingly beautiful, and that therefore she was a hallucination. Someone gorgeous enough to be a beauty pageant winner did not look meaningfully into your face as if it was a camera and then announce the death of the person you most loved. Of course, the desire for a delusion ensures that you cannot have one: the little story I told myself dematerialized long before it ended. It was not until much later that I summoned up the face and remembered how much I had once wanted it to be proof that I was having a nightmare. So okay: my brother's girlfriend had reminded me of the long-ago, beautiful messenger of death whose words changed my life forever. That still left the real girlfriend, the one who phoned me when her relationship with my brother ended, to see if I could shed any light (as she put it) on his abruptly dumping her and disappearing. She called *begging* me to meet her for coffee.

I had been working on an article about drag racing—my copyediting job is a wonderful way to gather trivia, which is sometimes useful in conversation, though it more often appears, bizarrely, as bleeps in my dreams—and had spent the morning preceding her call reading up on "red-lighting," the term for handicap racing, practiced by the driver profiled in the piece. I had been taking notes to make more accurate the writer's description of the helmet the driver wore, getting the terms right (eye port and vent port were, as I suspected, two separate things), when the phone rang and, through the answering machine's screening device, I heard Serena's voice and knew instantly that something was wrong.

In agreeing to get together with Serena, I didn't pretend to myself that empathy motivated me. It was more a matter of expedience; my intuition is good, and I could pick up many levels in her voice—enough that if I didn't do what she wanted I knew she'd call back and become hysterical. My job, too, can be seen as an outgrowth of being self-protective. There was a time when I could sit at a desk amid colleagues and tolerate their eccentricities, listen to their problems, catch their colds, sympathize with their being misunderstood by the boss or by their husband or even by their cat. I enjoyed the dullness interrupted by sudden crisis; I took pride in being the person people came to with copy that needed to be sharpened immediately with whatever *You fill in* was missing. I'm still in contact with my former secretary, who lives in Seattle and works for Microsoft. I am the godmother of her youngest daughter and send the child pop-up books that she thanks me for with crayoned pictures in which everyone floats. They visited me two years ago at Thanksgiving, and we had a wonderful time hiking around in the snow, laughing and remembering old times. This friend met my brother on that trip back east and never indicated the slightest interest in him, beyond noticing the family resemblance, which might have been the first time I realized that I was always waiting for such a thing to happen: that my brother would put the moves on Darryl, or that Darryl would begin flirting with my brother. But there appeared to be zero chemistry. So much so that I wondered if something might have been going on behind my back. I remembered how oblivious every single student at our high school had been about Andrew's affair—a silly word for teenagers, but that's what it was—with Patty Arthur.

When Serena called I had just burned the toast and then spoken to an author in Stowe who had included in his book on Vermont life a number of recipes that apparently couldn't be reproduced, though he steadfastly maintained that they had been passed on to him by a retired baker. Angry readers had written the publisher, who had forwarded their complaints, along with the request that I find someone to test the recipes before the second edition was published. I suppose they thought I'd call my good buddy Julia Child, since she lived in the same town? What I did was re-create the recipes myself, making substitutions any cook could see would make more sense. How the writer mistook baking powder for yeast I'll never know, but that alone made some recipes bakeable, if not exactly delicious. As my improvised muffins were cooling, I put two slices of rye bread—my usual breakfast—in the toaster, because the muffins had turned out fine, but unlike everyone else on the planet, I preferred toast to muffins. As I was taking a quick shower, the toast burned, popping up black and smelly, the smoke permeating the house. It gave me a headache, and by the time Serena's call came I was already thinking seriously about just going out to clear my head before I started in on the afternoon's work.

I agreed to meet her, though I didn't want to. I did my best—in our brief conversation—to make sure that she understood that I knew perfectly well that there were two sides to every story, but that my loyalty was to my brother. I said I could assure her that he was not known to be impulsive, and had no history of being self-destructive (answering her two primary questions). I told her that I did not want to discuss Andrew's shortcomings, though I believed he had them. I suggested a place to meet. I added that I was sorry and that I liked her very much, personally. What I said was no longer entirely true, though by then at least I knew that my revised, queasy perception of her had to do with something that was not her fault at all. Before she was the messenger of death, she'd been the person who shoveled my walk, and subsequently included me many times when they went out on dates, as well as going out of her way to develop a friendship with me. She had invited me to a fashion show at Louis for which a model friend had given her tickets, and another time to a private tour of an exhibit she knew I wanted to see at the Gardner.

When I walked into the coffee shop, Serena was already there. I ordered at the counter and brought my cup of tea to her table. She smiled wanly. She said: "I respect the fact that you're loyal to your brother. I asked you to come because I thought I could make you see things my way. The thing is, Andrew's disappeared and I don't know what went wrong. I guess what I was wondering is whether you could tell me whether there might have been something I missed."

"Relationships are complicated," I said. That was such a vacuous remark that I added: "He and I aren't confidants. About something like this, he wouldn't necessarily say much of anything to me." I had still given her nothing. "I don't know anything it would help you to know," I said finally.

She looked up and asked: "Do you know about the baby?"

This question told me significantly more than I wanted to know.

"You didn't know we dated several years ago, did you?" She didn't wait for my answer. "I never know what you do or don't know," she said. "I got pregnant by accident. I knew he was involved with somebody else. You probably know who it was. In any case, I didn't know him very well, and I'd just started my first job. I didn't want a baby, and he was . . . well: he was horrified. I mean . . ."

I leaned forward, though I wanted to withdraw.

"I wouldn't say anything about this now, except that in some odd way it created a bond between us, and he kept in touch when I moved," she said. "Then he wanted me back. I was living with a composer in Denver, working for city government. I told you that. But he said he'd thought a lot about me. What I thought he'd thought about was the mess we'd gotten into, because that was what *I'd* thought about. But I did fly back for a weekend. And he swept me off my feet. When I went back to Denver, it was to pack my stuff and move. I wasn't here two weeks, and he wanted to marry me and have children. He didn't care which came first—my getting pregnant or us getting married. And it scared me, because it seemed like he wanted to pretend the past hadn't happened. At the same time all of it was some intense, speeded-up version of our past, he . . ." She took a sip of her cold espresso. I let my tea sit there. "This time—what? It was going to be like the other stuff didn't happen? The two years I'd spent with another man, his relationships with women, the abortion . . . so I asked him to come with me to this psychologist I'd seen just before I decided to go out to Denver. We went twice, and I think he sort of had the guy hood-winked, a little. He toned down all the drama and sounded very rational—well: he sounded like he really loved me, which now as we can both see, he couldn't possibly have . . . anyway: he's gone wherever he's gone, and I'm here to say good-bye."

"I'm really sorry," I said sincerely.

"I know," she said. "I know. I don't see why it had to end this way."

"I don't know where he is," I said. It was a half-truth. I knew he had been seeing some woman from work on the side, but I didn't know her name. I hadn't realized he hadn't been living in his apartment.

"I didn't have very warm gloves," she said, beginning another story somewhere in the middle, "and he came home that snowy, miserable day with a bag from Lord and Taylor with very nice gloves inside, and in one of them—you already know this, but you don't know everything—inside one finger was the ring, and I knew what it must be the minute my finger touched it. It took a few seconds to find the ring, and while I was doing that his expression changed from a—what would you call it?—from that sly smile of his to outright grinning, but then when I couldn't get it out right away, he grabbed the glove back and said, 'It's a sign that everything is wrong.' He shook it. The ring fell onto the floor. Then he started to cry."

This was not what I wanted to hear—that my brother had become so unhinged. Also, her story was too long in the telling—she was telling it to good effect, but she was making me suffer, just the way she had.

"I met you the same afternoon you got engaged," I said. "You both seemed very happy."

"We were! I *wanted* to marry him. But I'd never seen him so distraught. I thought: Does he really believe that a ring getting stuck in the finger of a glove is an omen, or was he worried all along? And don't you see—I was right. I should have taken it more seriously, but I pretended . . . oh, I don't know what I pretended. That I'd ruined his surprise in some way, by being clumsy. He was embarrassed about getting so upset. We kissed and made up. Then nothing would do but that I put on the ring and the gloves, and a jacket, and we visit you. He was like a kid who'd made something in school, running home to show it to Mommy."

I realized that she was speaking metaphorically. Neither Andrew nor I could stand our mother, so her analogy wasn't a good one. More likely, we would have dropped our drawings in the trash.

"Do you know how he broke up with me? He left a note, coward that he was. He moved out while I was at work. All he said was that I would be happier without him—which decoded meant: he'd be happier without me—and that in big ways, and small ways, there was just too much sorrow between us." She stopped. "You wouldn't have an aspirin, would you?"

I rummaged in my bag, glad to provide something. She shook two pills from the little bottle and went to the counter to ask for a glass of water. When she came back, she said simply: "Thanks."

We sat there. For a few seconds I felt it was urgent that I think of some way to respond, and then for another few seconds I did my old trick of imagining myself floating above the scene. I peered down into the corridor of intensive care. In all the time I said nothing, she fiddled with her espresso spoon.

"I have no idea what goes on inside his head," I said. I couldn't resist: "Does the psychologist have any perspective on this?"

"I haven't gone back," she said.

"Maybe that would be someone to ask," I said gently.

She pursed her lips. She shifted, sat up straighter. "Right," she said.

"That was stupid of me to say. Cowardly, like my brother," I added.

"Right," she said again.

"I really don't understand it. Even if I asked, I can't believe he could account for himself in any way that would make sense."

She looked at me. This was an intensely unhappy person. "I'm sure there's no simple explanation," she said, "but do you think that because your mother was so passive, he assumes women are just there to be acted upon? Do you think this might be some baroque way of getting even?"

"I don't . . ." I had been about to repeat what I'd already said to her. I thought of our mother buying clothes that she intended to wear to night school, where she planned to study nursing. How uncharacteristic that she had once done something that might have brought her closer to our father. Or maybe our parents had been closer in a time I couldn't remember. Maybe he had wanted her to work in his office. She had not even finished the first year of school. I was not sure whether the drinking made it difficult for her to study, or whether her inability to focus on the work had made her pick up the bottle. Andrew maintained that he remembered a fight in which my father screamed at her, over and over, that one did not learn nursing by sitting in a movie theater. Andrew went down the hall. Our father had our mother cornered. "This is not *this*," Andrew remembered him saying, pantomiming a silly dance step, then pantomiming giving an injection. "This is not *this*," he had apparently said, kissing an imaginary lover, then touching his ears with an invisible stethoscope to listen to a heartbeat. He took himself so seriously. Maybe Andrew's problem—or part of it—was that *he* did, too. At the very least, he eventually made sure, in every significant relationship, to do something that would necessitate the other person's taking him entirely seriously.

"I'm going back to England to work in my family's business," Serena said. She unzipped the fanny pack she wore around her waist. Perched on the stool, she looked vulnerable, her silky hair falling in front of her face, her mouth set in determination. She took out a business card. "That's where you can reach me if you ever come to London," she said. "I'd like to see you. I didn't exactly get around to saying all I came here to say, but I don't want to take any more of your time. Don't give the card to him—it's just for you. I enjoyed our friendship, even though it was just beginning. And the other thing—and then I'll go—is that I have to confess to at least one person that I am the stupidest woman on the planet. I'm going from here to a clinic to have another abortion. You're going to die from shock, I'm so full of bad news. I'm sorry. It's unbelievable how stupid I was. But your brother, I have

Things to do while waiting for Friday...

Purple Violet

Edward Burns
Patrick Wilson
Selma Blair
Debra Messing

75.25

91.25

75. 25
4 .00
7 25

Debit 51.30   9761
27606.00   4.00
Deal 11:50   ACH 498.91
2753 - 8209   ACH 6.00
                            51.30

1,145.26
71.25
1,074.00

886.35

1945
1070.
975

to tell you, is a monster. I know I'm overstepping my bounds, but I had to say it to someone, and I don't know where Andrew *is*."

I didn't know where he was, either. At his job, with its flexible hours, where he was valued so highly? His job at the computer company, where he always said they liked you more, the less you liked them? Playing handball with Hound at the gym? Pumping himself up to look great in another woman's arms? He had a way of being omnipresent, though he was almost always somewhere else. That was Andrew: on the way from something, on the way to something. He gave the impression that his life happened in the transitions between activities, in his movements from person to person.

Serena put her hand on my shoulder as she walked away, and under the light touch I felt so heavyhearted, so flat-footed that even though my impulse was to follow her, even though I debated running after her long after she'd left, I only sat there, eventually taking up the same spoon she'd fiddled with and placing it in the empty espresso cup.

Outside, people crowded the sidewalk, hurrying wherever they were going. A glum-looking teenage girl in platform shoes clomped along on spindly legs, coltish and unsteady, her eyes as black-rimmed as a raccoon's.

As I walked home, I tried to think what I wanted to say to Andrew, but the more I obsessed about it, the foggier I became about what *should* be said. I'd told her the truth when I said I couldn't read his mind. No one can read anyone's mind, except that certain people can have a pretty good idea of what goes on in certain other people's minds when they've

known them all their lives. So I guessed that she was right—
that he had been trying to atone for the past by reenacting it
as part of the present. He did have an impulsive streak, I
decided.

Though he'd never prefaced the story by saying that he'd
dropped everything to do whatever he'd done, or that the idea
had struck him like a bolt of lightning, eventually I came to
realize that on the day he'd flown off to reunite with a girl from
high school he'd been at work in the morning and halfway
across the country by dinnertime. He presented these ren-
dezvous as somewhat harried and comic, as if he were a clown
stooping to scoop up his hat, instead of boarding a plane and
disembarking to rent a car and drive to the home of someone
who was for all intents and purposes a stranger. He was
strange, but so was Serena. I began rationalizing Andrew's
behavior, but reminding myself of the very things I'd said to
her: that there were two sides to every story; that if asked, I
doubted whether he could shed much light on his actions.
Stronger rationalization set in later: I wondered if there wasn't
something problematic about a woman who got pregnant
twice by the same man, when she did not want his child. And
really: swept off her feet? No difference whether they married
first or the pregnancy preceded the marriage? She was as
impulsive as he was.

By the time I put the key in my door, I was better. Shaky,
but calmer. But I should have left a window open: the sharp
smell of burnt bread still permeated the house, and my
headache resumed immediately.

✦

A month or so after Serena's departure Andrew began dating a woman he said was very special. I always got confused, unable to remember whether she was Jeannie or Janey. If I'd been able to put a face with a name, I might have remembered, but he hadn't brought her by and, frankly, I wasn't very interested. I had met a lot of his girlfriends over the years, and with the exception of his wife—whom I knew less well than some of the women he'd dated—he'd never had a long-term relationship with any of them. Then he dropped into conversation that Janey was the sister of Miriam Pendergast, with whom we'd gone to high school. I was two classes behind my brother, and Miriam was my age but had skipped two grades, so that as a fourteen year old she was in my brother's tenth grade class. She didn't quite fit in with the tenth graders, but she was so intelligent that she had little in common with the eighth graders, either. She sort of went back and forth between the groups, like a messenger confused about where to deliver her message. It was a surprise to everyone that she didn't get into her first- or her second-choice college. I forget where she did go, but in any case, she wasn't there long. She flunked out after a year, or maybe it was a semester, and there were rumors that she'd been hospitalized. I remember being in the room when our mother asked our father what he'd heard about Miriam. Because he was a doctor he tended to know about any disasters that befell people in the community, even if they happened in absentia—but his version of things was only that Miriam had decided to take a year off to decide what she wanted to major in. Even if he'd known otherwise, our father tended to make assertions that would end conversations, rather than further them.

Now Andrew had found Miriam, many years later. She was unmarried, living in a house in the Hudson Valley with several other women. He assumed she was gay, though none of the women seemed to be her companion. He had gone to see her not long after he and Serena parted. Her younger sister, Janey, had been visiting that weekend, and the three of them had gone out for dinner at a Chinese restaurant. At the end of the evening, he had kissed Miriam on the cheek, but he'd palmed her sister his business card. "Listen," the sister had said to him, as the business card slid into her hand at the end of dinner, "I don't do things behind my sister's back. If you want to see me again, maybe we'll get together, but this isn't the way to go about it." She had held the business card up like someone flashing her paddle at an auction. Miriam, he said, had seemed more embarrassed than he was. So he had been very surprised when, later that night, Janey had called his motel room and invited herself over—it was the last thing he thought would happen, though he did remember having mentioned the name of the motel. Janey had come there after midnight with a pint of Courvoisier and a box of chocolate truffles, wearing a raincoat with only underpants underneath. It had frightened him—if I was to believe his story. He had insisted that she tell him what was going on, and it had all spilled out: her sister's two hospitalizations; the family's constant worry that Miriam would stop taking her lithium; the crazy childhood they'd had, being beaten by their mother and coddled by their frightened father. Janey herself (so she said) was the only child who'd emerged unscathed. She presented herself as someone up for having a good time, while her sister aspired only to further repression, and their brother, the baby of the family—well: that was a story for another night. *But listen*, she'd told Andrew, *you can't choose favorites in front of her, because it makes her crazy. Paranoid crazy. So keep the business cards with your condoms: don't bring them out unless you're sure.*

I was amazed—I was often amazed—by Andrew's stories. He seemed to move in a world that only vaguely resembled life as I knew it. I was willing to believe all the clichés: that it was a jungle out there; that nobody worthwhile was ever available at the time you were looking; that all the men with any sensitivity were gay. I'd married young, and then been so traumatized by Mac's death that for years I had to force myself to leave the house. I wouldn't date, and when I eventually did I was so explicit about wanting nothing, and offered so little, that men quickly drifted away. I lost friends because of being so defended. One friend who was always curious about new men I'd met got angry when I lectured her about the futility of all the nonrelationships, as if she, herself, had been my suitor. She thought I had no perspective on how lucky I was, being attractive and not having to go to a job every day. She had bad skin and was always on a diet, and only married men would have anything to do with her, and then not for long. She saw me as a Cinderella who preferred to go barefoot, unescorted. In her view, I could have had a fairy-tale life, and I'd chosen to exchange that for sequestering myself and disdaining would-be princes. This was a figment of her imagination, of course. She was angry and depressed and, worse yet, not wrong about herself and her chances. Another friend, who was her exact opposite—girlish, optimistic about the right people finding each other in the world—stopped being optimistic when her husband slept with their baby-sitter, and the baby-sitter's family sued for statutory rape. She faded away from my life—as she faded away from her own—with no exit line, optimistic or pessimistic. I suspect that if her children hadn't already been old enough to speak, they would have learned very little language from their mother. I did get depressed, seeing what was going on around me. I'd had my share of wildness when I was younger. I smoked pot, dropped acid, and when I was in college I thought the most interesting aspect of dating was finding someone inappropriate. But the moment I met Mac, I had no more desire to act out. I only wanted to be by his side. As silly as it sounds, being with him was so comfortable that it seemed inevitable—a kind of closure, as well as a beginning. While he studied, I read detective novels; while he played basketball, I watched from the stands. When he went out with the guys, I sat in his chair watching TV or reading until he returned. Andrew joked that I would take up knitting next, and I did.

I had not been as close to my brother as I became during the years I was married to Mac—and we married six months after we met. It was Mac who used a cousin's connections to find Andrew his first job in Boston; Mac who liked Andrew so much, himself, that he asked him to be his best man. One of the ways Andrew and I became closer was through being Mac's coaches; we would stay up late at night to quiz Mac on highlighted passages in his medical books, while Mac would want to digress, asking Andrew and me to tell him stories about our childhood. He couldn't believe we were serious when we told him how much we disliked our parents. It was true, though we realized the tendency to want to top the other's stories only made us monstrous and humanized our parents. Well, yes, Mac had an uncle who'd been alcoholic, and he could understand how if one's mother. . . . Or: Mac's own father had been absent from the house much of the time, but didn't we believe that that generation thought differently about parenting? We never agreed with him. We would insist that our mother was drunker than other drunken mothers, and have the story to prove it; we would name my father's girlfriends, getting sympathy from Mac by enumerating the cruel ways other kids let us know that our father wasn't loyal to our mother, since the mere fact of his philandering didn't much impress Mac. "But you both came out of it intact," Mac would say. And secretly pleased that he thought so, we deferred to his opinion, felt better because of it. We both very much wanted him on our side, always, so we would only make moderate protests: my insomnia, Andrew's lack of motivation to focus on a career, my tendency toward passivity, Andrew's tendency to take our father as his role model where women were concerned.

Except for their noticing us perfunctorily, often just long enough to punish us, we had sensed before we could articulate it that we were extraneous in our parents' lives—drunken accidents, for all we knew, or more likely symbols of our father's sexuality. They missed our graduations; they never gave us a birthday party; they pretended to be poorer than they were as a way of insisting we couldn't have the things other kids had, when the truth was that both of them preferred their private pursuits to their children's, so that they did not enjoy shopping for us. They disliked each other and that dislike extended to what each had produced with the other person: devious children (as my father always said); two self-absorbed piggies (my mother). "But you see, you proved them *wrong!*" Mac would say. He was five years older than I, three older than Andrew. He was an only child, raised by an aunt after his parents died in a fire. He had gone through college on athletic scholarships. Family life fascinated Mac. He insisted upon seeing our pranks as necessary childhood rebellion; he interpreted our poor schoolwork as meaning that two obviously bright children had been failed by the system. He was, I suppose, the dream parent any child might wish for, though of course we could tell him more than we would ever have dared tell our parents. We even told him stories we didn't quite have a fix on ourselves, such as the story of Patty Arthur.

Patty Arthur was Helen Fox's daughter. Helen had given birth to her when she was sixteen, and in our community she was Hester Prynne, and Patty Arthur was Pearl. When the Foxes arrived, suburban lawns were suddenly bordered by a deep forest. Everyone who mentioned what was called "Mrs. Fox's situation" whispered, and the mothers were all very kind to, even solicitous of, Helen Fox, including our mother. Patty was always known as "Poor Patty Arthur." There was a family, two brothers and a baby sister, that had come after Patty, from Helen's marriage to Mr. Fox. How did we know so much about the Foxes? How had their secrets become so public? Our father worked at the hospital with Mr. Fox. He was an administrator, though, not a doctor. Whatever they did, the Foxes were never as good as everyone else. Even if they had their lawn landscaped, which they did, the bushes were inferior to everyone else's bushes. Girls were cautioned not to let happen to them what had happened to Mrs. Fox. When she walked down the street, people pointed at her (thinking they were doing it subtly) as a living example. Her daughter Patty came in for even worse treatment: kids who knew perfectly well what the situation was taunted Patty by asking why she was so much older than her parents' other children. On Halloween the Foxes' house got pelted with eggs, whether or not they opened the door for trick-or-treaters. Patty was quite thin—now, I realize she was anorexic—and her hair was limp, with the barrettes always sliding out. She looked defeated, so of course the mean kids set out to defeat her. She was picked last for teams; if she gave a wrong answer to a question, there was giggling, though there was indifferent silence if anybody else screwed up. I was never mean to her, but I was never nice, either. At least, not until she returned one September after spending the summer at what my father would describe only as "a special camp" ("Don't give those piggies any ammunition!" my mother's retort) and looked much better, with a nice haircut and bangs. Also, she had gained weight. I complimented her as we walked toward the school bus. She looked nice, and something made me say so. You would have thought I'd crowned her queen: she drew herself up, smiled, while looking into the distance, and said quietly, "Thank you very much." It confused me, and I didn't have anything else to say, so I walked on. But that night she called and invited me to her house. She sounded nervous, and not at all regal, on the phone. In the background, I heard the baby crying, and also, I thought, her mother's voice, quietly urging her on. I blurted out yes. I was to go to her house—to Poor Patty Arthur's house—that Saturday, at noon. The notion frightened me so much—even now I couldn't say why, but I do remember being simply terrified—so I asked my mother what I could do to get out of it. In spite of her condescending attitude toward the Foxes, all she would say was that I was an awful person, and that it was my genes, from my father's side, that made me that way. Then she poured a drink and dismissed me. I went directly to Andrew. He understood instinctively that of course I wouldn't want to go, but in his own confusion about what I should do, he suddenly volunteered to go with me. I doubted that what Patty had in mind was my brother and me, but I was so happy he'd volunteered that I jumped at the idea. Then I held my breath for two days, hoping he wouldn't change his mind.

He didn't. Only slightly grudgingly, saying that he was doing me a big favor, he got on his bike, and I got on mine and we rode over to the Foxes'. It turned out that no one was there except Patty. The whole family was gone, toys left behind, mess everywhere, dirty dinner plates on furniture in the living room, ashtrays overflowing. If she was surprised to see Andrew, she didn't let on. "Come in," she said, smiling her slightly remote smile. I quickly told her that my brother had come along because I wasn't sure where she lived. "Everybody knows," she said, refuting me. But she said it nicely. Even wryly.

And then our very weird afternoon began to unfold. She mentioned her brothers, who were playing at a house down the block, and she said that the baby was with a baby-sitter. As we followed her through the house, she mentioned that her parents had gone to Baltimore for the day. She added that her mother had left a pound cake, and that there was orange juice and Coke, if we liked.

Then we were in her room. It was small, with a big bed taking up most of the floor. On the bed were piles of beautiful pillows. It became the style, in the eighties, to bank pillows on one's bed. I had never seen so many, of all shapes and sizes, clustered together. Her aunt traveled abroad—to places like Morocco, she told us—and always brought her a pillow as a souvenir when she returned. Then she began explaining how some of the fabrics were made: with dye and embroidery. Some of them, though, had been made by Patty, herself. She said that she looked for art deco fabric at rummage sales. I had never heard of art deco, and couldn't decide whether it was interesting or ugly. I really remember that: standing in the room, absolutely mystified, but also interested, thinking: *Pink and gray is a very nice combination.* Andrew, it turned out, had recently read something about Morocco in a *National Geographic.* He began to talk to her about the stone used in Moroccan architecture.

The bed was not the only thing of interest in her room. She also had an aquarium. Her very own aquarium, with fish whose colors were so intense the Moroccan fabrics paled in comparison. Andrew turned out to know quite a few things about angelfish.

She showed us an album with pictures of the camp she'd gone to over the summer. It was quite amazing, with a big waterfall and a hay wagon on which people were taking a ride. I could see her, smiling. She pointed to someone she identified as "my best friend"—a blonde with sunglasses on top of her head and crinkly eyes. She handed me the book to flip through. Andrew was staring into the aquarium.

I remember my feeling of confusion as I stood in Patty's room. Everything seemed at once particular and impersonal, as if we were touring a museum. Finally, she asked again whether we wouldn't like some cake and something to drink. "Sure," Andrew said, and preceded us out of the room, down the hall to the kitchen. The kitchen was much worse than the living room in terms of dirty plates, but the cake was on a cake stand—it was a Bundt cake, not an ordinary pound cake—and there was a silver cake server next to it, which she used to cut us big pieces. The cake was marbled with chocolate, I saw with delight, as she cut into it. Also, there was some sort of glaze—a thin icing over the cake. I followed her to the kitchen table, but she passed by the table and went to a window seat and scrunched herself into the corner, patting the cushion to indicate that we could both sit beside her. We all ate appreciatively, though Andrew stood, leaning against the counter, looking past us, out the window, as if the view was as captivating as life inside the aquarium. Finally she gave me a little clue about what we were doing there. She said: "You seem more mature than other girls at school. I was glad that you said something nice to me the other day."

"Oh," I said, suddenly confused. "Oh, well—"

"I had heard that your brother was very nice," she said. She spoke as if he wasn't there. I could see that her remark got Andrew's attention.

"So," she said, "if you two want to be friends, it's my goal to make friends this year, and you're the people I'd most like to be friends with." Had she taken a sudden shine to Andrew and included him, or had she known that I had an older brother?

"Sure," I heard Andrew say.

She smiled. I nodded yes. This was, to my way of thinking, a pretty odd encounter. It had that remote, superpolite tone my mother sometimes used when she was angry.

"That is a very, very conventional school we go to," she said. "I'm not just being stubborn when I say that most of those people aren't worth getting together with."

"Yeah, some of those guys can be real assholes," Andrew said.

He had finished his cake and was helping himself to a second slice. Who, I wondered, did he have in mind? What exactly had one of them done that had made him an asshole?

"I sort of led you to believe that my mother made the cake," she said. "Actually, I made it this morning. From a recipe in *Gourmet.*"

"You did?" I said. It was excellent cake.

"Uh-huh. Sometimes I'm afraid it might seem like bragging if I say what things I'm interested in. Like baking," she added. After a little pause, she said: "Morocco."

"I'm friends for life with anybody who can make this cake," Andrew said.

"I hope so," she said. "That would be wonderful."

I almost said that *so was I*. But I suddenly realized that my feelings weren't the issue. She had known I had a brother. What good fortune made him accompany me she probably couldn't account for any more than I could, but in that instant it came clear to me. She was playing it cool, but this was the scenario she'd most wanted to happen. He couldn't take his eyes off her. I didn't know what to do, dizzied by a combination of insight and instinct. And something else, which I wouldn't have expected: the realization that I *did* like her—that if it was my brother she was interested in, I would try to give him to her.

"I'm supposed to be somewhere!" I said, looking at my watchless wrist. This was the best I could do: get out of there as quickly as I could; become the White Rabbit. If I'd been wrong, of course he could have left with me. But I wasn't wrong.

For the rest of high school my brother and Patty had what might have been the only secret relationship in the entire school—at least, I never heard the slightest bit of gossip— and, of course, because of what I'd done, I had impressed my brother with my great loyalty. It was part of the reason he was so loyal to me, always. I had only been looking for protection, but they had seen me, instead, as the one who determined things.

I remember knowing that something had changed in my life forever, feeling more lonely than I had ever felt before, picking up my bike from the front lawn, where the kickstand hadn't held in the deep grass. My brother's bike stood upright. I looked at it for a minute before setting out. It was a melancholy feeling, riding home alone. Maybe the first time I'd felt melancholy, which until that point was only a word I'd heard my mother use, on the rare occasions I'd asked her, futilely, why she had to drink.

✦

The same week I heard Serena's sad, bizarre story about her relationship with Andrew and the dastardly way he had behaved toward her, I was sent a book-length manuscript to edit—no research required; just a straightforward editing job—on the subject of people who had survived a serious childhood illness. The first essay was by Josephine Bower Epping. I passed over the name, but by the time I had read the first few lines, I realized that I had been sent a book that contained a piece by a person I knew. Nothing like that had ever happened to me before.

I had a funny feeling as I began to read. I wasn't at all sure I wanted to know what Josie Bower had to say, though illness itself rarely made me squeamish. My intuition told me that there was going to be something about Andrew in the piece. I felt almost as if I were snooping. Or worse yet, that fate had sent this particular manuscript my way deliberately, to throw me a curve. I was torn between walking away from it—physically walking away—or reading as fast as I could. What were the chances that Josie Bower would write about her cancer, and that twenty-five years later, someone who had known her—someone whose brother had probably screwed her—would be handed what she'd written to edit?

The essay began matter-of-factly. She described the way the tumor was found: on an X ray, after she'd fractured her ankle. She described the difficulty of treating such a tumor. She described the surgery and the radiation, during which all her hair fell out, and then her shortened leg, when it came out of traction. She hated not the limp so much as the lift in her shoe. She said she had tantrums, wanting the lift to be taken out. Whenever possible she would go barefoot, to exaggerate her limp. She said that in hindsight, she could see it had been very difficult on her mother, whose show of support included throwing away all her own high heels and wearing only flats. This was Josie's point of departure for saying that it had made her feel ashamed because her mother had been defeminized by the surgery—that she had realized *that* before she had thought about her own situation: the perfect daughter had been revised; the mother's own assumptions about femininity needed to be changed. The essay was going to be about her mother, as Josie had seen her as a child, and her mother as Josie came to think about her as an adult.

I read that Adelle Bower had been having an affair with a doctor in the town. The day Josie was hurt, Adelle ran into him—her lover—in the corridor of the hospital. She was upset, but not terribly upset. Still, he hung around and tried to calm her when it appeared there was something irregular on the X ray. A mass. He was not their doctor, but Josie had seen him before because she had been at parties with the doctor's children, when he had come to pick them up. She digressed to say that the doctor's wife was an alcoholic.

So then the concern, the confusion, remaining in the hospital for further tests, which her mother's lover patiently tried to explain to her. My father was kind to his patients, but abrupt with his family. Josie's father was away on business; at first, a fractured ankle hardly seemed reason to return. But at the end of the day, his wife called and he returned immediately. Then there was a new doctor at Josie's bedside. Her mother had told her not to mention Dr. X to her father. Not even to say that he had visited the room. To Josie's question about why not, her mother had replied that if Josie wanted

Mommy and Daddy to stay together, the best thing she could do would be to say nothing. If her mother had said nothing, Josie doubted whether she would ever have had reason to ask about the doctor. But her mother's admonition had resulted in a mystery, and perhaps because she needed something to distract her, she needed to requestion her mother time and again. *Already learning the ways of being women*, Josie wrote.

The essay, itself, was suspenseful. I was sure I would have been riveted even if I hadn't known her.

Much more about the discovery of the cancer. And then: one day, when the surgery was over, the doctor—Dr. X, about whom she wasn't supposed to talk—came into her hospital room, bringing with him his son. A boy that age was not allowed in, but because he was the doctor's son, the nurses looked the other way. The doctor had brought her daisies. Daisies, or some other flower. He seemed concerned. His son hung back, alarmed at the machines and the intravenous tubes and other hospital paraphernalia. She remembered recognizing him, and his faintly acknowledging her. He had been carrying a glass of water, in which the flowers were put, though it was the doctor who placed them on the bedside table. His son was reluctant to move close to the bed, and Josie was embarrassed because he was a boy . . . and then suddenly Josie's mother was in the doorway, surprised—not happily surprised, it seemed—to see her daughter's visitors. Josie's mother and Dr. X ended up quarreling. Right in front of the children. Now, Josie wrote, she realized that her mother had felt that Josie's illness had come as punishment for her affair, and she had tried to end her relationship with the doctor. There had been an argument, with her mother

slapping the doctor, and the doctor whispering harshly, grabbing her wrists, trying to hold her as the boy ran out of the
room. Finally things calmed down, but then there was
another problem for the doctor. Where had his son gone?
Josie had been frightened, and in an effort to calm her, her
mother explained the situation to her: that she and the doctor had fallen in love some time ago, but that it was over now.
That was why she had asked Josie not to say anything to her
father, and that was why she and the doctor had struggled in
the room—because Mommy wanted to be with Daddy, but
that was not what the doctor wanted.

What Josie had to say in the rest of the essay was that having the emotional trauma of her mother's situation as well as
the physical trauma of her own had been a terrible burden.
When her mother tearfully said that if her daughter would
never again walk in pretty shoes, then neither would she,
Josie had not protested, because in some ways that seemed
fair: that her mother be punished. It was not until years later
that she realized Dr. X was the person who prescribed the
pills her mother took too many of.

One day, the doctor's son was in her house when Josie
returned from school. It was years after Josie's surgery. He
had come bearing a bottle of pills from the doctor. Just as if
she'd walked in on a drug deal, and that was what the doctor's son had been doing—handing over a bottle to Josie's
mother, who had been crying, slumped in a chair, still in her
nightgown, though it was late afternoon. The doctor's son
had been the delivery boy, and when he saw Josie, he had
looked even more uncomfortable than he had in the hospital
room. It was not until they were teenagers that they ever

spoke of it, and even then obliquely, as they stood in line waiting to see a movie. "My mother hated your father," Josie remembered telling the doctor's son. And the doctor's son replied, "We hate him, too." A week or so later, with no contact except in passing at school, they had paired off at a party and Josie had had sex for the first time. She knew that what she was doing was different than having a real boyfriend. But what Josie took away from it was that she would, someday, have a boyfriend. That knowledge had made her happy, but from her mother she had been withholding, secretly glad that her mother walked in ugly flat shoes.

The author's note said that Josephine Bower Epping lived with her husband and twin daughters, Mira and Maureen, in Fairfield, Connecticut, where she taught history at a private school. There was no mention of the twin kittens, no mention of the fact that just recently, Josie had seen the doctor's son again. She must have thought it was fated: that at certain intervals Andrew was bound to reappear, and that there was a silent understanding that she would couple with him. After all, she taught history. She no doubt had some interesting thoughts on how people repeat the past.

It would be an understatement to say that I was stunned. I could not even pretend distance from the piece. I was, of course, going to have to reread it, to see if there were any mistakes of spelling or punctuation—but one go-through was enough for the day. The idea that I might query anything struck me as mordantly funny. *Note to author: Did my father really bring flowers?* The image of my ten-year-old brother in the hospital room was all too vivid. I'd been allowed to travel back in time to see a scene that had determined the way my brother approached the world. It was like some old movie about time travel, on late-night TV: the reluctant boy hanging back, the sick girl in the bed; the angry woman fighting with the man. It was instructive, but at the same time it seemed information I shouldn't have—the way you reflexively avert your eyes if you glimpse a stranger naked, or the way you stare at, but do not quite focus on, a highway accident.

I turned the pages over, putting them facedown on the desk. How many times had he run the odd errand for our father? He had been clever enough to elude "Dr. X," but how had our father gotten him to go to the hospital in the first place? By playing on his sympathy for a classmate, or by bullying him, which was how he usually got his way? It made me sad to think of Andrew forced to go there, so upset he ran from the room to hide, suffering who knew what punishment afterward.

Josie's essay had the rather ponderous title "Not Just a Child's Illness."

By the time Andrew mentioned another girl from high school, I had been feeling so sympathetic toward him that I'd almost forgotten how exasperating it was that he'd been on his single-minded quest. It had been months since he'd talked about high school girls.

He had rediscovered someone special, he told me. "I know. I know. I know I've said that before, but this time I think you'll be interested to hear who I've found," he said. We were at my house. He'd brought over a movie to watch on the VCR, and a plastic container of take-out sushi. Little dishes of soy sauce sat on the floor like dying lily pads. We were on the floor because the table was covered with papers from the project I was working on, so Andrew had decided we'd better have a picnic. We had often made ourselves picnics as children, which we ate in the woods behind our house, but they consisted of peanut butter and jelly sandwiches, and Hershey's kisses Andrew won in some card game he played at recess. We could hardly wait to finish our sweet sandwiches so we could eat our sweet dessert; if we could have had all our meals in the woods, we would have. This meal he had provided was an adult treat—so adult that there was *no* dessert. It had been good of him to get food and bring it over; if I'd told him how much I'd like some Hershey's kisses, he would probably have gone out to buy them, but I had learned in childhood that you should not ask for things. Old habits died hard. I was also not sure whether it was the candy I wanted or the pleasure of his pleasure: his favorite candy was Hershey's kisses; mine had always been Mounds bars. Why—when he had done such a nice thing, when he was so happy and relaxed, and when I was, too, really—why all of a sudden was it on the tip of my tongue to mention Serena?

"Who is it?" I asked.

"Rochelle Rogan," he said.

Rochelle Rogan! Rochelle *Rogan*! I let my incredulous expression say it all.

"Oh, come on," he said, opening a Kirin from a six-pack he'd put on the footstool. He handed the bottle to me and opened another. "Come on, you're not going to say that you still have some grudge against Rochelle."

When she was fourteen, she had fainted at her stepmother's memorial service. It was the first such service to which I had ever been. Behind the flower-flanked podium her voice had quavered and she had fallen like a rag doll to the floor, upstaging her stepmother even in death. Not one girl in the audience thought she had truly fainted. Not one of us believed it, because she had said days before that she was sure she was going to faint. She had announced that she was going to take one of her father's tranquilizers, but that she was still sure she wouldn't get through it. Someone suggested that she stay home and not try. Someone else, behind her back, said that she bet Rochelle had already bought new underwear. Rochelle had "fainted" when making out with Richard Lippe and ended up swallowing a bottle of sleeping pills when he found another girlfriend. She had her stomach pumped in the emergency room. If she hadn't been so silly about her desperation, people might have responded. But as it was, she thought she'd become invisible if, even for a moment, she wasn't noticed.

"Just don't marry her," I said sourly.

He stopped eating. "What do you know about Rochelle? You haven't seen her in over twenty years. Okay—so maybe she showed off a little. We were all maneuvering for position back then. We all did whatever we needed to get attention. You were perfect?"

Had he invited himself over to insult me? I said: "I wonder what attracts you to her now, when you could have been with her back then. Any boy could."

"Women are so vicious about other women. Did you hear what you just said?"

"Women are vicious? Think about how you treated Serena," I said. "She gave me a little debriefing before she left town, you know. She had a delightful story about the note you left her when you split. She told me about pregnancy number one and pregnancy number two. She was off to have an abortion the same afternoon I had coffee with her."

"She told you that?" he said. "What did she do that for? She was always trying to insinuate herself with you, but that was going too far."

"I'm not sure she was trying to insinuate herself, as you put it. I think she might have felt close to me, and she might have needed a friend," I said.

"She didn't leave without tracking me down and telling me what she thought of me. She stalked me, Nina. She waited in the lobby of a friend's apartment for me to come down in the morning, and the doorman and I had to restrain her." He had squeezed his hands into fists. He looked at them. He got up quickly, went into the bathroom, and slammed the door. For a long time, I didn't hear anything. I tried to imagine what it would be like: to have a brother who dwelled for a long, long time in my bathroom, like a mushroom growing under a log.

"Listen," I said, getting up and walking toward the bathroom door. "Andrew," I said more loudly. "Listen, I'm on your side. I just don't want you to make more mistakes, and you're right: I don't know her today, I just remember that I couldn't stand her then." I couldn't resist adding: "I was hardly alone."

Silence.

"Come out," I said.

"Why did she have to involve you in our problems?" he said sadly.

"You didn't exactly handle the situation very well," I said.

He opened the door. "Aren't women supposed to respond with some story about how they've done the same thing or had the same experience?" he said. "What's this about how badly I handled a complicated situation?" His eyes were red. His hair was a mess.

"I don't think I can come up with a similar experience," I said.

"I apologize for her," he said. "She got together with you to bust my balls."

"Come back to the living room," I said, as if coaxing a child. He responded by putting his face in his hands.

"Come on," I repeated, turning away. I thought it was fifty-fifty whether he'd follow, but he did. "There's another bad thing I did," I said, sitting down on the rug again. "I should have gone with her to the clinic."

"I can understand why that would have been difficult," he said.

We sat in silence. Finally, he curled onto his side: "I wish she hadn't found it necessary to drag you into this."

"So drag me in yourself. Tell me about—" I paused for dramatic effect. "Rochelle," I finished.

"You don't want to hear."

"Well, it's awkward now not to hear about it. So go ahead."

He sat up again. He picked imaginary lint off his pants. "She's lost that baby fat," he said. "She used to look sort of soft, but she's angular now. Her face. I don't suppose you care about a physical description."

I shrugged.

"You know, maybe it's because I'm getting older, but so

many kids nowadays look amorphous. Do you think people want to see more distinct features as they get older?"

It was nonsensical. I shrugged.

"Okay. She was living in Germany. She was married to some guy in the military. I talked her into flying back to see her father. I pretended to have really admired her father. He was her favorite, so I'd pretended back in high school, too. The most meaningful thing the guy and I ever did was to untangle the garden hose. I don't kid myself that she was dying to see her father, but I planted the idea in her mind as a way to see me."

There it was again: she'd been happily married, and he'd decided to undo it, as if marriage was nothing but a ball of string.

"And you were worried *Serena* said things that disturbed me?"

"Rochelle was always the one I couldn't get out of my mind. You probably thought it was Patty Arthur, didn't you?" he said. "As a matter of fact, she'd kept in touch with Patty. You know, Patty could never figure you out, because she knew you knew, but you never told anybody. You never even said anything to her about it. She wanted to be your friend, but you wouldn't let her."

"I think her interest was in you, if I recall correctly."

"So what? Did that mean you couldn't be her friend?"

When I was an adult, and when one of Andrew's girl-friends particularly liked me—as Serena had—and when that liking went both ways, then sure: I could be her friend. But it would have been awkward in high school.

"Have you noticed that you just don't answer questions you don't want to answer?" he said.

"What was the question?" I said.

"I asked if that meant that because Patty was my girl-friend, you couldn't be her friend."

"Give me a break. I didn't know how to act around some girl my brother was in love with. I've been friends with quite a few of your girlfriends. You know, making friends with your girlfriends is a little bit like befriending a snowman when the sun is peeking through the clouds."

"Thank you, Miss Simile," he said. "You know, you might use your talent for words to write something. Write some-thing of your own, I mean, instead of spending your life cor-recting me and everyone else."

"I was honest with you about what I thought, and you're taking it out on me that I won't just nod my head and never challenge you."

"It seems to be a family trait to direct criticism at me," he said.

"I'm nothing like them. You're trying to confuse the issue."

"You know who you're a little like, with your oh-so understated clothes and your uncombed hair? Rochelle Rogan, you might be amused to know. She's got your blond hair and your blue eyes, Nina. She has a lot of presence, like you. She's got your way of being casual and intense at the same time. And she's like you in one other respect, too. If you cross her, she fights mean."

He had said enough. He was antsy to leave, and I didn't at all mind his going. I let him have the last word; I simply watched him as he got his jacket and picked up his wallet from the floor and turned his back on me and walked out. As

I closed the door behind him I gave serious thought to the fact that my brother was a self-justifying, compulsive, chauvinistic asshole. It also seemed perfectly clear that what he was doing wasn't satisfying enough if he didn't drag me in. He was the kid showing Mommy his drawings, as Serena had so aptly put it. And the drawings were of pretty girls, circa the 1970s, about the same age, wearing their mod skirts and their flared pants and their tie-dyed tops that looked like a gigantic burst blood vessel in an eye, and their oh-so demure pearls and their class rings from their football-playing boyfriends, and of course their silver and gold and wooden and filigree and enamel crosses. What did they look like now? But really: did I care what Rochelle Rogan looked like? She must still be pretty, if he was so interested in her. It was all so easy for Andrew: as he said, their marriages were no obstacle, their sisters were fair game, distance meant nothing. As for his own sister, I suspected that deep down he had a patronizing attitude toward me: he thought I was a lost cause. He could plant ideas about how I should comb my hair, or try to make me think I was a tyrant who had to have her own way about things, but the conclusion that underlay all that, which was never articulated, was that I had mourned away my life, while he thoughtfully diverted me from my sorrow by providing me with cheap thrills, filling me in on all his amusing adventures.

"Grow up," I said, out loud. I directed the remark to myself, not to him. What was I doing, wasting my time conjuring up images of girls from the past, wondering what they looked like in the present? It was as pointless as reading tabloid gossip; it left you swimming in lies and speculation.

He was out of control, and what I needed to do was to stop being open to it. Tell him I'd had enough, instead of implying it with my questions. Leaving aside our father, everyone had always trod so delicately with Andrew. Why hadn't Serena persevered? She should have talked to him; she should have made him explain. He owed her something. Why had she run off like that—run right out of the country?

I finished my beer and opened another. I was surprised at how upset I was. He had a way of doing whatever he wanted, leaving it to others to pick up the pieces. I had let him tell me too many stories about too many women. I was to blame for having been seduced into living vicariously. Maybe that was something I'd been grateful for after Mac's death, though it had outlived its usefulness. I intended to tell him that. I was going to tell him that he'd been playing a game with more than the high school girls. That I was no longer going to listen, and then be criticized for disapproving.

But before I had a chance to talk to him, he did an Andrew. Doing an Andrew, as it was called, meant simply disappearing. This consisted of not returning calls, so that people wondered what they'd done, worried whether he was all right. Doing an Andrew meant not showing up at arranged places, at arranged times, to underscore the message.

Andrew's best friend had had enough of that behavior, and so had I. He hadn't returned Hound's calls, or spoken to me after hearing how dismayed I was about his looking up Rochelle Rogan. Two weeks later, Hound and I picked up the three tickets we'd reserved the month before and stood outside the ART until the last moment, knowing we were wait-

ing in vain for him to join us, then went inside to see the per-
formance. Earlier that day, Hound and I had made a pact not
to talk about it anymore. We'd decided on the phone that our
wondering aloud about Andrew was futile—that as long as
we talked about the things he did, he was still manipulating
us into making him the center of attention. We agreed that
this night we wouldn't talk about anything pertaining to
Andrew or to our personal problems, either; no complaints
from Hound about his possibly soon-to-be ex-wife; no pithy
remarks on my part about the absurdity of my work.

Hound had moved into a two-bedroom condo in Arlington, with high ceilings, cross-ventilation, and a redone bath
and kitchen. It left us with not a lot to say. For a little while,
we kicked it around about how much we wished we had
stock in Starbucks—which was where we went after the play.
Then he told me about a book he'd just read about a white
guy and some Indians who'd been arrested for stealing
orchids from a swamp in Florida. Hound told me about his
shrink's unshakable cough, and how worried he was for the
man. Hound, it turned out, had gone to college with someone whose twin had died of a bee sting.

Outside the noisy Starbucks it was a cool night, so I
accepted Hound's scarf when he offered it. Wound around
my throat, it made me warmer, but also left me slightly anes-
thetized by the faint odor of aftershave. He asked if I wanted
to see his condo, but I wasn't up for the ride; it had been a
long day. Hound said he understood, but I could tell I'd disappointed him. The strain of not being in touch with
Andrew was something I didn't intend to mention, but
worry had worn me down. After another two blocks we found

a bar with an empty table up front. Without either of us saying so, we had both been looking for a place to have a drink. I unwound the scarf as we sat down. "I'm going to try to get back together with her," Hound said. "Get back together but live apart, if you know what I mean."

"No," I said.

"Not give up my condo right away."

"Oh."

"She probably won't do it, anyway," he said. "Let me ask you something, and I'd appreciate it if you told me the truth. Can you imagine being married to somebody like me?"

"What do you mean?" I said.

"I'm dull," he said. "Isn't the bottom line that I'm dull?"

The waitress put down a dish of nuts. We both ordered scotch on the rocks.

"Hound," I said, "you're a nice person and a good friend. If you're feeling so shitty that you don't know your good qualities, they include loyalty, generosity, and an ability to take the miseries of life in stride. Also, you still read books."

"She doesn't want to be with me because I'm dull," he said. He ate a nut. "Could I ask you one more thing?" he said.

What was this going to be? The question that changed everything? I had already lived through the statement that changed everything. Every day, since that day when the policeman stood in my doorway at the carriage house, ever since saying, "Yes?" I had been braced against significant moments. "If it has anything to do with being in love with me, which I'm sure you aren't, please don't ask," I said.

"Jeeez," Hound said, waving his hand in front of his face as if he'd just been set upon by flies. "I'm supposed to report what you said to the *shrink*. He's not going to believe you came up with a response like that before I even asked my question. *Jeeeeeez*," he said again, gripping the table with his fingertips. "Give me a break here. It's not about love."

"What is it?" I said, a little abashed.

"It's that I'd like it if you didn't call me Hound. It makes me feel like a dog."

I couldn't help myself: I doubled over, laughing. The waitress knew better than to set my drink in front of me. She put both glasses in front of him and went away quickly. "Oh, God, forgive me," I said, "I mean, if you're serious, then . . ." Laughter overwhelmed me again, and this time he leaned back in his chair and smiled. "Yeah. Funny, huh?" he said.

I grabbed his hand. "Henry," I said earnestly. "From now on, it's Henry."

"Well, you know," he mumbled. "You say 'Hound,' and most people conjure up a dog. The shrink said, 'Why do you go around with a nickname like that? Why not wear a sign that says KICK ME?' "

"Absolutely," I said.

"You don't feel like maybe something is going to be different between us? Like it was just a nickname and suddenly you see how hypersensitive I am, taking everything too seriously?"

"I can understand not wanting a nickname," I said.

"If I can be totally honest, I feel a little naked without the nickname," he said.

This was the person Mac had once pronounced on by saying he was too nice for this world, and—behind Hound's back—also saying that because of that, the world was sure to get even. That hadn't happened—he'd been treated no worse than most, better than a lot—but my husband's empathy for Hound, his matter-of-factness about seeing Hound's future when he didn't see his own death . . . my frustration was with Mac for seeing wrong. Seeing wrong and then being done in, himself, by a world that proved people wrong if they thought they could anticipate anyone's destiny, including their own. Hound—nice *Henry*—was muddling along, consoled more than he let on about a condo in Arlington. That was what middle-aged excitement had come to, and my husband was gone.

My research, the day I found out from Henry that Andrew was okay, had consisted of information gathering about dirigibles. Going into the library, I had only the sketchiest notion about them; emerging, I could have told anyone who asked that "blimp" and "dirigible" were interchangeable terms, but that the construction of the interior caused variations in them because of the ballonets—the technical term for air bags—which determined the blimp's shape. I had already written a note about the distinction, lightly, in pencil, as a note to the *You fill in* author, who had now come up with a muddled piece about alternate forms of travel. I considered, as a little joke, suggesting to the author that he talk about witches and brooms.

It was October, and the air had started to get colder. The light had changed. I walked home, worried about my brother, reflecting—as I had a bit, lately—on what a reclusive, odd existence I led. I thought, again, about my father—

whom I could now think of only as Dr. X. When I got home, I opened the gate slowly so it wouldn't squeak and almost tiptoed past the big house. Inside, Mary Catherine was recovering from another episode in which she'd lost consciousness. Thirty-five years old, seemingly in fine shape, and now the doctors were puzzled. Justin had been sent to his aunt's. Wanting distraction, I hit the play button of my answering machine before I even took off my coat. The scarf I was wearing was Henry's: it had become my new favorite thing, an adult security blanket. So I was thinking about Henry when I listened to the message from New York—complicated: I'd have to call the editor, Angie, back—and then Henry's voice came on: "Hey, this is Hound. Jeeez! What did I say that for? Look at what I put my friends through, then I . . . listen: there was a message on my machine, so I wanted to let you know he's all right. He left it in the middle of the day, and he didn't try my work number, either, so you can bet he didn't really want to talk. Jeeez—he up and quit his job. He's got some mumbo jumbo about relocating out west. How long is this tape? He's with that girl, and there's more, so call me. I'll be home around eight. Got to see the shrink and now probably waste the whole damn session talking about thinking of myself as Hound. *Jeeeeeeez*."

I was relieved. First, because he'd heard from Andrew, and second, because I'd expected worse. Now that I knew he'd reported in, I could let myself become angry. Andrew's actions seemed tiresome, compulsive, impossible to sympathize with. All the womanizing, as well as my willingness to listen to his stories, had made me introspect. The person I found inside me was a person intent upon hiding out, not as different from her mother as she'd like to think. Though I'd assumed our mother had become a drunk in order to be a stay-at-home, there was also the chance that the desire followed the drinking. Afraid that I'd been genetically encoded to hide, I forced myself to put my coat back on and take a late-afternoon walk.

I wore a heavier jacket with Henry's scarf. As I went toward the square, I noticed how much things did not change in Cambridge. Mac and I had moved there because it was close to his school, but I didn't doubt that I had stayed on— in the house, with all the memories—because Cambridge existed in a sort of perpetual time warp: the plain but pretty long-haired girls; Birkenstocks worn with socks in winter; the backpacks; the street performers, scruffy and overly animated. There were signs that it wasn't twenty years ago, such as the proliferation of coffee places. I went into my favorite, needing a jolt of something. I looked around and decided that another big change was the babies. The long-haired girls pushed strollers now, or carried a baby in a Snugli. People were getting married younger, again. Having babies earlier. Or later: there was a woman in her midforties with an infant. All around me, women with babies. They must have been there, too, the day Serena met me on the way to her abortion. I had developed the habit of not noticing, unless a child shrieked in my ear. The truth was, a handsome dog sometimes got my attention, but I barely noticed people, let alone babies. Cambridge, being so crowded, with so much activity going on, conspired to let you tune out.

One particular publishing house in New York was keen on getting me to move there to take an in-house job. It would be an adventure, and certainly it would be even easier to disappear in New York than in Cambridge, but I always turned the suggestion aside, as if it were a joke. After several failed attempts during the last year, my friend there had finally said, quite nicely, as if I would surely take no offense, "If it reassures you, everybody who works here is nuts, Nina. You could definitely continue to be the Mystery Woman."

It was an insulting remark, but she was also right. I was a mystery to myself, most of all. Tethered to my brother, always fearful about how much I resembled my mother, I acted like my family existed purely as a curse put on me.

I finished my chai tea, went outside, and bought a frivolous fashion magazine that I tucked in the deep pocket of my jacket. The sky was blue-gray, not a blimp in sight. My mind did a little riff, from conjuring up the Goodyear blimp, to my friend in New York, who was always wishing me "a good rest of your day" on the phone as her sign-off. Right: and a good rest of my life. Angie was an intelligent woman; it was too bad she'd been corrupted by society's formulaic sign-off banalities. I thought about it again as I got closer to home: good rest of your day, good rest of your life, good funeral, good afterlife. The notion of an afterlife did not compute at all. All that was left of my husband was in the house: this many years after his death it consisted only of his massive desk, which I had never felt comfortable sitting at, preferring the kitchen table, and some descendants of the plants he'd grown under special lights. At least he'd had a hobby, which was more than I could say for myself.

My friend in New York, Angie, had an ex-husband who had recently moved to Cambridge to work for an ad agency.

She'd given me his number and asked me to call him. She said he knew no one in the area; he'd gone to Cambridge not only because that was where he could find a job, but also because his daughter from his first marriage was in graduate school at Harvard. Angie seemed to have only kind thoughts about her ex-husband. The way she told it, they had decided to divorce because every summer he wanted to spend his vacation sailing, and Angie hated to sail. By the time she disembarked the second year, in Camden, Maine, she'd known the marriage was over. Was it possible that things really happened that way? So capriciously, but so simply, at the same time? Maybe that was the way things happened: you decided something, and then found a reason for it. Feeling a little sorry for the man who had been left because he liked to sail, I flipped through a folder and found his business card. She had sent it to me recently, clipped to a manuscript, her handwriting covering the small card in lavender ink: *Jim is a neat person and could use a friend! Call!*

So for the hell of it, I did, thinking he might like to come by for a drink. It would be something different, since—leaving aside business calls—I couldn't remember the last time I had called anyone who wasn't already a friend. Jim Burnham was not home, though. His answering machine picked up just as I was about to hang up. I thought about leaving a message, but decided against it. I was already backpedaling. If I was in the mood for socializing, I could wait until eight and see if Henry wanted to get together, or I could go visit Mary Catherine.

When the phone rang, I looked at it suspiciously. It might be Andrew, and I didn't want to hear about his latest exploits.

I hesitated a moment, then picked it up on the chance it might be Henry. Instead, it was Henry's wife, Kate. It was one of the few times she had ever called me. They were still living apart, though they spent weekends together and had begun seeing a marriage counselor. "I'm embarrassed that I never call you except when I want something. That time I had you look up that word in the thesaurus. The time I asked if I could park in your neighbor's driveway."

"How are you?" I said. "Cut to the chase: what's the favor?" I tried to say it lightly. I didn't know her well, and had never felt drawn to her—though that might have been because I knew she caused her husband so much grief.

"I was wondering whether we might get together." She cleared her throat. "I don't want to put you in the middle or anything, but I've been thinking that in some ways you might know my husband better than I do. You know we're thinking about giving it another try," she said.

"Yes," I said. "Yes, he's been unhappy without you."

"He has?"

"Sure he has." It was only fudging a little: he was unhappy without their boy, but I didn't think he'd go back just for that reason.

"Could we have lunch?" she said. "I'm free all week, because Max is with his father."

"What are you doing now?" I said.

"Right now?" She sounded alarmed.

"I'm not doing anything," I said. "Actually, I was going a little stir-crazy earlier."

"Well, I don't mean to call and impose myself," she said.

"You're not," I said. "Not at all." I gave her directions to the house. The coffee shop where I'd met Serena had developed bad associations for me now. And I'd always considered lunch a waste of time. I hoped she didn't assume I had any insight into her troubled marriage, though. Or any particular insight about her husband. She'd never sought out my company before, preferring not to come along on any of my outings with Andrew and Henry, but I was in a strange mood, and I was willing to hear whatever she had to say. My friendship with Henry went back years—longer than she and he had been married.

When she came into the house she seemed so nervous that I wondered whether the bottle of wine I opened for us was a good idea. Kate was windblown. Her hair, one of her best features, was tousled and curly. She had on dark pink lipstick, but no other makeup. I realized for the first time that I was still wearing the sweatpants and stretched-out turtleneck I'd worn to Widener. She was wearing black pants and a white shirt. She looked like someone from one of the pages of the magazine I'd bought earlier. I poured each of us some wine and gestured toward the sofa.

"Is this something I shouldn't be doing, coming here to talk to you?" she said.

"Why shouldn't you talk to me?"

"Well, because it's always seemed you were more his friend than mine, and maybe this could seem like I'm doing something behind his back."

"It's all right to talk to me," I said.

"Did I offend you? I mean, I envy you, being the Three Musketeers. My best friend lives in Idaho, and the people from work I knock around with . . . I mean, I like them and all that, but I don't feel terribly close to them."

"I don't have many friends, myself," I said. "It's nice to see you."

"Good wine," she said. My matter-of-factness—though I did not feel particularly calm—seemed to have put her at ease.

"Thanks," I said. It was one of several zinfandels I'd bought after copyediting a piece on new California wines. The wine was very good.

"Could I come right to the point?" she said.

So much for hoping she didn't have a particular agenda. "Why not?" I said.

"Well, I . . . I really feel like I've *offended* you."

"You haven't offended me. I just hope you don't think I'm a good resource about your husband. We really aren't the Three Musketeers. My brother's decamped for somewhere out west with his new girlfriend, and Henry knows it's upset me, so he's called a couple of times."

"Hound," she said.

"He asked me not to call him that."

"I never did call him Hound," she said.

Having no idea what to say, I waited.

She crossed her legs. "Where did you say your brother was?" she said.

"I'm not sure. Somewhere out west. If he hadn't called Henry, I wouldn't even know that."

"He's thoughtful, isn't he?"

"I presume you mean Henry."

"Henry. He has such a low opinion of himself, though. An inferiority complex."

She was right. He did. I said: "It's unfortunate."

"And I haven't helped him," she said.

So this was going to be a confession.

"In that I made the mistake of sleeping with his best friend," she said.

I had been about to take another sip of wine. I didn't.

She looked at me. I could not quite decipher the look. Was she puzzled that she'd confessed, or puzzled to have done such a thing in the first place? "Andrew?" I said, needing to make sure.

"Yes. He's his best friend, isn't he?" She looked unhappy. "I thought you knew," she said, taking a sip of wine. "When you're guilty, you assume everyone has X-ray vision."

"I don't," I said.

"It was a mistake," she said. "You can't be seduced if you refuse, right?"

I decided not to answer.

She slid down in the chair, looking away from me. "He's out west?"

"So Henry says."

"He told me you and he had had some sort of fight. You and Andrew, I mean."

I tried to think how to summarize my frustration and anger with my brother. "He's been looking up girls from high school," I finally said. "It's his new hobby. I got sick of hearing about it." As soon as I spoke, I realized that the information might have offended *her*.

"If I thought my son would grow up to be like Andrew, I'd kill him," she said.

I wondered how much she was going to say. Andrew and Henry's wife: didn't it just figure.

"It happened some time ago. When Henry went to Chicago. Andrew was worried about Max. Max had a fever, and it wasn't going down. Andrew came to check on things."

"Is this what you came to tell me?"

"I can't tell what you think of me," she said suddenly. "There were times when I thought I should have everybody over. Before what happened between us, I mean. I thought: Why don't I invite Andrew and his sister over to the house? But Henry was so proprietary, and something just . . . I just decided to prove to him that I wasn't jealous of his having a friendship with a woman. Which I really wasn't jealous about. I mean, I very well might have been. I was always a little intimidated by you."

"Intimidated," I said, singling out the important word.

"For no real reason!" she said. "Because you lived on your own and you seemed to have such an interesting job. I felt very insecure years ago. I saw a psychiatrist, myself. Oh, you'll think I'm an alcoholic and that Henry and I are these pathetic people who rely on shrinks to—" She stopped talking.

"I don't disapprove of people seeing shrinks," I said.

"No. No, I'm sure you don't," she said. "I think the other thing is that I have a brother, myself, and we don't get along. You know: you have such a devoted brother, and my own husband likes you so much. I mean, I wasn't jealous of you, exactly. I was more envious."

I raised my eyebrows. "My husband died," I said. "I have no romantic relationships, I'm estranged from my mother, who's in a nursing home because alcohol rotted her brain, and I have a philandering brother—I'm sorry: I don't mean anything personal by that. But it's a little hard for me to think of myself as intimidating."

Kate put her fingers to her lips. "I'm——" She cleared her throat. "I probably shouldn't have come over here and dumped all this on you. Believe it or not, I had some notion of coming here to apologize. This was just my way of apologizing. When I'm in my right mind, I don't think anybody has a totally enviable life. I came here thinking I should apologize for never having made an effort to know you, and then it seemed like I needed to apologize for sleeping with your brother." She looked at the floor. "That bastard," she said softly.

"Kate," I said, "I don't have any control over Andrew, you know. I actually try to stay out of his business."

"Oh, I know it has nothing to do with you," she said quickly. "I didn't in any way mean to say that his actions reflected on you."

When I said nothing, she got up to pour more wine. "Oh, and you've got a kitchen table just like the ones I've always wanted," she said. "I really am a petty, envious person. Can you believe it? I invite myself over and dump all my problems on you, and then I even admit I envy you your kitchen table." She caressed the wood. Then, dejected, she walked back and sat on the sofa. "Neither one of them wants me," she said. "I knew long ago that it was over between me and Andrew. Henry's trying to persuade himself that he wants the two of us to get back together, but do you know what that really is? He misses Max."

I didn't feel that I should mislead her. It seemed to me she was probably right. What I really wondered was whether this was the way people talked to each other. Whether, if I'd known more people, I might have had such straightforward and surprising conversations more often.

I deliberated giving advice I hadn't been asked to give. Finally, I said: "Give it another try with Henry."

She tucked her legs under her. "I know what you mean," she said. "I should make more of an effort."

I was thinking: *The Three Musketeers were a bunch of guys with plumes in their hats.*

"Excuse me?" she said.

Worse yet, I had mumbled it. The wine had gone to my head. I said: "The Three Musketeers were a bunch of guys with plumes in their hats."

She smiled. "A cheap candy bar," she said. She finished her wine. She was as tipsy as I was. "Can I ask you one last thing?" she said.

"Fire away," I said. I thought this response might have some of the braggadocio of a Musketeer.

"Over there. On that chair." She tilted her head. "It's his scarf, isn't it?"

My lips parted in surprise. She thought . . . she had jumped to the conclusion that there was something between Henry and me. She had been sitting there all the time she was confessing, assuming that.

"That's what I thought," she said, when I didn't answer. "But really, why should I sneak around behind his back and not expect that he might do the same?"

"Kate," I said, fixing her with my eyes, "we had coffee a couple of weeks ago and he gave me his scarf because I admired it. You know what a nice person he is. It was completely unexpected, but he gave me his scarf."

She ran her finger around the rim of the empty glass. Finally, she looked at me.

"I'm telling you the truth," I said.

There was another long pause. Then she said: "Okay. I'm not going to doubt you."

"Good," I said. "In my life, coffee isn't a euphemism for anything."

You have an insight like that—realizing that your life is lived too much on the surface, on too literal a level, and that what you've been doing is sipping coffee—and you have two choices: settling for the way things are or seeing if they can change. I phoned Angie the next day and told her I'd decided to fly to New York to discuss the possibility of taking the job. Then I began the process of reinforcement: I told someone else I was thinking of making a move. It was just Mary Catherine, but still.

When Henry phoned, I said nothing about Kate's visit. Only that I'd had a real moment of truth and that now I saw more clearly what he and everyone else close to me had tried to convince me of: that I had dropped out of life, and that I needed to find a way back into the world. I couldn't bring myself to say the words "New York." He could tell from my voice that something was wrong—that it wasn't only an enlightening moment I'd had—but he knew better than to press it. I gave no explanation. (Should I have said, "Getting to know your wife, and getting smashed with her"? Or: "Hey: what about Andrew and Kate in the sack? How did that make you feel?") I told him that if he heard from

Andrew again, I didn't want to know about it. I was angry at Andrew, and I needed time to sort out my thoughts. Wherever he was, he was probably lobbying some high school girl to come to his side, so he could cheat on Rochelle Rogan. Half an hour after Henry hung up he called again. "I don't get the feeling that things are going great," he said.

"How could they, with a brother like Andrew?" I said sourly.

"I know. He's got his faults, but you've got to sympathize, because the guy is really his own worst enemy."

Amazing; Andrew had found a best friend who thought Andrew was Andrew's worst enemy, not his own. Even cuckolded, Henry was siding with Andrew.

I paced around after we hung up, as angry as if Andrew, himself, had called with his double-talk and his self-justifying explanations. I thought again of Serena, who had fallen for him not once, but twice, and of all the high school girls he'd already worked his way through.

What did it say about me that the person I had been closest to was a rat? I sat at the kitchen table, tapping my foot. I wanted to change my life right that second. I wanted to have an unlisted number that Andrew could not call, even if he was so inclined. I wanted to be in New York, living on the Upper West Side, or in the Village, or *anywhere*. I hadn't realized what a symbol it was, my little house in the shadow of the big house. Inadequate, constraining—the house of a person who had given up hope, so that in her forties she was still spreading her papers out on the kitchen table like she was doing her homework, throwing her clothes on the furniture like a messy adolescent instead of using the coatrack. Was there even one person whose life he had affected positively? I concentrated, trying to see if I could come up with anyone. Henry, of course, was simply so insecure, or so shell-shocked, he'd come up with an explanation of Andrew that would make things less painful. Andrew had gone to our father's funeral—the funeral of Dr. X—but now that I thought about it, that had probably been to hit on women. The whole funeral had probably been a big fern bar to Andrew. He had even left my husband's funeral with a weeping woman, ostensibly helping her into a cab, but probably arranging a date later that night. And if he could impregnate her, so much the better. Instead of tea, I had opened, just for myself, another bottle of red wine, and instead of drinking it from a water glass I was pouring a thin stream into a crystal wineglass. Drinking from a water glass had been our mother's way of pretending she wasn't drinking.

The realization did not stop me from drinking, however. Common sense finally stopped me, because I knew I could not get blitzed two nights in a row. I put on water for tea and went into the living room and picked up the clothes draped over the back of the sofa and hung them up. I moved the sofa to the opposite side of the room, slowly, a bit at a time, careful not to scratch the floor. It was heavy, and I let it down with a thud. Then I rearranged the chairs and fixed the rug and stood back to consider the changed room. I moved the chairs again, so that they were facing the fireplace. It wasn't a very good place for them, in the center of the room, but it did change the way things looked. When the teapot whistled, I brewed some chamomile tea, thinking that would calm me.

Eventually, watching some dumb sitcom on TV, I did

calm down. For a while I forgot everyone, Andrew included. And when I started to remember him again, I took a warm shower, put on my favorite nightgown, which I removed from the laundry hamper, and climbed into bed with a Hershey bar and a mystery. The mystery made me agitated, though, and the caffeine in the candy bar made me alert. I had to put the book down, and then take a sleeping pill—I was partial to the same pill Mac had taken in medical school, which a friend of his phoned in prescriptions for when I was running low. I awoke in the middle of the night with a headache and the need to pee. I flicked on the light and went to the bathroom, barely remembering anything I'd thought before I'd fallen asleep. Some bizarre dream about butterflies funneling above muddy ground. I was my own personal Nature Channel. The magazine I'd bought was on the bathroom floor. I glanced at the cover and yawned, eyes half-closed, until I realized that a little light show was happening in my bathroom: blue lights revolved around and around near the ceiling, like color tossed off by a rotating wheel. I saw trouble before I heard it: an engine idled outside, and voices were crisscrossing. A two-way radio emitted more static than words.

An ambulance and a police car had squeezed into the driveway, though the police car was really parked on the lawn. The big house was lit up, and while I stared, aghast, my hand froze on the doorknob so that I lacked the dexterity to open the door. What was it? What was wrong?

I found myself on the lawn, barefoot, panting rather than breathing, my hands dangling numbly at the sides of my faded red flannel nightgown, on which bears wearing bow ties danced around beehives. Blinded by the lights, I looked down at the bears. Then Justin was being thrust in my arms and his father was gone—he said something that was probably important but that I didn't understand, because the baby was crying; I still thought of him as a baby, even though he'd just turned four. I was standing there holding Justin's suddenly quite heavy body against mine, saying something that sounded calm and rational, though I had no idea what, exactly, I had thought to say. The policeman was speaking to me: "I assume you're all right with this?" I answered him, answered yes. What, exactly, had the policeman said when I'd opened my door in the middle of the night so many years before—the policeman who came to tell me that Mac had been hospitalized? I had tried to remember, and I had tried not to remember, so many times. What had he said, beyond asking my name? Why had he come to the house when Mac was not even dead? Didn't that happen with servicemen killed in a war, not with interns hurt in car accidents? This policeman, too, was asking my name. He had already asked if it was all right to leave Justin with me—wasn't that what he'd been asking? Because certainly he couldn't have been asking if I was all right with the fact that something bad had happened to Mary Catherine. Twice, he said her name.

There was Justin, reaching for me in the chaos. I must have taken him in my arms. That was what had prompted the policeman's banal question. I was trying to say calm things to Justin, at the same time hardly able to breathe. I'd been fooling myself for years, assuming disaster couldn't come to my door a second time. Pollyanna, assuming Mary Catherine would be fine. She was thirty-five years old. She jogged every morning. Most every morning. I found myself alone on the lawn as all the vehicles left in a great hurry, gripping the child as hard as he was gripping me, trying to figure out how many mornings she really did jog, since I knew it wasn't really *every* morning.

Sound trailed behind the police cars and ambulance—a sound that seemed to flap and flail as it became airborne, like a runaway kite. Voices cried after it, and then everything was gone. The police and the ambulance were gone. There was only a man running up, asking what had happened. He had on pajamas and an unzipped leather jacket and sneakers. His fly was open.

"His mommy," I said over my shoulder, jiggling Justin more than was necessary.

He looked so horrified, I almost went back to reassure him, but I had started toward the house and needed what momentum my shaky legs still had to get there. There was a neighbor I'd never even seen, who obviously knew Mary Catherine? I was light-headed; I needed to blink away dots that floated in front of my eyes. And then I thought, as everyone eventually does: At least it isn't me. This time. Once I had needed every bit of strength I had to walk to a police car to be driven to a cabstand. Why had they done that? What had the policeman said, what had been the succession of events that led me not into his car but into a cab driven by a sleepy driver who took off, assuring me, as if we were good friends talking about something already well understood, that there would be little traffic between where we were and the hospital. Things couldn't have been the way I remembered. People didn't get awakened to get shattering, inconclusive news, only to have some policeman put them in a cab and send them off, like they were off to the airport to get a flight. I could not remember getting from the cab into the hospital. The hospital I could remember distinctly, so brightly lit in the dark, at once hot and cold inside, warmed by the body heat people gave off in a cave they were used to living in.

The door to my house was open, and the night air had made the house frigid. The temperature change would not be good for Mac's plants, I thought, then marveled at what a stupid thought that was. I had actually expressed so many stupid thoughts when Mac died. I think I had tried to coerce Andrew into telling me that there was such a place as heaven, and that one day I would go there to join Mac. The day after Mac died, a whole group of doctor friends had come and knocked on the door, and I had cowered in the bedroom, afraid that letting them in was synonymous with admitting more bad news. I was so relieved when they went away. I think they might have called to tell me they were coming, but I don't remember. I do know that their knocking became the signal, in bad dreams, for a mysterious group of men who were coming to take me somewhere, and that the way I ran from them in nightmares—the ways I morphed and the superpowers I possessed—couldn't have been invented by the wildest minds of science fiction. "It's okay," I said to Justin. "Sometimes people get sick suddenly, but that doesn't mean they're not going to be okay. You know how sometimes things happen very quickly? Like the way there are a few raindrops and then suddenly it's raining hard? Or firecrackers? You remember last Fourth of July when we looked at my

TV and the fireworks got launched and there was that big pink flower?"

I was talking fast, confusing him even more. He was sniffling, though, looking at me attentively, willing to tolerate whatever I did because in that moment I was all he had. In the hospital where Mac died, I must have listened, wide-eyed, to any number of people. Who had they been? People who knew my name, though I did not know theirs. The beauty pageant nurse—had I seen her before the time she told me Mac was dead, or had that been our first meeting? "Remember the fireworks?" I said to Justin.

"Fourth of July," he said warily. He looked up at the ceiling. We both looked, as if expecting explosions. A large cobweb dangled from the corner.

"Mommy is going to be okay," I said.

"Where's Daddy?" he sniffed.

"He went with Mommy—to take care of Mommy," I said.

He snuggled closer, almost toppling me. I did not know what I was going to do to keep the conversation going. "Do you want a candy bar?" I heard myself say.

He shook his head no.

"You don't?"

The surprise in my voice convinced him. "Okay," he said.

"Okay," I echoed. "We're just going to wash our faces and dry these tears first."

"When does Daddy come back?" he said, his bottom lip quivering.

"Soon," I said, lifting him in my arms instead of holding his limp little hand. "Here we go," I said, walking in the direction of the bathroom. The light was still on, the toilet unflushed. I flushed it. The pinwheel had stopped turning. It was, I saw by the bathroom clock, 3:30 in the morning. He squinted hard against the washcloth, and shook his head from side to side, trying to avoid the towel. I thought everything he did was eminently sensible. Why wipe tears when there are going to be more? Why cut off what air you're able to inhale by clapping a towel over your nose? I could remember something I had long forgotten: a tantrum I had had with Andrew, plucking Kleenex after Kleenex out of the box on the table, crumpling them and letting them float to the floor like mangled parachutes. I think Andrew had only just arrived, bringing food. I remembered that he had put his hand on my arm, and that I had recoiled, confused by some thought or memory I couldn't articulate. I remembered my face in his cupped hands, which seemed much more satisfactory to me than crying into a Kleenex.

I hiked Justin onto my hip and carried him into the kitchen, trying to remember why I'd decided to walk in that direction. Of course: the candy bar. I looked out the window and saw that the man next door was talking to several other people who had gathered in the darkness. I got the candy bars out of the drawer one-handed and gave them to Justin to carry, keeping my eyes on the people gathering outside, as if they might look through the window and think I was being frivolous. I took him into my bedroom and turned the light low, sliding in beside him under the covers, eager to open my candy bar just so I would have something to do. I broke it nervously into little squares and pushed them one after another into my mouth. I left the light on and stared into space as he chewed his, then became drowsy and quiet. I remembered that the phone was turned off and very slowly slipped out of bed, so as not to disturb him. I tiptoed into the living room and switched the ringer on, so I could pounce on the phone the second Jack called from the hospital. It would be too terrible to think that anything really serious might have happened to Mary Catherine.

Amazingly, somehow, eventually, in spite of the suspense, I fell asleep. I had terrible dreams in which silver mountains crumbled, and I rushed after the liquid silver, trying . . . but what was the problem? What was I trying to do? Outrun a river? Be the boy who put his finger in the dike? In my crazy dream, I found myself back in the corridor of intensive care, staring at the polished floors, knowing that below them flowed silver. There was no one to tell. I woke up parched, but fell back asleep without water, confused because—half-dreaming, half-awake—I thought all the water had turned to silver. Justin and I had fallen asleep by the time his father returned and knocked on the door, calling my name and saying over and over, "She's okay. It was some awful allergic reaction, if you can believe that. Nina, *open the door.*"

I grabbed Justin tightly, sliding lower in the bed, utterly terrified until I sorted out that it was Justin's father's voice. That Jack stood at the door, waiting for us.

It was Cambridge outside, not some wilderness with spooky silver mountains.

At eight o'clock in the morning, in blazing sun, Justin was carried home.

✦

I didn't leave my house at all the next day, and the few times I could focus on my work, I was thankful to be involved in something that distracted me from the neighbors' problems. I screened calls and did not pick up when I heard Angie's friendly voice, wanting to know when I planned to come to New York. The only other call, all day, was from a David Scolkowski, whose name meant nothing to me, though by the time he'd finished leaving his message, I realized he must have been the man on the lawn.

Things were not back to normal, because after something like that, things never entirely return to normal, but my problems had been put in perspective. I was glad Henry didn't call, because the aftereffect of my talk with Kate had been my realization that I'd gotten too involved in their lives. It was still hard for me to believe that Andrew had done what he'd done, and that Henry had decided to find a way to make it acceptable. I sat in a chair, looking blankly toward the bedroom as if time had stopped, and Justin and I were still back there, in bed asleep. My thought was: What if I were still a young woman—what if I was Mary Catherine, with a husband and a little boy—and suddenly my life was threatened? A tiny corner of my brain had sometimes envied her, the same way Henry's wife said she had been intimidated by me: Mary Catherine, out in her running clothes, dashing off with her long legs, or leaving her son at my house before she and her husband disappeared Chagall-like, in evening clothes, off to some benefit or ball. I wasn't alone in trying on other people's lives for size, but I had let the game depress me too many times, unwilling to admit that the lady in the fancy clothes could be suffering menstrual cramps, or at wit's end because her dashing husband threw his underwear all over the floor, as Mary Catherine had confided in me Jack often did.

I didn't know what kind of life Mac and I would have had, because he'd died not long after we began. Of course, all I could do was imagine it. At our wedding reception, Bonnie Daley, a woman I'm no longer in touch with, had caught the bouquet. Andrew had flirted with her: he had tried to get the flowers. One of my strongest memories of my wedding was of my brother's wide smile, and Bonnie Daley's sparkling eyes. Had they gotten together? Knowing Andrew, they probably had. In those days, he didn't tell me about women he went out with. When I was married to Mac, he talked only to Mac; I wouldn't have known that, though, if Mac hadn't said to me that he was flattered by my brother's confidences. I had felt left out, then; through the years, it made me even sadder to be Mac's permanent stand-in. My other memory of the wedding—a regret, more than memory—was about my wedding dress, which my mother said she would take to the dry cleaner to have cleaned and boxed. It was ruined when she decided, instead, to clean it herself, and scorched it with an iron.

The night Mary Catherine returned from the hospital, when I was deep into self-pity because it had stirred up so many painful memories, I got a call from Jim Burnham, Angie's ex-husband, who had pushed *69 and found out who hadn't left a message. When I answered, he greeted me by name, so obviously Angie had also sent him my phone number, and told him to call me. He had a nice voice. An unfamiliar but nice voice, which was not something I often heard. Also, since he did not know Andrew, my brother would not be a topic of conversation. That alone was a good enough reason to talk to him.

We discussed his move to Boston, and then he invited me to a screening. He suggested that afterward we might go out to dinner. I liked that idea. Whatever happened would be a new experience, not fallout from an old experience, or information from my friend's wife, filling me in on things I didn't know and didn't want to know. It was also unlikely that when I was with him, there would be any crisis in the middle of the . . . okay: I was going to call it that . . . *date*. I said yes. I agreed to see him two nights later. The screening was being held at the Brattle. He offered to pick me up, but I pretended that I would be busy until the last minute and said that I would meet him there. I did not get my hair done or buy new clothes or obsess about the evening to come. I did get a manicure. That was it. I wore black pants and a gray cashmere sweater. At first I had put on a black turtleneck, but that made it seem as if I was still in mourning for Mac. I took that off and got another sweater out of the closet. I felt awkward, unattractive, and greatly lacking in confidence.

Jim was standing outside the theater, looking closely at the faces of people walking by as if he knew what I looked like. All that I'd told him, jokingly, was that I would be the woman wearing an autumn leaf. There were plenty of leaves underfoot, though my jacket sported only a small rhinestone songbird on a branch. Since he was the only person searching the crowd, our eyes connected quickly. I gave a tentative wave, and he rose up a little on his toes, returning the wave. Jim Burnham was not a large man, as I'd imagined from hearing his name. He was about my height, dressed elegantly in a long black coat. He was probably sixty. A very attractive girl stood at his side. I tried not to look surprised. I tried to appear unthreatened by the presence of the girl, whom he introduced as his daughter. She, too, was meeting someone and going to the screening.

Jim had a sincere smile, and the manners of an older generation. He cupped his hand under my elbow and began explaining his relationship to the filmmaker as we walked. Both had gone to RISD in the fifties, though Jim had dropped out and gone to Yale. Jim was preoccupied with the fact that he should have met me at my house; twice, he said that not picking me up just hadn't seemed right to him.

The first person to say hello to me inside the theater was Sue McCamber, sitting with a man who turned out to be her husband. I was happy to see her, though at first it had caused me a moment's panic that Andrew might be there. "This is Nina, the sister of a man I used to date," she said to her husband. "She was my son's favorite baby-sitter of all time." She smiled, exaggerating my beneficence. "He had such good times at your house," she said. She had cut her hair and looked more businesslike; also, she was wearing a suit. *Good*, I thought. *Good that you got away from Andrew.*

Jim and I moved away, toward the front, close to the screen, where there were still seats. A young woman in a sparkly minidress handed out photocopied pieces of paper, which turned out to be the filmmaker's ideal review of the film, which he had written himself as a joke. There was much laughter as people caught on.

"Is this a very Cambridge evening?" Jim said quietly, helping me off with my coat.

"I've never been to a screening here," I said. Actually, I had never been to a screening.

"Who was that woman you said hello to, if you don't mind my asking?"

"A woman my brother didn't manage to ruin," I said. It just slipped out.

The lights were dimmed, then extinguished. The film began. The night before, I had been so anxious and afraid, and tonight, sitting next to this man, I was pleasantly excited. I looked at my hands. The nail polish shone in the dark, ever so slightly. I guessed that Jim would not take my hand, and he did not. When the movie ended, though, and we were applauding, the shoulder of his jacket touched mine, and there was a little jolt that took me back to adolescence.

He had made reservations for dinner at Harvest. Harvest was not the sort of place you'd go alone for dinner, so I rarely went there. It seemed to glimmer with sound: muted conversations and the clink of glasses placed on shiny trays. It seemed surreal, in juxtaposition to the events of two nights before. I waited for him to order a scotch on the rocks. He ordered an Amstel. I planned to order a glass of wine. I ordered a Bloody Mary.

Jim talked about his daughter, who was getting a degree in architecture. We talked about Boston architecture we liked: I. M. Pei; H. H. Richardson. He asked about my work and I told him I enjoyed the freedom of being freelance. It seemed a good way to bring up Angie's name. I said that I was grateful she sent interesting jobs my way. "I can't remember. Did you and she work together in New York?" he said. I told him that we were, as I put it, "phone pals." He smiled. He said that he could see that working at home would have its advantages, but that every time he'd done it, he'd gained weight. He quickly added that I had a lovely figure. Then his face clouded. I could see that he thought it was a mistake to have mentioned my body.

We sipped our drinks immediately when they came. He did not—I was happy to see—offer a toast to anything.

Before our dinner arrived, he told me about the man he called "the mad genius," the twenty-six-year-old CEO of his ad agency, and I told him, sketchily, that two nights before had been pretty distressing at my house.

We did not stumble and bumble. We had a good dinner, after which—barely arrived in Cambridge or not—he gave the waiter his business card and asked him to see if the chef could come to our table. When the chef came out of the kitchen, he broke into a big smile, as Jim jumped up to shake his hand.

"How is—"

"*Fabulous*," I said, smiling at my almost empty plate.

"I had the sea bass, which was spectacular," Jim said.

"Good choices," the chef said. "But what is this that you didn't let me know you were coming? I can at least send over an after-dinner drink."

The whole evening was so unusual, so *pleasant*, that I stopped thinking of "pleasant" as a dismissive word. Back home, I wondered if it had all happened. It was the sort of evening many people had much of the time, but it was not the sort of evening I ever had.

Henry called to say that he'd found someone to sublet the condo in Arlington. He and Kate were going to give it another try, but he was hedging his bets, holding on to his new place. I half hoped he'd want to make plans to get together, but he was only calling for corroboration that he was doing the right thing in moving back in with Kate.

As I was exiting Widener a few days later, Jim's daughter greeted me warmly as we crossed paths near the entrance. It took a second for me to remember who she was. Did I pick up a change in her expression that might mean she wanted to say something else, beyond our too polite banter, or was I imagining it, wanting to think there was more to tell me? My life in Andrew's orbit had made me always poised to hear something important—at least, important to someone else. I thought that might be why I hung on Jim's daughter's words, though we had nothing much to say after exchanging our reactions to the film. I knew enough not to linger, so she wouldn't report to her father that I'd acted strange.

Mary Catherine often came over in the afternoon for tea. In September Justin had started preschool. She told me that sometimes she got frightened in the late afternoon, when the light began to fade. Jack had also mentioned that to me privately, so I had gotten into the habit of calling to ask her to drop by. In spite of the fact that we'd been neighbors for years, I knew her son better than I knew her. Having people in—having any routine—was something I resisted, but I couldn't stand to think of her in her house feeling sad. I had mentioned the screening to her, and the dinner afterward.

"Do you think I should invite him over? Take the initiative? Popcorn and a movie on the VCR—that sort of thing?" I said.

"The world hasn't changed as much as you might imagine

during your retreat," she said, with no hesitation. "Wait until the guy calls you."

He did not call. Andrew appeared on my doorstep—my wet doorstep, muddied with leaves and shoe scrapings—about seven o'clock one night, almost two months after I'd last seen him. Nothing he could have said would have made me want to let him in—I'd rehearsed what I'd do if he arrived as he did, but face-to-face I could remember none of the lines I'd come up with.

He didn't say anything. He just stood there, looking older, needing a haircut. He had a black eye. He thought that when I took a step backward I was inviting him in.

Chopin's Nocturnes was on the tape deck, and I was baking myself a chicken dinner. I had just gotten off the phone, still needing more details for the interminable piece on alternate forms of travel that had been turned back by the senior editor at Angie's magazine. Earlier, I had spoken to a woman who had ridden five hundred miles on a camel. These situations were so odd that they made the world seem discordant. Out my window were the leafless trees, the small, muddy yard—the scene of so much unhappiness—that separated my house from the neighbors'.

Andrew looked around as if the place was unfamiliar. The chairs—perhaps that was what it was. Or had the house itself been tinged by the crisis next door? That could happen to places: a memory sometimes hovered, as if something that had transpired within had taken shape to haunt you the way a restless ghost would.

Of course, under the microscope even dust has life.

He went to the coatrack and hung up his coat. He was wearing a blue sweater and jeans. He had on cowboy boots, which struck me as ludicrous, like a tourist coming back from Mexico with Kahlúa and an enormous sombrero. So he'd been out west, playing cowboy. I went to the sofa and sat down, pulling the robe I'd thrown on the back of the sofa earlier over my legs. I hadn't yet started a fire, and the house was drafty. I did not feel it necessary to avoid meeting his eyes. The tightness of my mouth must have told him I was perturbed.

He sat in one of the chairs and looked over his shoulder in the direction of the kitchen, raised his eyebrows, and rubbed his stomach. Then he pointed his finger at his chest.

I pantomimed a gracious gesture of receptivity to the idea: You show up after all this time and want a chicken dinner? Why not.

He patted the skin beneath his eye. A nasty bruise.

He dropped his hands in his lap, his mute show-and-tell session apparently concluded.

I slid a bit lower on the sofa and closed my eyes, as he had. I did very much enjoy Chopin. I felt an almost numbing reluctance to say anything, because whatever I said would cast me in a role I didn't want. To my surprise, though, now that he was in the room, I felt less rancor toward him than I would have thought.

He said: "To begin with, I'm sorry."

I turned my head in his direction.

"Come on," he said. "I don't know what to say."

When he said nothing else, I gestured to my own eye.

"She decked me," he said.

I had guessed that, but I hadn't been sure.

"I learned a lesson, if you're willing to believe me. I was in way over my head. She stopped taking her medicine."

"Wasn't that the problem with Miriam, too?" I said.

He frowned. "I wasn't dating Miriam," he said. "What? You think I'm attracted to loonies? Is that your point?" He stood up. "Being judged by you isn't one of my favorite things," he said.

"Forget being the invincible older brother," I said. "We both grew up."

"Is that what you think? I'm upset by the way you're acting, so I must want your approval, don't you think, Nina?" He got up and grabbed a potholder and inspected the chicken, bending to look into the oven for a long time. "It's okay," he said. "Chicken's okay, even if your brother isn't."

"Andrew," I said, offended that he thought all I cared about was sitting in judgment of him, "how about not telling me the story. How about the two of us having dinner and listening to this tape, and maybe you'd want to make a fire."

"Sure," he said. Dejectedly. Then he asked: "Is that because you have no curiosity?"

"I have no curiosity," I said, trying it on for size. The truth was, I didn't have much.

"I should have listened to you," he said. "One thing I realized coming back was that it was wrong of me to think that running away would be a harmless form of entertainment. She knows karate, it turns out. And when she goes off her meds, her favorite sport—along with real paranoia about men—is the first thing that comes to mind."

"Andrew," I said, "that's talking about it. I was suggesting—I was quite seriously suggesting—*not* talking about it. I have a life. This place is not one big confessional. I was about to have dinner and quietly spend an evening listening to music. Do you get *that?*"

"Yeah. Sure. No. I understand," he said.

I got up and brushed past him, going into the kitchen to check the chicken myself. I was so angry, my hands were trembling. I opened the oven door carefully and pierced the breast with a fork. The juice was clear. I closed the oven and took out two plates and a carving platter. I pushed my papers to the far end of the table.

"Can I help?" he said.

"Yeah," I said, walking away from the drawer I'd just pulled open. "You can set the table." I went to the wine rack and took out a bottle of wine. I couldn't bring myself to ask him what he'd like to drink, I so little wanted him as a dinner guest. I knew that I should calm down, but I was furious that he'd pulled an Andrew and then come back, expecting sympathy. I opened the refrigerator and set out a liter of water. Let him have water or wine—whichever he wanted. I put out two place mats and put two tumblers on them. He picked up the silverware he'd put directly on the table and put it down again on the place mats.

"What's going on with Hound and his wife?" he said.

"He isn't called Hound anymore. His shrink pointed out to him that that was something you'd call a dog."

He gave a snort. "How are the two of them doing?" he said.

"Did you care this much about the state of their marriage before you screwed his wife?" I said.

There was a long, silent pause. "He told you that?" he said.

"She did."

"How did she happen to tell you that?"

"By coming over to my house and telling me. That's what women do if I'm not meeting them for coffee. They come to me, if I don't go to them. They want you back, or they want you obliterated from their memory, or whatever it is they want. They just call me and talk to me, as if I have any control over you. As if I have any insight. I should stop talking to them entirely, except that they'd probably beat down my door, you leave them so miserably unhappy."

He maneuvered himself into the chair. "I'm going to have a very difficult time getting back into your good graces, I can tell," he said. He rested his head in the palm of his right hand, elbow on the table. He said nothing, shoulders slumped. "I called that shrink Serena and I used to see," he finally said. "I called him on the way back from the airport."

"That sounds like a good idea," I said.

"It's the Cambridge way."

"I wouldn't indict a community because you have such severe personal problems," I said.

"What's the matter with you?" he said. "You're this bent out of shape because I didn't call for a couple of weeks?"

"Whether you believe this or not, once I knew you were safe, I didn't want you to call."

It was what I had been thinking about Jim Burnham, too: the fewer calls, the less complexity, the better. It was all I could do to deal with real crises. I had not slept well since Mary Catherine had been hospitalized. Just that day, she had asked me, as we were having tea, whether Jim had called, and I had realized she had her own fantasy going about the two of us. I had all but told her to drop the subject.

"I don't believe you didn't want to hear from me," he said.

I raised my eyebrows, suggesting that he would do well to believe it. If Jim Burnham *had* gotten in touch again, I would have said the same thing to him. I lifted the chicken onto the platter and handed Andrew a carving knife. Finally he got up and stood in front of the platter. As he used the knife to remove one of the chicken's thighs, I had a sudden image of him as a boy, standing at the stove, intently cooking our breakfast eggs. He was squinting with the same concentration. From behind, his shoulders were slightly stooped. Still, I was determined not to sympathize with him. I said: "Can you imagine . . . no: you can't. But if you *could* imagine anything from anyone else's point of view, could you see that it is dismaying to hear, over and over, that your brother, the person you have considered yourself closest to, is a person who uses and abandons women, letting those supposedly nearest and dearest to him deal with the fallout? But those people can take care of *themselves* when the wife of their brother's good friend comes over and explains how an affair with Andrew ruined their marriage. Or if they're off for an abortion—surely your sister, who will never have a child herself because her husband is dead, can offer consolation at no personal expense. Do you see what I'm talking about? It's a compulsion, Andrew. I don't know what it's about. Maybe just incredible ego. But this quest you're on makes no sense at all. All the women you've looked up have been nuts, by your own admission. What's in it for you? You used to have a life that wasn't just about dating girls from the past. You used to date women from work. Women from—" I had no idea how he'd met most of them. "From *Boston*," I finished. "Maybe we shouldn't talk about my life, if it upsets you so much," he said. "If you spent a little more time in the world, you might be surprised that it's not only the people in my life who have problems. What am I supposed to do? Stay at home like you, put myself under house arrest? You think people never make mistakes? You think that if you turn up the music and go from the chair to the table, and the table to the chair, that's a sort of incantation that will keep the world at bay? Well, I have a job. I have friends. I have lovers. I make mistakes, yes, but no more than other people. Take a survey, Nina," he said bitterly. "I dare you to meet enough people to take a survey."

The telephone call from Eugenia Manzetti came as a surprise. She was in Boston for a wedding, and she wondered if we could get together for lunch. She had gotten my number from Sylvia Richards. I had no idea how Sylvia knew the number. Sylvia Richards had been another one of Dr. X's conquests. She was the subject of the last big fight my mother had with my father before he died. She had been particularly hurt because she had considered Sylvia—another person with a drinking problem—her friend, until Sylvia confessed her long-ago affair. I wouldn't have known, except that my mother felt so bad about some of the things she'd said to my father, as he lay dying in the hospital. She told me on the phone, trying to instill guilt because I had not rushed to the hospital when his condition worsened. I tried to think why Eugenia Manzetti—Mrs. M—would call me. It didn't take long to decide it must have to do with Andrew's looking up her daughter, even though she'd said nothing about that on the phone. Eugenia—though she'd asked me to call her by her first name, Mrs. M came more naturally—had not sounded upset, but I still had my suspicions.

When I went to the restaurant of her hotel, I saw that she had put on an enormous amount of weight. She had on a navy blue dress with a white eyelet collar, and she wore bright red lipstick. I could feel the smear of oily lipstick she left on my cheek.

We talked with the awkwardness of two people who didn't really know each other, which made me feel as if I was with Jim Burnham, whom I'd not heard from again. It was chitchat, which I had never had any talent for. Impatient for the conversation to take off or, more likely, turn to Andrew's latest escapade, I made a preemptive strike. I said: "My brother and I have had a falling out. If there's anything you want to say about him, I should tell you that I don't discuss him any longer."

"Oh!" Mrs. M said. "Well, I don't think there was anything I particularly intended to say."

When I said nothing in reply, she began to talk about the old neighborhood. She segued into her husband's death, and how much her life had changed. What would that be like, I wondered: to have your husband become an old man and then die, without your ever hearing a knock on the door?

She fiddled with her wedding ring, which she still wore. "I'm so glad I got up my courage to call," Mrs. M said. "You shouldn't bother young people, you should let them fly the coop once they've grown, but I really do remember you so clearly. You were such a thoughtful girl, and so talented, too."

My face must have registered my surprise.

"Of course you were. I always used to wonder how you'd combine your many talents."

"Are you sure you're remembering *me*?" I asked.

"Of course. And it was such a pity that your parents didn't take the interest they should, though I do believe that old adage that people who live in glass houses shouldn't throw stones, and every parent lives in something of a glass house, I think. If nothing else, we're transparent to our children."

She ordered a cheeseburger. I asked for chicken salad.

"I *liked* Josie, I certainly was fond of that girl," Mrs. M said as soon as the waitress turned away, as if we'd already been discussing Josie all along. "And of course, that poor child's health. You know, when she was operated on some of the boys started calling her 'the Dead Girl,' as if going into the hospital meant certain death. I'm not superstitious, but it upset me that they went around saying that. I'm glad she and Alice have become reacquainted as adults. You can't make children be friends with someone just because you like that child, that's something a mother learns."

The restaurant was nearly empty, except for two Asians eating at a corner table and a few businessmen talking earnestly.

"But I don't want to talk about Josie," she said. "I'm interested to hear more about you. From what you told me when we spoke, it sounds like you're a research librarian who also writes?"

"That's pretty much it," I said. "Most people doing what I do are on the Internet. I'm old-fashioned. I like to go to the library to do my research."

"I was fascinated by that piece in *The New Yorker* about the card catalogues getting thrown out," she said. "It was written by that man who wrote the book about phone sex." She took a sip of ice water. I started to feel less anxious, because I'd figured out that she did not expect answers to her questions; in fact, the way her eyes glazed over as she hurried to the next statement made me think that she would be unhappy if we did stop to discuss anything.

In her own peculiarly animated way, Mrs. M was as adept as my mother at shutting out what she didn't want to hear. Having a real exchange had always been what my mother liked least; she never wanted to know what you thought, or anything that happened in your life. Neither did she ever seem to introspect about her own. Though perhaps she had had some willingness, if the topic was impersonal; she had briefly gone to school to study nursing.

"I think back to those girls—it's terrible of me, but I always assumed the boys would turn out fine, one way or the other, but I worried about some of the girls," Eugenia said, as the plates were brought to the table. "If I ever found myself in Chicago, I'd like to see Andie Bornstein again. Such obvious talent as a painter, and her parents only paid attention to her brother. I do wonder if she continued to paint."

Andie was someone from high school whom, to my knowledge, Andrew had not yet screwed. That was my only clear association with the name. Eugenia was enjoying her cheeseburger, plopping French fries in her mouth like a late-night slot machine player.

She wiped her lips. "Josie Bower was so upset that they called her 'the Dead Girl.' Well: I was an adult, and I was upset, myself, that those nasty boys called me 'the Witch'!"

"You knew about that?"

"Everyone *always* knows a nickname that's said behind their back," she said. "You know, your brother was one of the boys who defended her. He was quite friendly with that other bully for a while, that redheaded boy whose father did everyone's taxes. I think they stopped being friends because he was so mean and he wouldn't stop picking on Josie."

I thought wryly that Andrew's defense of Josie had not been part of Josie's essay. Had she even known? I wondered. I had an image of Andrew holding the flowers. Our father placing them on her bedside table. All of it a seduction. All of it meaning something other than what it seemed.

"Alice has always had such good manners, but that's different from being courageous, of course. She never rushed to Josie's defense, and she still feels bad about it, she was telling me the other day. But here we are talking about a dead girl who lived, when I've come to hear about you." She leaned across the table. She said: "Tell me the truth. Is it exciting, living in Cambridge?"

I almost laughed, it was so unlike what I was expecting. I forced myself to be serious. I explained that it was a place—like San Francisco, like Paris—you couldn't disabuse people of romanticizing, because it had a charming facade that made it seem at once open, yet mysteriously remote. I spoke on the subject of Cambridge as if I were responding to the lame writer's *You fill in*. Perhaps this was how people talked at lunch, I thought. Perhaps this was why I avoided getting together with them.

"Alice's husband is having a midlife crisis," she said. "He has wanderlust. That expedition with that socialite to the Himalayas, where so many people died climbing that mountain. . . . I gave him the book, and it made the exact opposite impression from what I hoped. He loves an adventure. He's off on his motorcycle even in the worst kinds of weather. I think she'll divorce him," Mrs. M said. "Between you and me."

"That's too bad," I said, not knowing what else to say.

"But I said to Alice, I said, at least he says good-bye. You remember poor Patty Arthur? Such a lovely girl in high school, and she goes off and leaves a letter for her husband that she's tested positive for HIV—just disappears. She left her little baby with a baby-sitter, wrote a note, and vanished! So I suppose you could also say poor husband."

I stopped eating.

"Josie and Alice had been back in touch with her—at least, until she disappeared. I must say, in my day, the doctor having to talk somebody's wife into taking a penicillin shot when the husband had caught syphilis was the most shocking thing imaginable, but then you look at Patty and you wonder: When she wrote the note—what kind of person must she be, to do that?"

I stared at her. It was another rhetorical question, so no answer was required.

"Am I a horrible old woman, gossiping? Josie told Alice

that Patty had seen your brother recently, so I assumed you knew."

He'd seen her? I thought that telling me about everyone he'd looked up from the past was part of his game. Then it hit me: Andrew saw Patty Arthur. My mind raced, yet at the same time it stood still. It was an all too familiar feeling. I had had it the many times I'd overheard our parents' fights. I'd had it when I'd looked through the chain pulled across the front door of the carriage house. Mac had insisted I never open the door without attaching the chain. I could remember carefully putting on the chain as whoever was on the front step repeatedly knocked and said my name. Looking into the policeman's face, I'd had the same stomach-sickening realization I had now. It was as if I was being swept upward, my weight not enough to keep me on the ground. I'd had it, also, the night I'd gradually become aware of the lights revolving around my bathroom ceiling, at first convinced they were some dizzy projection of my mind, slowly realizing they signaled something bad happening over and over, whether or not I shut my eyes.

But I was in a restaurant; I was not airborne. *Open the door, Nina, everything's going to be okay*, Mary Catherine's husband had said. He had been standing at my door, wanting to reclaim his son.

Our plates were cleared, a grape still impaled on my fork, as we ordered coffee. Rather, Eugenia ordered coffee and I nodded numbly. I was overwhelmed by fear, but it got all mixed up with Patty's preoccupation with Morocco. Morocco's mountains were the tallest in North Africa: the Atlas mountains. There were earthquakes in Morocco. My mind wouldn't stop fixating on useless facts. Gazelles ran wild in Morocco. Macaques, which many people mistakenly thought were birds, were actually a kind of monkey.

Mrs. M didn't seem to notice that I'd been transported. She had delivered her surprising news, and now she wondered aloud whether dark chocolate creme brulee might not be a bit much. I couldn't think of dessert. Desert had one *s*, dessert two. Of course Andrew had not slept with Patty Arthur. Of course not. Wasn't that always what he said, except for those times he looked away and spoke vaguely, giving me to understand that he had?

After our coffee, before we left, I took down her number and promised to call if I ever visited Pittsburgh. Pittsburgh! I could recite facts about Pittsburgh, too, but I was still wandering through Morocco—the real Morocco, obliterating Patty's imaginary, young girl's fantasy. As I put my pen and the piece of paper in my handbag, I wondered if Eugenia had any idea how unlikely a visit from me would be, but decided that pretending we might meet again elsewhere was only a social form: no harm in pretending. Outside she kissed my cheek, telling me, again, what a remarkable person I was. "Remarkable" was probably a kind word. I was a zombie. Andrew had seen Patty Arthur? She had been married, had a baby? She was sick, had disappeared?

Walking down the street, I had an image of the bed in Patty Arthur's room: the pillows in their various shapes and fabrics. Then I remembered Andrew leading the way into the kitchen, remembered what it had felt like to straggle behind him, with her in the middle. My mind jumped to another scene: my bike fallen over, my hands on the handlebars to pull it upright. The whole world had changed, and I was supposed to bicycle home. It was as futile as standing outside in your silly nightgown while a crisis unfolded. My bike had two wheels, and I was the third. I had been the third wheel all my life—so afraid of being unwanted, that except for the time I was with Mac, I kept to myself. I was always happier seeing Hound on my own, without Andrew. Without his wife, either. And those pleasant but awkward evenings, tagging along with Serena and Andrew. I knew I shouldn't have agreed to go along, but couldn't help myself.

I walked some distance before I called Andrew from a pay phone. He was back at his job, where they had forgiven his disappearance, not only because he was so good at what he did, but because when you worked with people your own age, everyone assumed that midlife crises were as common as colds.

He was not there, his secretary told me; he was at lunch. She loved to give disappointing news. If Andrew was out, or busy, the measured, false regret in her voice had a tingly quality that betrayed her pleasure in disappointing me. Years ago, he had had a brief affair with her. He'd told me that one of the things she held against him was that he was more devoted to his sister than he was to her.

I walked to the subway, not sure if wind or misery made tears roll from my eyes.

Seen, I thought. "Seen" was so often a euphemism for having sex.

Whereas "had coffee with," as I'd told Hound's wife, was not in my life a euphemism for anything.

His secretary did not pick up when I called from home; he

got the phone on the first ring, sounding harried. "I heard you called. I'm glad you're speaking to me again," he said. "I'm just about to walk into a meeting, though. Can I call you back?"

"It's about Patty Arthur," I said.

There was a silence. "Patty Arthur," he repeated. "Okay. What about her?"

"You never told me you'd seen her."

"I got the idea you were a little exasperated that I was looking up some old friends—or did I get the wrong impression, when you called my seeing people a compulsion and presented yourself as Goldilocks, with women coming over to huff and to puff and to blow your house down."

"Andrew—did you have sex with her?"

"As more of my ongoing *quest*, you mean? Part of my *compulsion?*"

"Just answer the question," I said, so light-headed I was dizzy.

"Can I get back to you to discuss my sex life in about fifteen minutes?" he said.

"Andrew—do you know that she's sick?"

"What do you mean?"

"She disappeared," I said, not able to get to the point.

"Disappeared?" I had his attention. "How would you know that?"

I wanted to tell him what I knew, but I didn't want to say the words. When we were younger, I had never needed to use words. I had used my eyes; I had been able to communicate with him by making the smallest gesture. I had let him know I was sad by disappearing from his sight, but other times I had drawn close, attached myself to him even when we didn't touch. I remembered, suddenly and ridiculously, the pound cake—the special pound cake, with the cake server lying beside the cake stand—Patty Arthur's white lie about who had made it; the cake's thin white icing. Then I saw my bicycle again, on its side in the grass. Andrew's was still standing.

Andrew was talking to me. "Listen—" He lowered his voice. "I'll call back in ten minutes, okay?"

"No, it's not. Andrew, this is important. She—" I knew I had to say something, or he would hang up. I heard my voice, shakily saying, "She had a baby."

"What's so surprising about—ooooh, I get it. You think it's mine. You think I'm Mick Jagger. She was pregnant when I slept with her, Sherlock."

The phone toppled from the table and I knelt on the rug, still holding the receiver to my ear. A glass filled with pens had toppled with it. Pickup sticks, I thought: pens facing every which way. The rule of pickup sticks was that when you picked them up, no stick could move any other.

"You slept with her," I repeated.

"I did. As part of my compulsion."

"I have very bad news," I said. "I had lunch with Mrs. M today. Alice's mother."

"You had lunch with Alice Manzetti's *mother?* You're putting me on!"

"Andrew, please," I said. Then I could not think what I wanted him to please do. "She told me she was HIV positive," I said.

"*Alice Manzetti's mother?*"

"No. Patty Arthur. Jesus, Andrew. Patty. And she disappeared."

There was a long pause. "That can't be true," he said.

"Why can't it?"

"Because she . . . there's some mix-up. Look: she's sort of a pothead. She wasn't—"

"Andrew, she wrote her husband a note. She abandoned the baby."

"There's some mix-up," he said. "I know Patty."

"What if you *don't* know Patty?" I said. "Call Josie, Andrew. She's the one who told Alice."

"Let me close the door," he said. I could envision him walking the length of his office. He was still alive. Walking. Even if he had slept with her, that didn't mean he'd caught the virus. It was the first reassuring thought I'd had.

"Can you call Josie?" he said, when he came back. He sounded perturbed, as if he was only indulging me, until he spoke again, and I heard his voice crack. "Will you do that? Let's try to sort this out, okay?"

"Why don't *you* call Josie? You slept with her. Call her yourself."

"For your information, we didn't have sex. I haven't touched her since high school. It was a harmless get-together, but she's married to such a tyrant she had to see me behind his back."

When he spoke again, his voice was more serious. "All I know is that Josie lives somewhere in Connecticut," he said.

"She lives in Fairfield. Her married name is Epping. E-p-p-i-n-g. Your memory was so good that you even told me what *pets* she has, Andrew."

"Why are you yelling at me? She told me she had twin girls and twin kittens. What of it?"

"You weren't there?"

"No. I saw her in Brattleboro, when she'd gone to visit her aunt."

"You got together with her in Vermont? You'll do anything, you'll go anywhere to screw these girls. They're all desperate, and they'll all get involved with you. And it might have gotten you in very, very bad trouble."

"Nina—get a grip," he said.

He seemed almost superrational, considering the news. What was he trying to prove? That I was the prudish, hysterical female? That he was the wise older brother? What did he think—that assuming those roles, you could bully death?

"I *know* Patty Arthur," he said. "She isn't a deceptive person."

By the time I got the letter from Eugenia Manzetti, Andrew had spoken to Josie and had been proven right: it was not Patty who had tested positive, but her husband. Everything else, though, was true: she had left the baby with a sitter and never returned; she had written a note to her husband, saying that it was over between them. Six days later she had been found dead in a New York City hotel room. Apparently she had not been married to the man she called her husband. At the autopsy, multiple drugs were present in Patty Arthur's body, but there was no sign of HIV. *I am sorry I relayed vicious gossip about a person who obviously had enough problems*, Mrs. M wrote. *I suppose there is always a tendency to want to place blame in these situations, and I am inclined to say that the man she lived with should have noticed if she was depressed and needed help, but he certainly had problems of his own, so for all I know he did what he could,* she wrote. *She is not a person whose mind can be fathomed, if she left her own child in that situation. I hope in the future to write to you about something other than tragedy, but because I realize bad news does not always travel fast—and that bad news can be wrong in its specifics—I needed to write to give this sad topic closure.*

Bad news can be wrong in its specifics; that was almost as good as *You fill in.* Awake at night, my insomniac memories were almost always about how much Patty had wanted to go to Morocco. If there was a heaven—which I didn't believe—she might be there, drinking strong Moroccan coffee, lazing in bed, propped against an enormous collection of pillows, waiting for her life to begin. As she had been that day, though none of us would have made an analogy between those odd surroundings and heaven. The pound cake—the ordinary, yet exceptional cake she lied about and then confessed to having baked herself—that had been heavenly, though of course it had nothing to do with heaven.

I was so sorry that I told you so abruptly about Patty's disappearance, Eugenia Manzetti wrote, at the end of her note. *The death of another is always a lesson to all of us that we should value this world while we can, for life's but a fleeting shadow, as Shakespeare wrote. I am moved to say that you have capacities you have not yet experienced, and if you will forgive unwanted advice from an old woman, petty quarrels, such as you are having with your brother,*

*will only sidetrack you from the most important matter of all: that
of recognizing, and expressing, love.*

It was quite the note. But when it became flowery, it
reminded me of the many sympathy notes I had received after
Mac's death. I read it through once and put it aside. It was
not until several evenings later that I picked it up again, to
show it to Mary Catherine, and that same night to Kate,
when she stopped by to apologize for intruding in my life
with what she called her "quandaries," bringing a bottle of
wine I knew she wished I would invite her in to drink.

So we did that: Kate and I had a glass of wine, and she
filled me in on Henry's move back to the house, her son's joy,
her own confusion. "She writes eloquently," Kate said, handing it back to me. "She must think very highly of you to
write such a message." By now, she had settled herself in my
house comfortably, curling onto the sofa. If I wanted a new
friend, Kate seemed willing to be that.

"It's not going to work, I can already tell," she said, by
complete non sequitur. Except that nothing is a non sequitur
to the teller, if that is the thing they've come to say.

Why refute her? If that was what she thought, she knew
more about her relationship with her husband than I did. I
said: "At least you tried."

"You don't seem surprised. I suppose you saw it more
clearly than I did."

"I don't know what's going to happen, Kate," I said. "I'm
just accepting what you say."

She looked around the room. "When something like this
happens, does it—I shouldn't ask, but when someone close to
you dies, it must bring up all the emotion about your hus-

band's death, doesn't it? I know that when my uncle died, it made me think about my mother's death all over again."

"Death dominoes," I said. Most times, she was right—all too many things took me back, consequential and inconsequential—but this time I had been so overwhelmed with worry about my brother that I had never really dwelt on Patty Arthur's actual death. Instead of thinking of her as a grown woman, in the present, I had frozen her in time as a yearning adolescent, masquerading as a grown-up. I hadn't been so intelligent, as Eugenia had suggested. I was only shy and withdrawn, so I made books my friends as a way to hide my nervousness, while Patty had been both a pretender and the real thing. She aspired to something—even if that thing, that state, was a young girl's fantasy.

I thought about the whole issue of Andrew's looking people up. A big part of it was sex—he wasn't going to make me think otherwise—but he could have had sex with anyone. *Did* have sex with many women he hadn't gone to high school with. It seemed more likely—it was an idea Serena had first planted in my mind—that in trying to reconnect, he'd been trying to work his way back to something. Bodies held history. You didn't exactly have a relationship with someone you'd known in your youth and rediscover the past; but in the script, so to speak—in words that might be spoken—or in deeper feelings that might register inadvertently, in spite of what was said, I thought it was possible that having sex with them was an attempt to arrive again at that point where your desire was so obvious, you didn't need to articulate anything. Our childhood remained puzzling, but also preoccupying. What to make of those years? Though we

survived them, it would have been likely we'd become alco-
holics ourselves. Violent people. I continued to think about it
long after Kate had hugged me and left. There were so many
unknowns; there had been so many mysterious incidents
between our mismatched, loudly and silently warring parents that we'd never know why they stayed together.

It seemed clear that our father and mother did not love
each other, but had they had anything else, in place of love?
Their lives couldn't have been only the crises or the standoffs
Andrew and I remembered. Their marriage had seemed not so
much like a battle as the day of defeat after the battle was lost.
We had kept out of their way—not that our father was often
present—but we had developed the habit of coming in the
back door instead of the front, of not even flushing the toilet,
so as not to draw attention to where we were. My mother
called us piggies, but we had our own, private reasons for the
things we did. What had we learned, growing up in the house
of Dr. X? Craftiness. Deception. To pretend that things that
were happening were not happening. How to make an end
run around them: Andrew practicing signing their names on
our report cards; neither of us passing on information about
events at school. She would have come drunk, and he would
have put his patients first and not come at all—a situation
that was inevitable with doctors, though I had heard too many
rumors about the mothers he fooled around with to believe
that he was ministering to anyone but himself. Patty Arthur
had not been the only girl who'd been taunted in her youth
because of things that had happened to a parent. Why was it
that the girls were taunted, but never the boys? Because it was
assumed that boys were separate, that girls were bound to

their parents in a way boys were not. If anyone confronted Andrew about our father's womanizing it was always another boy, and the questions or revelations were delivered with barely disguised admiration. And our mother? Boys did not talk about other boys' mothers. Ever. Neither did girls— except that I knew they gossiped behind my back, and worse yet, that some of them pitied me.

At home, we were meek when we were not lucky enough to be absent. So our father must have been all the more surprised the time he came upon Andrew and me in Lucy Roderick's rec room. I had been waiting to see, when Andrew began looking up high school girls, whether he'd go so far as to look up Lucy Roderick. As in a bad comedy, all of us— Andrew, me, Lucy, and Lucy's visiting cousin, Dianne—had assembled at the Roderick house to do something furtively. Like our mother, Mrs. Roderick drank. She drank bourbon in Coca-Cola, sipping from a straw as she vacuumed, taking a Coke bottle with her as she drove around.

We'd known she would be away on a long errand the day we assembled. I was to be the photographer. Andrew had taught me how to use a camera. He had heard about a magazine that paid for sexy pictures, and he wanted us to cash in. It was so crude—so unlike Andrew. I never believed for a minute that he really wanted to do it for the money, but since I didn't know why it was so important to him, I guess I went along hoping I'd find out. We never discussed the intimacies between him and Patty Arthur. So since we did not do that, why did he want to subject me to such a parody of what I assumed was his real love for her? All I knew was that, somehow, it was a test. It was pointless; he knew he had my loyalty. I've never understood pushing to the limit people who love you. In that, I suppose he was his father's child.

Lucy was the first to take off her clothes. She had big breasts, but her cousin's were even larger. Andrew had ripped pages from one of our father's hidden copies of *Playboy* so the girls could imitate the poses. He also provided the marijuana, so the girls could loosen up. Dianne said that she had once smoked hash. She twirled her shirt over her head, then tossed it on the floor. Things were beginning: eventually we would have a roll of film of Lucy and Dianne stripped down to their panties, cavorting.

I had not easily been convinced to go along with the plan. Quite frankly, being in the presence of girls posturing through re-creations of porn shots seemed embarrassing. I knew that Andrew and Patty Arthur had had some argument, and I asked him if that was why he wanted to do it. I talked around the subject and did not even use her name, but he knew what I meant and simply tossed the question aside as if it did not deserve an answer. It also made me nervous that he was smoking more grass, and doing it more daringly. I'd had a few tokes before, and knew how strangely it could make a person behave. But he really wanted me in on the action; he wanted me there as much as he had not wanted me in on his relationship with Patty Arthur. He all but told me that my being there would be the factor that would really make things happen. If Lucy and Dianne saw that I wasn't shocked, they would eventually give up their reluctance.

Lucy went along because her cousin always had a more exciting life than she did; it pleased her to think that this time, she could turn the tables. Dianne—whom Andrew and

I had met once before, sneaking out of an adults-only movie with her hoody boyfriend—had a reputation for being a girl who liked to do things just for kicks. Andrew had a friend whose older brother had agreed to develop the film.

I helped Andrew convince the girls that the pictures would make them famous. It was all a big joke, really. They didn't believe it any more than we did, but Dianne had a crush on Andrew, so she was eager to be persuaded. Lucy had already promised Andrew in school that if I was there, she would go through with it. She obviously never thought I'd really join him. I had let Lucy down, in supporting my brother. Once there, she was so amazed, and Dianne was so excited to see that someone else was in on it, that I wasn't about to lose face by flinching.

We ran upstairs to watch Mrs. Roderick's old Buick pull away. On the way back downstairs, Lucy detoured to show us that her father also had a secret stash of dirty magazines. They mostly featured people in the military, without any pants. Dianne insisted on taking one of the magazines downstairs, though Lucy kept trying to grab it away from her. Dianne was the most nervous. All of us, including Lucy, lied to Dianne, saying that we had taken pictures like the ones we were going to take before. We were so united in what we said, and we said it so straight-faced, that I began to believe it, myself.

Andrew put himself in charge of the music. They huddled and smoked grass—I didn't, because I wanted the pictures to turn out—and as everybody got sillier, Andrew changed the music, switching between songs that were fast and slow before the music really had time to register. He reminded me of our mother, drinking after dinner, fiddling with the radio dial until I thought it would come off in her hand.

I did not smoke grass because I already felt peculiar enough. It was strange, to be a girl her brother considered one of the guys. I felt that what he was doing should be part of his private life, but at the same time, I was flattered he wanted me there.

The record Andrew put on sounded dated; the music was slow and too romantic—it might even have been a record the Rodericks danced to, since Lucy said her mother and father sometimes danced late at night in their rec room. The grass had made everyone giggly. The girls cracked themselves up by pouting like the men in Mr. Roderick's magazines. We all knew nobody would buy the pictures. We were doing it as an excuse to act up, and to express forbidden desires through sexual pantomime. We were doing it because things had progressed to a certain point, and no one wanted to back down. Eventually the magazine had nothing to do with the poses Dianne and Lucy struck. They became rather inventive, as each tried to top the other. I took a reading with the light meter, the way Andrew had taught me, and backed up, trying to find the best vantage point from which to photograph. They wouldn't listen to me and hold still, so I began taking pictures while they were in motion. I took most of the roll of film and then, the way all of a sudden a wind comes up that lifts the hat off your head and leaves your hand patting the air, a chill descended over the room as we heard a key inserted into a lock, and our father walked in through a door leading from the patio to the basement.

He stood there with the key in his hand, as surprised to

see us as we were to see him. I was on a footstool, aiming down at Lucy and Dianne, who had stopped cavorting a few minutes before to line their eyes with a black pencil and to put red lipstick on their lips. Their faces were not what I looked at, though. Each had the nipple of one breast touching a lava light that sat on a candlestand Andrew had pulled into the middle of the room. The candle sat forgotten, in the corner. The lava light sent up mesmerizing gobs of green oil.

He had the key, of course, because he'd been carrying on with Lucy's mother, but at that moment, I thought that he'd followed us—and I continued to assume that as he stood in front of me, so surprised that his mouth dropped open. I had never before really seen him rattled. Furious, but not rattled. I tried to think how he'd known where we'd gone. When he finally recovered himself enough to close his mouth, he turned instantly toward his son. "Andrew?" he said. We all chimed in. We were so frightened, we couldn't let Andrew be our spokesman. We felt we had to explain, immediately. Our desperate attempts all came out in a rush: the money someone was offering for photographs; immediate, tearful apologies; the girls grabbing each other and scrambling away, as if there was anywhere to go. You would have thought our father was Charlie Manson, there was so much pandemonium. Within seconds, he was cursing Andrew, and the words were so vicious, so ugly, that I was more frightened than I'd ever been in my life. The only advantage I had was that I was not stoned. Andrew was, and as astonished as he'd been, he also found our father's astonishment funny. It was the smirk of the prisoner going to the gallows. Which was not a bad analogy, because in a way, he was about to be killed. When Andrew did not answer his questions, our father became even more enraged. He chased Andrew through the house—for once, he was so filled with adrenaline that he actually caught him—and dragged him back to the basement where only I remained, sitting on a sofa, bugeyed with fear. Andrew came into the room propelled by my father's kick, flailing until my father pounced and pinned his arms behind his back. "Where are they?" our father said to me. "Get those girls." My legs were shaking so badly I couldn't stand. "Get them," he repeated, this time shouting into Andrew's face, before once more kicking him from behind. Andrew fell and lay sprawled on the floor. He slowly curled into a very tight ball.

"I knew it," our father whispered. "So now I see. The adolescent version of the boy who plays doctor. Is that what you do? You have someone undress, so you can examine them?" He pushed the toe of his shoe into Andrew's side. "Are you playing doctor, or are you pretending to be a big, important movie producer, maybe? Is that what you think you are?" He leaned forward and spoke to the back of Andrew's head, his voice veering crazily. "Well, I guess I should at least give thanks that you found yourself two little sluts besides your sister," he said. He turned to me. "You'd do anything for him, wouldn't you?" I knew him well enough to know that whatever he asked, he would be dismayed to hear any response. He became a frenzy of motion. He threw open the basement door and charged outside.

The girls were not far away. They were so terrified, all they had done was go into the yard, pulling on what clothes they could, to shiver behind a bush. Our father dashed back into the house, grabbing Andrew by one arm. "Round up your little whores," he said. Andrew flinched as he raised his fist; somehow, Andrew managed to avoid the blow and also back up through the door. I have no idea what Andrew did to make Dianne and Lucy re-enter the basement, or why he even came back, but he did, and they did. Lucy turned and started to run once our father put out his hand. Andrew was on his feet, wavering, but standing. Andrew caught Lucy by the wrist. In a trembling voice, he tried to tell my father that what was going on was not as bad as it seemed.

"That's what I'm always told, but I'm a doctor, a smart doctor, and I know otherwise," our father said. "Your mother's not here now to protect you."

He wouldn't listen. Every time Andrew started to explain our father raised his fist in a threatening way, and said, "Is my son playing doctor? Is that what he's doing? Is he exploring girls' bodies? Is he getting his jollies with two little sluts?" He looked at me. "With *three* little sluts?" he said. Andrew had long ago stopped smiling. "What kind of boy doesn't have a hard-on when there are pretty naked girls?" he said. "Do you have a hard-on, or do you have a limp dick that pissed your pants when you fell down?"

Lucy was crying so hard she was sobbing. Dianne looked at our father as if he were an alien who had just landed, speaking some frantic, repulsive language. Only the tip of her nose quivered, making her look like a frightened rabbit. "Back to your positions!" he said. The girls clung to each other, backing away. He moved faster than they did; he slammed shut the door from the basement to the upstairs. "Sweater off," he said to Lucy. "Just the way I found you. We need to get this picture for your mother. Come on—off with it." Lucy pleaded to be allowed to leave the room. When she ran out of words—when it became clear that he would kill her if she did not do what he wanted—slowly, her head hung in misery, Lucy removed her sweater.

"Take the picture," he said to me. I knew he wasn't kidding. I picked up the camera and looked through the viewfinder. I saw the stain on Andrew's pants. This was a nightmare. How could he ever, possibly have known where we were? He never knew where we were. "What's the matter with you?" he said, turning to Andrew. "What's your role in this? This was your idea, wasn't it? Aren't you the boy who loves to play doctor? I hope this was at least your idea, that you aren't just some pansy pretending to be a man."

"You bastard," Andrew said. He elbowed Dianne aside. At first I misunderstood; I thought he was upset with Dianne. But he had already seen that my father was done with talk and was about to spring into action, and tackle one of the girls the same way he had tackled him. Andrew and our father struggled on the floor. I thought he was going to kill Andrew. I thought that I was watching the murder of my brother by my father. Eventually—in not much time at all—Andrew lay there so still, I thought he must be unconscious, or sleeping like an owl with open eyes.

"Do what you're supposed to do in a situation like this," my father said, pulling him up and pushing him against the wall. A picture fell and broke. That was what happened when our father was angry: things broke. "At least put your *hand* on it," he said, exaggerating every word, grabbing his own crotch to show Andrew what he expected. "Look at the mama's boy," he sneered. "He's such a pansy he won't touch it." Maybe I looked. I don't remember. Maybe we were all looking at Andrew, or maybe no one was except our father, but our father's gaze could have bored a hole through Andrew's head. Slowly, I watched as Andrew's shoulders slumped. He was a veritable statue, he stood so still. Except for the blood from a cut on his cheek, he was as white as marble.

One last time, our father spoke his epithet for his son. One day before, Andrew had turned fifteen.

The note I received from Jim Burnham was different in tone from Mrs. M's, and was written on an embossed note card. The postmark was Minneapolis, Minnesota. It said: *I am afraid I have had to relocate. In Boston, I thought I was out from under, but losing my job a second time has made me come to my senses, so I am here to dry out. I hope that you will not hold this against me, and that if I should return to Boston, you might still be willing to have that long-promised dinner, though I'm afraid water will have to replace the wine. Thank you for your friendliness and generosity.*

It was illuminating, and right to the point. The thing that bothered me was that I hadn't suspected. It made me wonder—after all the training I'd gotten in my childhood— whether there was something thickheaded about me, so I failed to see what was happening in front of my eyes. I understood that I would never see him again; something written between the lines let me know he knew that, too. I threw the note in the trash. A little later, when I put on my coat to go out, I opened my door to find a tall carton shipped by UPS sitting on the step. I took it in and unpacked an orchid plant, its single blossom conch-shell pink, delicately flecked with lavender. The plant had been carefully wrapped in a cocoon of excelsior. I expected the note card to be signed by Jim Burnham, but instead the plant had come from the grateful author of the interminable piece I had finally signed off on the week before. He didn't have a chance of impressing me with a gift, or anything else, after the note from Jim. I didn't want to have anything to do with men. Andrew and I were on good terms again—nothing like thinking someone might die to reinforce the bond—but other men? Forget it. I didn't want to hear Henry's sad story about how things were falling apart; I didn't want anything from anyone except to be allowed to disappear again. The drama and deceptions, the sorrowfulness of other people's lives was nothing I could do anything about. Furthermore, I had decided I was not going to take up the subject of Jim and his drinking with Angie, who I could only think must have been pimping for her ex-husband. I was not going to ask her about her recommendation that I look him up. Neither was I going to ask for the writer's address. It had been a nice gesture, but I had also spent an unusual amount of time on his piece, adding to it so greatly that I had almost written it, myself. Not only that, but the orchid was just another thing that was going to die on me. The carriage house did not get good light. Mac's plants—what few were left—never bloomed.

I left the house. I walked and walked, closing my eyes sometimes, because I knew the sidewalks so well. I could go blind, and still walk those paths. In a way, I had gone blind: I was impervious to what went on around me; I had developed the habit of ducking my head and hurrying toward my destination.

I made myself slow down and stroll. I met people's eyes, those few times their heads were not also pointed at the ground. A woman in a pale blue coat smiled as she walked by, and I remembered myself when I was her age: how much I had liked the place where I lived; how automatically I had smiled when I looked into someone's face. I did not come from an expressive family. My father never smiled; my mother narrowed her eyes when her lips turned up, as if happiness caused her discomfort. Andrew did smile: a slow, almost dreamy smile, his face so relaxed he might have been falling asleep to sweet dreams as he looked into your eyes. I never saw that expression except for the times we were alone. He and I had our private world, as children always do. We lived a parallel reality to what was going on. For years—for years and years and years and years now—our most private expressions, our most sincere expressions, had not figured in the way we related to each other. I've wondered sometimes if they are still there, below the surface, deep in the woods, or lurking in a corner of the attic. But even if I could bring myself to ask, how do you request that a person shine a particular smile on you? You might as well waste your time rooting for the sun to outrun the clouds or for the autumn leaves to return to the trees. For all the years Andrew's seemed to be happier than he was in his youth, for all the years we've now spent away from our parents, in all the time that anyone who didn't know him well would be sure he was happier and more content and more adventurous and filled with such self-confidence—in all this time that he's grinned so often, I've been less and less convinced, and I've missed his dreamy smile all the more.

Maybe he bestows his special smile on the high school girls. Maybe he smiles that way if someone shows up at his motel wearing underpants and a raincoat; maybe it's his expression when he greets anyone—even Rochelle Rogan. Maybe he's appropriated the smile from his younger self, and in smiling it again, he's filled himself with promise.

Near the newsstand, a girl in a sari and her tall blond boyfriend stood with their arms around each other's waists, closing the distance between them until their bodies fused. Young love. It was more noticeable in the spring than in the winter, but there were always so many sidewalk romances in Cambridge, you would quickly lose count.

I couldn't imagine myself anymore as the other half of a couple, so my thoughts went, instead, to Andrew. When he reunited with those girls from his past, did they walk down the street hip-to-hip? Did they stop for coffee or a drink as an excuse to sit close together at a tiny table and to look meaningfully into each other's eyes? Was it like high school again—painfully fraught with significance? Did they still believe in possibility, or had things come to seem less possible, and if so, did that realization make their relationship cozy and companionable, or something of a letdown?

I walked into the same coffee shop where I had seen Serena and ordered a cappuccino. As I waited at the far end of the counter for my order, I began to wonder about what Andrew had told me: Had he really only talked to Josie? Really? Not even a quick kiss on the lips? If that was true—which it might have been, he had sounded so emphatic—

then maybe it was because by escaping death she had become superhuman. A living miracle. Not someone he'd toy with. There was an explanation, I thought, picking up my cappuccino capped with its quivering dome of froth.

Getting back to a simpler time, for me, would not be by way of phoning around and sleeping with people from my past. It would consist of remembering how *not* to connect. Lately, I had been living outside my own life, involved in other people's problems, having people to the house as if I were the Queen of Hearts at her perpetual tea party, rushing out to meet people for coffee, for lunch. It was better to pretend to be busy, screening calls; setting limits with Andrew and with Henry, whose troubles I could sense gathering like clouds over Cambridge. There had never been anything romantic between Henry and me, though when we discussed Andrew, sex often became the subtext. Hound struck me as entirely asexual. He wasn't my type, in any case: a bearish man with defeated eyes and a down-on-my-luck quality he used manipulatively, to gain sympathy. For too long, I had let myself pretend that he and I had a stronger bond than we did. I had acted as if we were really connected—as if he really were a hound, and I was the moon.

I studied the faces coming toward me: college students, people getting off work, people hurrying home, hurrying to the subway, to the gym, to bars, to bookstores and music shops and restaurants and parking garages. None of them—none of them, ever—would be the face of Mac, though many of them would remind me of what might have been: the laughter; the affection; the concern. The *You fill in.*

In an attempt to cheer myself up, I went through my list

of things to feel good about: Andrew did not have AIDS—he had been spared; Henry was where he chose to be; and for all I knew, Patty Arthur might be reincarnated, living in Morocco.

Oh, I liked not believing in things, didn't I? It made me a dead girl myself, a person sleepwalking down a sidewalk in Cambridge. I tried it on for size, and it fit. Like Henry's scarf, which I was wearing, it was long enough, and supple enough, that it couldn't help but fit.

*T*he ghost and the fairy flew quietly into the attic. There were musty things you would not want to touch and old toys stacked here and there. They were super careful not to be heard so they did not look through boxes.

The ghost could be invisible but the fairy could never hold her breath long enough to truly disappear so she only became teeny tiny. The ghost could disappear by willing it but she worried that someone might come up and swat her if they mistook her for a bug.

The fairy and the ghost were careful not to be discovered. In the summer they played in the woods but in the winter they made caves out of old coats and blankets eaten by moths then crept inside and curled up tightly. Sometimes in the cave when it was dark enough the ghost would let the fairy look right into his eyes though his eyes were always blurry because she was so close.

One time in the attic they discovered poor butterflies that had been put in frames. They took them into their cave and examined them. It made the fairy cry because it was so sad. The ghost did not like the fairy to feel bad so he told her to play the game where she imagined everything was the opposite of what it seemed. The butterflies escaped from the frames just like a person squeezing through a tiny crack in a window and disappeared into the woods where they joined the other butterflies and fluttered in the sunshine.

IN MY GENERATION, marriage and motherhood were supposed to be the culmination of a girl's dreams. What if I didn't have any dreams? Or, excuse me, I had them, Dr. Freud—I had real, complex, baffling, sometimes frightening dreams—I had *real* dreams, not silly dreamy dreams, in which my husband and I clasped hands and walked toward the sunset, and in the next sequence we walked right through the dazzling color, and found ourselves smiling on the other side, each clutching a baby's hand: a boy for you, a girl for me, as the song goes. Get out the Brownie and take the annual Christmas card picture. And for emphasis, sign it "Dr. and Mrs.," along with the children's names. You've married well—you're, let's face it, a little better than everyone else, if you're a doctor's wife.

Thinking about colorful skies, I remember one of the first books Nina had as a child. There were little birds, each a different color, which got together at the end of the story like the June Taylor Dancers and arranged themselves into a rainbow. The red birds. The orange. The yellow. Birds in every color of the rainbow. Nina was fascinated. Now, they'd take the same idea and make it a pop-up book and it would be much more exciting, but no matter: Nina never failed to create her own excitement. In fact, as the smallest child, she had scorn for whatever fun I tried to instigate. She always preferred to have her nose in a book, reading about something make-believe. The only person who could distract her was her brother. If Andrew wasn't around, she'd turn to the stories of the witch or the dragon, or to Bucky Beaver. Her father and I were just poor stand-ins for the fictional characters she believed in. She looked down on us for being so dull and so . . . human. I'd rock her, when she was a baby, trying to get her to sleep, but if my voice went out of key she'd scrunch up her face to let me know I'd blown my audition. I was always auditioning with Nina. She was never an easy person to feel comfortable with. She let me know long before she could talk that I was nothing but the sum of my deficiencies.

I thought about being a singer. My model was Billie Holiday, and I loved her as much for her gardenia as for her voice. For the style it conveyed, I mean—not that putting something pretty in your hair is the same as having been blessed with a magical voice. The exquisite perfection of that flower! There she was, in real life, down and out, drug addicted, but oh, she never neglected style. She embodied style. And what those transgressions did for her singing! You can listen to her every day and still be uplifted by the quality of that voice. She was her own chameleon. She just turned another color when the music demanded it—went from red velvet to a lump of coal. The idea of someone opening her mouth and singing that way—using one's life for a jazz improvisation . . . it reassures you that people can make harmony out of chaos.

Which was a trick esteemed by my mother's generation,

and passed on to mine. We were supposed to deal with complexity by taking the components and whipping everything together into a Jell-O mold. Once solidified, hold briefly under warm water and unmold. The triumph I felt when it slipped to the plate, perfectly shaped, prettily concocted. How could I ever have been so silly? By the time you caught on, all those Jell-O molds had relegated you to a life of service to others, so that you served your husband, and your children, and your parents—everyone. You're tethered to the things you create, even when they're as banal—maybe particularly when they're as banal—as a Jell-O mold.

Oh, I lived in such earnest times. The war was over—that hard-fought, earnest war—and home came General Eisenhower, leaving behind his lover, Kay Summersby, the driver of his jeep, for his dull but proper wife, Mamie. And on his heels, soon to begin his lifetime of earnest apologies, Richard Nixon. They all shadowed each other: Nixon shadowed Ike; Pat shadowed her husband . . . Pat, always lingering in the background, except when she was trotted out in her good Republican cloth coat. Their little dog, Checkers, and Pat's cloth coat. Which dog was the real subject of discussion? you have to wonder. There she sat, like a sphinx. Who could imagine what riddle she embodied—her whole marriage was one big *Why* riddle for the women of my generation. It had hardly been love at first sight between the two of them. He used to drive her to her dates with other men, back in the days when she had a lion's head and a woman's body, before it got switched and her wings never opened again, and she had merely a woman's head on a lion's body. Odd creature that she was, she didn't prowl very far: no farther than the liquor cabinet for much of their marriage, apparently. But imagine the spirit she must have once had, to let him drive her to meet her dates and ferry her home, afterward: a woman unafraid to take the devil as her personal duenna. And Pat's little joys: Tricia and Julie. One so dark, the other so fair. In the Brothers Grimm, you'd know which would represent trouble, and which was intended to be the pretty, placid princess—but Nixon saw to it that life was no fairy tale, so nobody got to play their assigned parts. What a circus all of that was: Sputnik; the Cold War; Khrushchev banging his shoe.

I sent away one of Andrew's first shoes to be bronzed. That was what you did in those days: the bronzed shoe was every baby's personal bronze star. Some mothers put silk flowers in them, but more often they were empty, placed near the baby's picture. We had our little shrine to Andrew: our gleaming shrine to the boy who had once been a gleam in Daddy's eye. So had the baby I miscarried been a gleam in Frank's eye, but I lost that baby when I tumbled down the stairs. That was just like Frank, to think that all the king's horses—those sanctimonious geldings he worked with at his hospital—could put Mommy back together again. As a matter of fact, I did get put back together, but the Jell-O mold inside turned to mush. After that, I wasn't allowed to drink when I had relations with Daddy—this was in those long-ago days when no one knew how bad alcohol was for unborn babies. He and I only had sex cold sober after the accident, and when we started to have cocktails every evening after Frank returned from last rounds at the hospital, sex became less frequent. But it was fortunate that Nina came along so quickly. He was disappointed we didn't have another boy. Not so much because he loved sons as because he'd already judged Andrew a failure, at the age of two. Andrew and his father were entirely different, temperamentally—which was a blessing for me, because I couldn't have taken two tyrants. Andrew was quiet, and reasonable—later, Frank liked to torture me by insisting he was homosexual—and he was also my favorite child, because I had a better idea how to raise a son than a daughter. Which I think is because I knew I didn't want my daughter to be a replica of her mother, yet I didn't have a clear idea of what a girl could, or should, be; when you had a boy, that child was automatically different. All I had to do with Andrew was contradict Frank's harshness, and hope Andrew would turn out to be more compassionate than his father.

As a young woman, I mistook Frank's phenomenal ego for a positive quality. I thought it made him strong; the sort of man who could protect me. I didn't have a very clear idea of what he might protect me from—the irony is: what would have been worse than Frank?—but my mother had communicated to me her fear of the world. Girls of my generation were given their suit of armor, but instead of shields and spurs, we were issued bras and girdles that went halfway down our thighs—even a slim girl, like me, wore a girdle with stiff stays and dangling garters to keep her stockings up. I wore stockings with sandals! Every extra membrane was important; every man a potential Tom Jones, leering and laughing as he tossed up the hussies' layers of skirts. I was so reluctant on my honeymoon that Frank had to get me drunk on champagne—the first I'd ever tasted—before I'd even agree to lie down with him.

Those moments before losing my virginity stay with me.
I remember the room spinning. It was like a moment in a
movie when the transition is made from one scene to the next
by some clever technology the audience knows nothing
about: into the picture comes a little tornado, spinning
everything into a blur, the whole scene rotated, riveting the
viewer and disorienting you at the same time, eventually pro-
pelling you, like Alice, to the other side. "I'm late, I'm late"
became Frank's mantra. He was phoned in the hotel room, in
the middle of our first sexual experience. Today doctors all
wear beepers—or they have someone covering for them, so
they can go into the world unencumbered—but then, the
phone rang, and everything stopped. As Frank spoke with his
calm, reasonable voice, which I would later realize was only a
veneer to cover his rage, the day's events began to regress. I
went backward in time, back to the spinning scene, and from
there, back to the church, and from there back to my parents'
home, which had always been—I had this revelation, there in
the hotel room—it had always been the place you stayed
until you could leave, a wallpapered version of the womb,
from which you were ejected after a certain period of time. I
had been pushed out at twenty. Gestating longer could have
caused complications for my mother, who had married too
young, herself, and who wanted to get on with things. My
childhood was all about getting through my childhood, getting to the life that awaited me. That life began to evolve out
of a boozy swoon in a hotel room, and was christened by my
throwing up on the floor.

Ah, romance.

Mary Catherine, my clandestine correspondent, writes

that after all this time, Nina does, indeed, have a beau. Imagine it! The Ice Princess, beginning to thaw. Andrew mentioned the man to me, but of course he would lie to me outright to spare me unhappiness—so I had no reason to believe what he said about a romance in Nina's life until someone I trusted corroborated it. Mary Catherine has not seen the man, though. Both of us are pleased that he exists; Nina's life of mourning has gone on much too long—it has been so intense, and so exclusionary of others, that I think the capacity for lapsing into such a state must have existed before Mac died. Maybe calling it mourning only lends an easy explanation to her depression. If that's the case, she inherited her proclivity for misery from Frank. So many of these things are genetically determined, we now know. Frank's rages were fueled by alcohol, but I've become well enough informed that I believe the drinking was an attempt at self-medication. He couldn't account for his mood swings, would never face the fact that he, himself, needed doctoring. With the alcohol he seemed to level out into being a petty tyrant, rather than raging one moment and trying to console the victim the next. How is it his patients were exempt from his behavior? When he apologized to me, I would dread the knock on the bedroom door because I knew it would be followed by tears, and more often than not, his dropping to his knees. It was so hypocritical, because Frank never believed for a moment in any greater being. He insisted that our marriage be performed by a JP, in my parents' living room, rather than by a minister in a church. He would always become pious after one of his rages. I would not have known so many of the things he did to the children if he had not come into my room and dropped to his knees, confessing his transgressions, as if he had transported himself to a church.

My room was not like a church. Instead of organ music, my radio would be playing. I liked Billie Holiday, but I played a little game with myself, resisting putting her records on the turntable during the day so I could be pleasantly surprised when one of her songs came on the radio at night. I knew which channel to tune in, of course.

It was not a church because instead of stained glass, there was the ugly broken windowpane from the time he struck the window instead of striking me. He never hit me. But he bloodied his wrist, and broke the glass, protesting my plan to study nursing. He was so insecure, he thought having a nurse in the family would be competition. He had to be the important figure. He pretended shock and dismay that I would think about leaving the children. He told me that was reprehensible. That was his opinion, while I was supposed to think nothing about his sleeping with his nurse.

It was not a church because instead of a crucifix was hung a print of a Norman Rockwell painting. Nothing Norman Rockwell ever painted symbolized suffering. My picture depicted two children, a boy and a girl, sitting on counter stools, sharing a soda. Frank ripped that from the wall in a rage, then began apologizing. He eventually replaced it with a picture of a boy and his dog, kneeling to pray. By then, though, we had reached such a point in our marriage, and with our family, that I despised such images for what he had made me see, through his actions, was their false, cloying sweetness. Our children avoided both of us and were devoted to each other—they were never two cute youngsters down at the soda shop having a treat. As hard as I tried, it was almost impossible to say where they were, because they would go off on their bikes the minute they got home from school. Before they were old enough to do that, they'd hidden in the house or played games in the vacant lot behind our yard. I was so preoccupied with Frank's infidelity—I would have left him, if only I hadn't had children—but at the same time, I hated myself and I blamed myself for his faithlessness. It became a vicious circle: he would not sleep with me because I'd been drinking, but I was so upset he preferred other women that by late afternoon I would wonder when he was coming home and begin to drink. Our marriage was a sham. I found out he was sleeping with many women, not just the nurse, so I decided I would no longer go through the motions of pretending to be the doctor's devoted wife. Let him create his own lovely home. Let him have his own Christmas parties, if that was what he thought necessary to keep up appearances. Let him shop for the children himself, if he found time to have affairs whenever he wanted. Let him plan their birthday parties. Let him cook his own breakfast. Theirs, too. Let them see that a problem was a problem, without their mother rushing in to fix it. In the long run, that would stand them in good stead. What good had it ever done me to have my mother pretend my entire childhood was nothing but a pleasant waiting period until the day when I'd walk down the aisle.

My parents—my mother, particularly—did everything she could to make sure I married well. That, I think, is because when I was gone, she wanted to feel no more responsibility toward me. Marrying well—what did that mean? To her, it had to do, entirely, with whether or not the man could earn a good living. Obviously, she did not think that she had married well. Her parents had to come to their rescue any number of times. My father was a salesman, and worked hard, but his life was filled with disappointments. All day long, doors were shut in his face, and then he would come home to find my mother's door shut. I thought I would never behave that way, but what recourse does a woman have? To scream like a shrew, to let everyone know her shame? Like my mother, I retreated into silence—which, I came to see, allowed you to retain a certain amount of power.

I pride myself on not being the bitter woman I might have become. I learned in childhood to create my own world and to dwell there peaceably. All children do that, but my world didn't close down when my crayon stopped coloring, or when the time came that I had to stop singing my cheerful little song. My mother, who cared so much about appearances, was only too happy to decorate my bedroom with lace curtains and a pink rug in the shape of a giant strawberry. There was even a violet plant—a real, dark purple violet, that she alone was allowed to water. When there were things she wanted me to have that they could not afford, she went to my grandmother. I had the softest deep pink blanket. I wonder, now, if it might have been cashmere. It was laid across the bottom of the bed. My mother folded it so meticulously, with the corners tucked under. I shivered some nights rather than undo it and have her berate me for not refolding it perfectly in the morning. When anyone visited, she would insist on showing them through the house, and my room was always the culmination of the tour. My best dolls were kept on shelves low enough that I could reach them, but because they were my least favorite dolls, I rarely took them down. There was also my mother's butterfly collection, which she passed on to me. Year after year, on my birthday, I would feign surprise and delight. The butterflies were hung higher than the dolls' shelf, because touching their frames, even if you were very gentle, might shake the butterflies from their mounts. There was a yellow-and-black butterfly, and a small white butterfly flecked with different colors, which I liked more than the others, though that one was the hardest to see because it was hardly bigger than a grain moth. My books were on a bookshelf my father had built when he was a boy, working with his grandfather. He was upset when my mother painted it pink to coordinate with the room because he felt it was wrong to paint over wood that was inherently beautiful. But the room was my mother's creation, and nothing could stop her.

At first, when I was a child, I liked the things she bought, but when I grew older I sensed there was an edge to it—that some drama was being played out in my bedroom that I didn't understand. I tried to get her to stop. That was impossible. She continued to look through magazines, make lists of needed things, insist that she and I browse, even though we did not have the money to actually purchase things. Finally, I withdrew from her frantic pursuit of more and more things. I wouldn't go to the stores with her; if she liked something in a catalogue or magazine, I said that I did not. When she bought the things anyway, I realized it was best to take a different attitude. I began to tell her I wanted things I didn't want, just to see if she would get them. I soon learned that asking for a fish in a bowl was futile—not that I'd wanted a fish, or any pet; pets are dirty and require too much care—I just felt the need to test her. If I asked for rosettes to tie back the curtains, though, or for an elegant little clock carved from ivory, or any number of other small frivolities, she was actually pleased I'd thought of them. I knew that the room was very important to my mother—it seemed more important to her than I seemed, and certainly more important than my father—though I really couldn't have told anyone, even if I'd had friends back then, why she took such an interest in it, and why I found that so torturous. She could have fixed her own room differently—put some nice things in there—but she never did. My parents' room contained twin beds with pale yellow bedspreads that were hand-me-downs from her mother, not patterned with flowers or pretty in any way, and two chests of drawers with peeling veneer. There was a large wardrobe in the corner. Except for a torchère and a table lamp my father had made from an old blowtorch on the night table, that was all the room contained. Nothing hung on the walls. There was a water stain on the wall by the windows, where rain had leaked through the roof. There were shades at the windows, but no curtains. It was a utilitarian room. Not even a rug on the floor. You would think, then, that my mother was living out her fantasies through my highly decorated bedroom, but the truth was—and it took me years to understand this—she did not like my bedroom any better than I did. She pretended to think it was unique and gorgeous, but in fact, it upset her. It was as if she'd created a monster that lived and breathed, whose four walls and ceiling and floor demanded her vigilance. She was always there, dusting and sweeping and polishing and fluffing pillows, turning the violet so it wouldn't grow lopsided, leaning toward the sun. The more she brought into the room, the more she tended it, the more she complained about how difficult it was to be conscientious about indulging a child without spoiling her. She would say to friends who admired the room that it was not easy to raise a daughter who had such high expectations. I didn't have high expectations. I thought the room was embarrassing. The froufrou things that proliferated, the crystal fan pulls and beaded lampshades, seemed to me so ridiculous, though so obviously representative of her taste that I couldn't resist letting her create her garish world.

When I was in the room with my door closed, I usually sat on the floor and played with my rag doll, Molly. Though my mother knew she existed, I kept her under the bed, the way a dog hides a favorite toy. When cleaning, my mother would take Molly out and put her on the windowsill, or on my dresser. For whatever reason, she would never put her back in her place under the bed. She never propped her up, but made her lie flat. I suppose she thought that if I was going to have such an ugly thing, no one should mistake it for something worthy of display. I would talk to Molly about how silly the room was—what I was really saying was how unhappy and pointless my life was—reassuring her that when I grew up, I was going to have a room with blue walls—blue was both Molly's and my favorite color. In that room, I planned to place her in the center of the bed, with her head resting on a pillow.

By the time I was a teenager, I no longer wanted blue walls, and one day I took the violet plant, which had grown leggy in spite of my mother's good care, and put it on the kitchen counter, without comment. At my insistence, my childhood books had been put in boxes, and I had asked my father to carry the bookcase outside so I could strip the paint off—I had done it with his blessing.

The butterflies were hung so high I rarely looked up, so I let them hang there. I put the blanket on a shelf in the closet, cramming it in. All this was done without consulting her, but she never carried the plant back to the room, or asked where the blanket was. She gave no reaction at all, until she saw me removing the paint in the backyard. She got it then, I think. Before that, she might have pretended to herself that I wanted the violet to get better sunlight, or that because it was spring, I no longer needed the blanket. And then when she saw me taking the paint off the furniture, she knew that until that time, I'd only been having a laugh at her expense, with all my requests for so-called beautiful things; that I'd only pretended to care about the things she cared about. I looked up and saw her at the kitchen window, and I felt triumphant. Without ever having to say anything, I let her know exactly how much I resented her.

And then one day I realized my doll was gone. For months, I'd rarely taken her out from her hiding place, but then for some reason I wanted her and when I reached under the bed, there was no Molly. "You don't play with dolls anymore. You're an adult now," she said. As she spoke, I saw that her eyes held the same resentment they'd revealed that day she saw me stripping furniture. She had thrown Molly in the trash. Fortunately, though, the trash had not been collected.

Furious, I went into the garage and rooted through until I found Molly underneath newspapers and opened cans, food stains smeared across her chest. I was delighted I'd found her, but so angry that I flung her at my mother. I threw her hard, and Molly hit the wall behind my mother's shoulder. She acted as if I'd hit her, as if I'd thrown a rock, rather than a doll. She cried hysterically, claiming that she'd always known I never loved her. She ran from the garage and didn't return to the house for what seemed like hours, during which time I apologized to Molly over and over, giving her a bath in the sink and drying her with more towels than were necessary, cuddling her, her dampness as horrible to me as blood seeping from a wound.

Ask yourself: What sort of mother throws away her child's beloved doll?

Ask: Should I have confiscated my son's naughty magazines, or did he deserve some privacy—some respect for his secret passions?

Ask: Was it wrong to throw out my daughter's ice skates, because deep inside I knew she must have stolen them?

What, exactly, determines whether it is fair to rush in and assert one's will, regardless of consequences?

My mother's retaliation took years, but she finally retaliated in a baroque way by finding the person she intended me to marry, knowing that that person would cause me unhappiness. She knew she had no power over me; I had become Daddy's girl, and like him, I was headstrong, so she couldn't have thought that I'd agree to an arranged marriage. Not many people would. But she was desperate to get me out of the house, as time eventually proved. So she gave me mixed signals: she introduced me to Frank, but she pretended not to be too taken with him, though he, himself, told me later that his mother and my mother had decided we were meant for each other. Just like the Queen Mother and Diana Spencer's grandmother! The old crones having their coffee klatch, planning ruin for everyone. Oh—we were hardly royalty. His mother was worried that Frank had never developed the right social graces. That he was blunt to a fault, with no idea of how to persuade rather than bully. She had tried to instruct him, but he had always had what she called "a hard edge"; rejecting the idea of having a childhood, he had spent his adolescence studying. He had started preparing for his career when he was still a child, playing with a toy stethoscope, taking his friends' temperatures with a twig thermometer, studying anatomical drawings long before he could pronounce the words.

Frank's father had been a dentist who died of a heart attack in Atlantic City, the week Frank turned seven. Everyone thought he was riding a wave when he bent suddenly and went down. When the wave passed, he was still floating. Frank had been playing in the ocean with his father, clutching his hand only a minute before. The waves began to roll in faster, and Frank became afraid. He couldn't swim, and the game his father was playing scared him. He stumbled in the undertow. He urged his father to stop. He stood where his father floated, seizing his shoulder, screaming and attracting a crowd when his father would not respond. My mother said that so many times, people never recovered from such tragic incidents, and wondered aloud whether Frank would ever be a happy man. His intelligence, his scholarship, his earning money were to his credit, as was—she said point-edly—his devotion to his mother. But my mother sensed the rage beneath his steady, hardworking resolve. There was also something else she couldn't put her finger on. Something about the way he kept his distance, when after all, wasn't he studying to go out among the people and be a doctor? She said these things to me indirectly, talking to my father in the front seat of the car, as we drove away from their friend's house, her mission accomplished. She had known Frank's mother for several years, but during that time Frank had been away at medical school; it was the first time my parents had met him. Of course she knew I was listening, in the backseat. She knew I never did what she wanted, so she was using reverse psychology in announcing her reservations about Frank. Or perhaps she believed what she said, but felt a last-minute desire not to throw me to the wolves. She was torn, and her desire to have me marry a doctor won out. A doctor was above judgment: her daughter would do well to marry a doctor. Any reservations anyone had, her own included, were just talk. In fact, if that doctor was not an easy person, so much the better, because neither was her daughter. I had sensed, myself, that his cordial manner masked his desire to keep his distance, but to a young girl, that had seemed intriguing. When he asked if he could call me before he returned to school, I said yes. He was handsome, and I liked the idea of being romantically involved with a man I knew my mother had mixed feelings about. My mother cared, above all else, how things looked. It mattered so much to her that people approve of her daughter marrying an accom-plished man; it was just a continuation of her need to have viewers look into the frilly pastel bedroom of her child and verify that her daughter was truly a princess.

I let my children make of their rooms whatever they wanted. Neither really seemed to express anything about their personality in their rooms, though. If Nina had ever wanted a more girlish room, she never said so. And Andrew was oblivious to his surroundings. He had his toy box when he was young—as Nina had her box of dolls—but neither ever fixated on toys, the way so many of the other children seemed to. They were never the sort who asked for every new thing, and even if they had they quickly found out that pleading, in our house, got you nowhere. They didn't care as much about toys as they cared about the games they played with each other, really. Until they got too old for it, Nina crept into Andrew's bed almost every night. Frank absolutely would not have the children in our bed. Soon after Nina's birth, we had separate bedrooms, anyway—but the minute she could toddle, Nina would head for Andrew's room. Scared of the dark, like most other children. I didn't mind that she did it—I was such a light sleeper; once awakened, I was awake half the night, so better she crawl in bed with her brother than with me—but when Andrew started kindergarten, I thought it best to make her sleep the night in her own room. I removed her from his bed the first few nights. I never had the right touch with Nina: I always woke her, and she always cried. It took Frank's going in and overreacting—he could be relied upon to do that; he had no tact, whatsoever—to end it. Poor Nina, being lectured with words she didn't even understand, in the middle of the night. Poor Andrew, too, who always got caught in the middle.

He was my favorite. I think he might have been afraid of the dark, too, but he would never want his mother to know that. By the time Nina started school, I would sometimes find him in her bed. He was so sensitive, he intuited that she needed him. I said nothing to Frank, because there would have been another awful scene. I pretended not to know, and let him creep around and do whatever he wanted. That made their bond indelible, I now see. They were together day and night. No sibling rivalry at all. Most parents I knew would have given thanks for harmony among their children—and I did give thanks, though I'll admit I felt more than a twinge of jealousy. Neither ever depended on me. It was as if I was just another presence in the house, and they learned young to make an end run around me, as well as Frank. If I'd left him and taken the children, would they have gradually warmed to me? As it was, they both stood in judgment of me, knowing that by staying with their father, I was letting them down.

But maybe that's not true. Maybe that's my own guilt speaking. They were polite, but I always sensed it was the same form of condescension I had toward my mother. You want children who are polite, but when their emotion runs no deeper . . . ? How are you supposed to really *be* the mother, when they prefer to take care of themselves?

My own mother left my father the year I married. All along, she had been in love with the butcher. She had waited and waited. Waited for the moment she thought proper. I rarely saw her after she remarried. They moved to Ohio, and my father moved, too—to Albuquerque, where his half brother lived. All those years I'd thought I was Daddy's girl, I had no idea his affection for me could simply come to an end. After their divorce, he sometimes sent me a card on my birthday, and on Christmas he might send some coffee-table book, but for all intents and purposes, I ceased to exist for him when his wife did.

What did their bedroom look like, in the apartment my mother lived in with the butcher?

What plant did she tend in her new life? Or did she let her plants become tall and leggy, always facing the sun?

To have parents who move away from you, physically and emotionally, makes for an odd situation. People ask you how they are, and you wonder, yourself, how are they? As a parent, you can explain, almost with pride, that your children have moved out of your orbit; people will nod knowingly, but when parents have lost touch with you, their adult child . . . people squint, as if they're watching an eclipse.

Not that very many people asked. One time early in my marriage Frank and I planned a trip to visit my father, but he wrote back, saying it wouldn't be convenient. Frank thought it strange, but instead of blaming my father, he wanted to know what part I had played in causing such a rift. That was Frank: always adding punishment to punishment.

Nina has some of his tendencies. Andrew is sociable and outgoing, but Nina is convoluted, like her father. I think that making only one attempt at a relationship has been a form of punishing herself. I understand that Nina loved Mac, but what can be assumed about a young woman cutting herself off from life so drastically? Like suicide, it was an act that also hurt everyone else. It hurts Andrew to this day, though he refuses to admit that. It hurts *me*, but then, when would Nina mind that? Her narrow life is a reproach of me, for being so deficient, so lacking in courage. She thinks I should have left Frank. Though naturally the idea of choosing is enticing to her—she, whom fate did not allow to choose.

There is something about me she deeply dislikes, but I've never been sure what that is. The drinking, the drinking, the drinking. I know that's part of it. Numbing oneself is not conducive to good mothering. She probably thinks I should appreciate her for her outspokenness, for being the one who had the courage to ask me to stop.

Helen Fox was the only person outside the family who had the nerve to approach me about it. If you can believe it, she thought that her having had a child outside of marriage was much the same as my then-current state of drinking too much! Any sin women committed, in those days, got jumbled together with greater or lesser sins. We were all supposed to be pert and perky Doris Days. Our hair was never supposed to be windblown; our lipstick was supposed to brighten our lips even at bedtime—though it must never smear the white pillowcase. We were to go to church—try getting Frank to church!—and spend our spare time making our washes whiter and our brownies a yummy chocolate brown. Domestic perfection would save the world. And of course a girl *always* got married before she even thought of having a baby.

Helen had been sent to a home for unwed mothers. All the time she was there, they worked on her to agree to give the baby away. That was what was thought best. It was such an American notion: make a mistake, invent a new identity, go on from there. Lucky for Helen, she had a strong will, and even trickery could not make her sign her baby away. Luckier still, the janitor—the janitor!—took a fancy to her, and not a month out of the home for unwed mothers, he tracked her down, going to considerable trouble to do so. It really was so romantic. He proposed marriage. She left her parents' house that day with the baby and never looked back. Or at least that was the way she told the story. In any case, Mr. Fox became devoted to her, even wanting to give her daughter his name, though some sort of perverse pride prevented her: Helen liked it when people asked about her daughter's surname; she was eager to tell her story to anyone who asked.

I first heard her story in the corridor of the high school, during a parent-teacher conference. I had never been to a conference before. Of course, Frank did not accompany me, because at the last minute his lover—that fat, oversexed nurse—called and pretended there was a patient emergency. He had her do that regularly: call and lie. But that one time I did go, and Helen and I struck up a conversation. We started by discussing the advantages our children had that we had had to do without. "More awareness," Helen said, opening the way for our discussion. I felt sorry for her. Her husband was right there, and she was telling me, as if she saw the absurdity of it herself, that the janitor in a home for unwed mothers had fallen in love with her, and there they were, this many years later, with Patty and three other children, and she pursuing a career as a florist, and her husband in a white-collar job at the hospital. She and I agreed that "awareness," as she euphemistically put it, was good. She told me that her daughter had eating problems and was very shy, even though she and her husband loved her and had provided a good home. "You think it may be God, visiting a curse on those you love, which can be even more painful than putting the curse on you," she said. I took note of her mention of God. I was not an atheist like Frank, but still: I was wary of people who talked outside of church about God.

I ran into her a second time at the liquor store. She was there buying a bottle of wine—nothing I ever developed a taste for—and a package of cigarettes. Outside, she offered me a Lucky Strike. We sat in the front seat of her car and smoked and talked. She told me that she gave thanks every day that her life had been saved. What she meant was that had she lost her daughter, she would have died. She had such depth of feeling for her husband and for her children. I felt uncomfortable; I cared for my children—by then, I did not care much for Frank, because I had lost almost all respect for him—but my children were not people I would speak in hushed tones to someone about, as if they were somehow sacred. Truth be told, they seemed like two other adults who lived in our house. I had to remind myself that they were children, they were so self-sufficient, and they kept their lives so private.

What Helen thought, though I did not find this out until another day, was that my son and her daughter would make a perfect couple. I laughed and told her about my mother's machinations, implying that things had not worked out well. She seemed to understand what I was saying, and let go of the idea. I was surprised, though, how well she seemed to know Andrew. It was because she had gone to some of the sports events, and to Parents' Day, which I always overlooked because Frank never went. I was amused that she had her eye on Andrew. I knew my son could take care of himself.

Andrew never in his life did anything other than what he was inclined to, with the exception of things said or done to placate Frank. I liked Helen Fox. She was a modest woman. Not self-centered. She wore her hair in a ponytail, and her fingernails were clean but unpolished. Her wedding ring was her only piece of jewelry.

When she had a drink with me at the house a month or so later—when I invited her over, after an unexpected phone call she made to me—she was a different woman. It seemed her doctor had recommended that Patty be sent away. It was Helen's worst fear, really; after having been so traumatized all those years ago, fearing she might not be able to keep Patty, Patty had developed a problem and was going to be wrenched away from her, after all. In those days, anorexia was not a word you heard. I doubt whether doctors even thought it was a disease. She did not use the word with me. She described Patty's wasting away. Her low energy. Patty's hair had begun to fall out. What was it? she asked me fearfully, though her doctor had already told her it was a nervous disease.

We sat in the kitchen, drinking coffee. Isn't it funny: I can remember the salt and pepper shakers—plastic ears of corn—and the little can of condensed milk on the table near the sugar bowl. Frank would allow sugar in the house, but no butter. If I'd wanted to offer her a bit of buttered pastry, I couldn't have.

Buttered pastry. Who am I kidding? If there was bread in the house, it would have been moldy.

"She'll be fine," I remember telling Helen Fox. "If the doctor thinks it's best to send her to a hospital—"

"No. Not a hospital. He wants her to go away for the entire summer. The minute she gets out of school. He's sending her to some camp a hundred miles away!"

Camp? It was the most peculiar thing. Someone who was ill, going to camp? But that must mean she was not terribly sick, after all. I said that to Helen Fox. She was so distracted, she wasn't listening. She wanted to discuss Patty's problem with Frank, it turned out. She did not want to offend their doctor, but she wanted a second opinion.

I assured her that she could and should speak to Frank. But the woman had no self-confidence, at all. She wanted her husband to speak to him, so she wouldn't misunderstand whatever he might say. All right, I told her; that could just as easily be arranged. Naturally I felt I could ask him to offer advice about our children's schoolmate's problem.

The meeting took place at Frank's office. Joe Fox went alone, and apparently left the meeting less heavyhearted than he'd been. Frank gave me only a quick description of the meeting, assuring me that what Patty had was treatable, agreeing with his colleague that the special camp might help to turn things around. He said it was run by a doctor whose daughter had the same problem as Patty.

And then I forgot about the Foxes. Life intervened. In spite of my children's dismissal of me as an inadequate mother, I kept the house clean. Months passed, and summer vacation began, and had I thought of her at all, I would have remembered that Patty had gone to camp. I was in school, myself, taking a course in nursing. I was surprised when Helen Fox called and said she had to see me immediately. My first thought was that Patty had died. Why else would she be calling in such a hushed voice? Why else would Helen be choking back tears? I asked her over immediately. My children would have it that no one ever entered our house, but Helen came to the house many times. Though she didn't accept my invitation, that time. She asked me to come to her house. I was busy—I would have preferred otherwise, but she sounded so distraught that I agreed. Braced with a drink of whiskey—with only *one* drink of whiskey—I drove to the Foxes' house.

We sat on cushions placed inside the bay windows. She had made no effort to clean up. Plates and food containers, cans and dirty napkins, were everywhere. She held the baby, who was suffering from a cold. She bounced him nervously, wiping away tears with her elbow. "What can be so bad?" I said. "Tell me what can be so bad."

"I'm so afraid you'll never speak to me again," she said.

"Tell me and let's find out," I said.

"There's no way to say it but to say it," she said. The baby twisted in her arms; her eyes were bright with tears. "He sent a bill we can't possibly pay," she said.

I was thinking so slowly, I asked who she was talking about.

"The doctor," she said. "Your husband."

Frank had sent my friend a bill? I had not really thought of Helen Fox as my friend until that moment. An acquaintance, yes—but really, she *was* a friend. I was embarrassed, since Frank knew their circumstances, that he had billed them. But perhaps I did not know how these things went. I could hear Frank, dripping with sarcasm, saying just that to me: that I knew nothing about how the world operated.

"I'll speak to him," I said. Somehow, I sensed that Helen was not just upset about the bill.

"Joe phoned him, and he was quite abusive," she said. "And then Joe and I had a big fight, because . . . well: because the meeting had been my idea."

"There's been a misunderstanding," I said. "I'll speak to him tonight."

"And then he called me," she said. "I know you're never going to like me again, but I like you, so I'm going to say something I never believed I could say."

"Frank called you?" I said.

She nodded yes.

"What did he say?"

"He made it clear that if he and I got together, there would be no question of any bill."

It was stunning news. The minute she said it, I knew she was telling the truth. I had no idea he would stoop so low. Really, I found him as contemptible as she did, but I was so humiliated, I couldn't speak.

"Joe will find a way to pay the bill," she said. She was almost whispering. "But I thought you should know," she finished.

The baby had remained quiet until the discussion was over. Then, immediately, he began to wail. She stood quickly, jiggling him against her chest, and almost ran from the room.

She never returned. Of course she was only upstairs, too miserable to come down, but I could not make myself walk up the steps to comfort her. What little anger I felt toward her was irrational, I knew. For a few seconds I indulged myself, but I was not able to convince myself that she shared the blame.

She had done one thing to prepare for my visit: there was coffee percolating—the smell attracted me, bringing me out of my reverie—so I went to her cupboard and took down a teacup and saucer. I poured a cup, imagining myself pouring two, carrying one upstairs. I knew she took milk in her coffee. Milk only, no sugar. I took both, but the effort seemed too great. I sat there with my cup of black coffee, drinking liquid that tasted as bitter as I felt. She was upstairs. It was my obligation—it was what any decent person would have done—to go up to her.

I sat at the table. If Helen Fox, who else? Anyone and everyone?

Eventually I made myself go home. It was almost three, and I did not want to encounter her children, returning from school. Neither did I want to see my own children, because they were all that anchored me to—as Helen called him— "the doctor."

He could not really have desired her. He had only done it to disgrace me.

I drove home shakily. In the driveway, I turned on the car radio. I had driven in silence all the way home, but I felt that I could not get out of the car without hearing some music. Anything would have done: the news, as well as a song. A song was being sung, but I could not concentrate on the lyrics. It just added chaos to my thoughts. I turned off the ignition and went inside, and there was Andrew, sitting at the kitchen table. It was five minutes after three.

"What are you doing back so early?" I said.

"I got sent home. I have a fever," he said.

I felt his head. "I'm calling the doctor," I said. Andrew's pediatrician was Frank's colleague, Davis Strumm. Instead, I dialed Frank's number. I handed the phone to Andrew. "I've called your father," I said. "Tell his nurse what you just told me." He tried to give me the phone back. Why did he always hesitate? I looked at his outstretched hand. His head had been burning. "Andrew is sick!" I screamed from where I stood behind him, so loud that Frank's nurse, Frank's whore, must certainly have heard me. Andrew pushed back the chair, clambering to get away. The phone fell to the floor. I picked up the receiver: "You tell Frank to come right home, that his son is ill," I said. My voice was trembling so much I could hardly get the words out. I hung up on her. I went to the cupboard and took out the scotch and drank straight from the bottle. "What are you doing? Mom? What are you doing?" Andrew said. He had returned to the doorway. I had made him cry. I began to cry, seeing how much I had upset him. "Stop it, Mom, stop it," he said. "What are you *doing?*"

Did she fail to give him the message? Or was he not there—had there been some emergency at the hospital? More likely, he was also two-timing her. Frank came home at the usual time, and pretended to be shocked when he found Andrew with a washcloth on his head, almost delirious on the living room couch. He thought what Andrew was saying to him—because sick as he was, Andrew immediately began apologizing for my hysteria—was delusional. But I told him. I told him why I'd gotten drunk in the first place. Frank and I had a bitter, bitter exchange. And where was Nina? Nina, who was always mutely off in some corner, watching. For once she was not welded to Andrew's side, but had gone off with a girlfriend. Some mother I had never heard of called to say that she had taken her daughter and mine ice-skating.

He didn't even try to tell me that Helen Fox had misunderstood. That night, in my room, he begged forgiveness. He said he had always been attracted to loose women. Wasn't that just perfect? He didn't even realize how insulting such a confession was. I felt I must defend Helen. I was angry that not only had Frank propositioned her, but that he had misunderstood who she was. I couldn't have known, that night, that Andrew was going to become so smitten with Patty. To tell the truth, while I knew Helen Fox had done a fine job raising her children, and while Andrew knew better than to do anything that could get him in trouble, with Patty or with any other girl, I was not comfortable with the idea of his seeing so much of Helen's daughter. Looking back, I see I was just plain jealous, because after the incident, I was too embarrassed to continue my friendship with Helen. When my son began to spend more and more time at their house, it put me on the spot. It was as though my friendship with Helen was continuing vicariously, through the children. I should have screwed up my courage and called Helen. I'm sure her standoffishness was just embarrassment over having to tell me about Frank. But instead, I let Andrew be my ambassador: my little gentleman, courting her nice daughter. Nina, I think, was quite thrown by Andrew's defection. Finally, their age difference did begin to result in their going their separate ways. But she would not discuss it with me. She would not discuss it with anyone, apparently, following Andrew's lead, because being the shy and private boy he was, Andrew wanted to keep his infatuation secret. Ashamed to be smitten, like any other young man. So much for Frank's ideas about our homosexual son.

Wouldn't it just figure that Frank would think a man with any sensitivity was homosexual. But for a moment, when he first said that to me, he did manage to plant the seed of doubt. People didn't even speak of such things as a distressing possibility back then. People—leaving aside Frank—said nothing at all.

Oh, he had sex with Patty, I suppose. In all that time, he must have. Helen knew it, too. Eventually we ran into each other in the grocery store, and she could hardly look at me, and I could hardly look at her. We were as inept as adolescents. I still have no idea what she thought she had to feel embarrassed about, since my son was the one who had gone courting. Girls had no ability to attract boys in those days. They do now, but they didn't, then. A boy either took to you, or he didn't. Here I thought she was going to be Nina's friend, but Nina never did make friends easily. She was probably glad Andrew lifted the burden. In the grocery store, Helen grabbed the bar of her shopping cart tightly. There was that baby, with its perpetual cold, sitting in the seat, the baby just as still as his mother. To avoid a discussion, I talked to the baby for a few seconds. I patted his soft hair. Helen blurted out that history was not going to repeat itself. She said that I had nothing to fear. It was the strangest conversation, if you could even call it that. I remember that a can toppled from a shelf and that she nearly jumped out of her skin. I suppose I might have taken offense at what she was implying about my son, but after all, I knew what she was alluding to. It was good Patty knew what to do. Frank had assured me that he had spoken to Andrew when he was five years old, and six years old, and on every birthday thereafter until Andrew finally asked him to please stop, because he had gotten the message long ago. So if both of them were using protection, so much the better. But there I stood with Helen, who used to be my friend, half-embarrassed and half-grateful that at least she felt she could speak honestly with me. I was not such a prudish person. I heard her out and then she simply started past me with her cart. I had to say something, but I couldn't think what. She looked at the floor for a few seconds, no doubt hoping the baby would make a fuss. The baby was just sitting there, watching—another version of Nina. It was so unnerving. The whole setting, the unexpectedness of it, her strangeness made for one of those awkward moments, but I had no idea how awkward, until she spoke. She said: "Have you been drinking? I know you drink." What was she talking about? I had not even had a cup of coffee yet that day. I thought to myself: Who is *she*, to say such a thing? In that moment, I saw her through Frank's eyes. "*You* should talk!" I said. Her hair was disheveled; she was wearing high heels, in the grocery store. She was the one who thought it was perfectly all right for two teenagers to have sex. She wasn't just looking the other way, she was condoning it. I made my voice low—though my inclination was otherwise, I had not been drinking and I was quite aware that we were in a public place—and I warned her to stay away from my husband. None of it was what I wanted to say. I wanted to ask her to come to my house for coffee. I wanted to ask her if she thought that what was happening between Andrew and

Patty was really love, and if so, whether we shouldn't be happy. I wanted to give her a hug and ask her to put the past behind us, but what she had said insulted me. Then she was hurrying away—running in her cheap high heels, pushing the cart with her sniveling baby sitting inside. When we crossed paths after that, we both pretended not to see each other. I gave myself credit for not involving Andrew in the problem. That encounter stayed a private matter.

I am a person entirely able to keep a confidence. That is not a thing you will find often in this world. It's rare to meet a person who does not eventually, if not immediately, share a secret with at least one other. Being a reliable person is a real virtue. If anything Helen Fox had told me had been said in confidence, it would have stayed with me, alone. I always felt that she did want to say something. That she and I were kindred spirits, which made her nasty, inaccurate judgment of me even harder to take—though who can account for the things people come up with when they feel the need to justify their own actions? Oftentimes, people tell you a secret because they wish you would repeat it.

I think Frank confessed his transgressions so he could be more at peace with himself. I never went to the children, saying, Oh, is it true he did thus and such? People need to take care of things among themselves, and if you rush to intervene, you are usually the one who catches the flak, while the people at each other's throats kiss and make up. I think the children became stronger and learned strategies to adjust to Frank's mood swings better because I neither condoned his actions nor pretended they didn't happen. Those times either of the children did report some unkindness of Frank's—it happened when they were quite young, more with Andrew than with Nina—I would explain that they must find a way to work out the problem directly with their father. You wouldn't have so many people suing each other today if that notion had been instilled in them as children. Andrew and his father did work things out. The truth is, they just had very different personalities. And while I would never speak directly against Frank— well, they knew about the other women; sometimes that was just too much for me to bear—I let him know Frank's lack of loyalty hurt me, though I tried to explain to Andrew that his father was not a simple man, and that there were more complexities—more good qualities—than were apparent. There were those letters he wrote me—I think Andrew was pleased to learn that his father had such a romantic streak. Without them, I would not have had much evidence of his affection, because Frank was not one to be publicly demonstrative. It was a different time then, of course. Physical passion was not enacted by decent people outside the bedroom. Then Elvis Presley arrived on the scene, with his sexual pantomime, to open the bedroom door forever. Pretty soon musicians were mimicking sex acts with their guitars and the climax of their songs became a crescendo of destruction.

I might have tried harder with Nina, though something in her eyes told me she wasn't likely to be persuaded. She didn't like Frank—such a sad situation for both of them—and certainly she didn't need her father the way she might have, had Andrew not taken his place. But then you consider Nina as an adult: she went right out and married a doctor, herself. There's Dr. Freud: noticing how people unconsciously repeat the past. Except that of course she thought she was improving on the past: she intended her marriage to be perfect. What would have happened if Mac had lived? He was a nice enough man. A little remote. Not much of a sense of humor.

The time the two of them came calling—the time Andrew and Mac came to take me to lunch—could have been such a happy occasion, if only she'd joined them. But of course she didn't know; they were doing it behind her back, so how could she have come? Mac had some idea about reconciling me with Nina. Frank had died the year before, and for years—for all her childhood, as well as when she was an adult—Nina had been lost to me. Some mothers might have been angry with their son for taking their daughter away from them, but I wasn't that irrational. She had attached herself to him like glue, not vice versa. So there he was, unglued—a little pun! It's always good luck to make an unintentional pun—there he was, looking so sheepish, with Nina's husband-to-be at his side, and Mac with a bunch of flowers. A gesture Frank never made, but it was such a conventional gesture; I'd hoped Nina's intended would be a little more original. My mother used to say: *Never look a gift horse in the mouth*, but really: a bunch of chrysanthemums? I was sure that the bride's nosegay would be filled with dainty roses and baby's breath, but there I stood, receiving my spidery chrysanthemums from Mac. Their smell was downright unpleasant; no way to sniff them and truly offer thanks, so I just took them. But do you know, he wanted me to put them in water immediately. He was so proud of his flowers. As proud as a child bringing home his drawings—which at least Andrew did. Before he started impressing his sister by casually discarding them.

Mac asked for a vase and for room-temperature water.
Room temperature! He wanted the water to be as neutral as his
flowers! He even asked for scissors to cut the stems. I looked at
Andrew, to see what he made of it, but he was as good as his
sister at not showing any reaction. I suppose I showed my irri-
tation, my disappointment, too clearly. Like his father, Andrew
would never acknowledge certain of my feelings. He acknowl-
edged them those times he thought them appropriate, but dismissed them, otherwise. What was I supposed to do? Dovetail
my feelings to theirs? Yes. That was what I was supposed to do,
because I was secondary. They were both of supreme impor-
tance to themselves, and I was silly and temperamental: worse
than that, they would claim I was a drunken woman, which
meant that I was a person who wouldn't conform well enough
to what they wanted. Well: as a mature woman, and one who
had had not one sip of alcohol prior to their arrival, I wasn't
going to ooh and aah about cheap flowers. Those chrysanthemums were silly, not me. People take such pride in the mag-
nificence of their gesture, though even when the gesture is the
right one, it's so often made by the wrong person. If Frank had
courted me with flowers, that might have been nice, but when
it was my future son-in-law, it was clear that he thought I was
some old lady who'd be easy to impress.

What did he have that should be so impressive? I wasn't
much impressed that he was going to be a doctor, that was for
sure. Did he count on winning me over because he was tall
and nice-looking? I'd found out by then—as everyone eventually does—how little appearances matter. Did he think I'd
be impressed that he might be willing to hear my side of the
story?

As it was, he didn't hear it. It was chitchat, chitchat. He sat there assessing me. In that, he was like his bride-to-be. *Like a buzzard on a branch*, Frank used to say about her, unkindly, and I'd say: *They're just little piggies, rooting around in the mud.* What I meant was that when they misbehaved, they were just doing what they were programmed to do. The genes explain so much of it. Nina was programmed to be shy. Andrew was also shy, but shyness in men is called charming, and as he matured, he became more self-assured. You always sensed the conflict going on inside Nina's head: should I; shouldn't I. It was difficult to know what she really wanted. I don't know if *she* knew, half the time. She knew she wanted to marry Mac—that she was definite about. And, as I might have expected, she did not want a big wedding. Who would she have invited? And there was to be no white bridal dress. She did everything she could to make the occasion as joyless as possible. She did not even consult her mother about her wedding. It wasn't just Frank; she disliked me every bit as much. She looked down on me—her own mother—as if I was extraneous. She might have suggested the chrysanthemums to Mac. Why not? Why not have him bring extraneous flowers? I remember trying to talk to her. Unlike Andrew, when I tried to remind her of pleasant things that had happened during her childhood, she would look at me as if I was crazy. Who can believe that a child hated every moment of her upbringing? Even Dickens's orphans didn't have that bleak a life. Every day contains so many small, happy moments. Even when I dwelled in my mother's fussy dollhouse of a bedroom, I had my rag doll under the bed, and I loved her.

Though I suppose that what Nina had was Andrew. More sibling rivalry might have given Nina some instruction about how better to get along in a complicated world, but she was no feminist, my daughter: she went from Andrew to Mac. They even looked alike.

Mac and Nina at their wedding, their expressions so radiant, as the cliche goes. They thought they would be together, always.

Andrew, intent upon finding someone to sleep with that night. You think I have a dirty mind? That the mother of the bride should notice only the loveliness of her daughter's wedding day? Nina later said I embarrassed the family with my drinking—a few celebratory glasses of champagne! It was Andrew-on-the-prowl, not me, who took the whole ceremony down a notch. Nina was his Molly, I think.

She hardly ever contacted me after the wedding. The one time I saw their house was after the reception. The reception was held in some restaurant in the suburbs, but afterward a chosen few returned to Nina and Mac's house. Wasn't I lucky, to be selected? Maybe I wouldn't have been, except that Andrew—tipsy as he was; I wasn't the only one drinking—was always so attuned to my feelings. He was the one who extended the invitation. Such a small place. Their living room reminded me of my own childhood room, the way my room became empty and purely functional, after I'd rejected my mother's clutter. It made me nostalgic. No—it made me sad. I went outside to get a breath of air. I was thinking of Molly, discarded by my insensitive mother. I only stopped being teary when I remembered that after all, there had been a good outcome: I had rescued her. But then what had happened? She had been in my hands, and then somewhere I had lost her. That was when Mary Catherine came down the path that separated Mac and Nina's house from her own. She registered my sadness immediately: my sadness, amid such happiness. Her husband continued on to the party, and she and I stood for a while, talking. She had only been married a year or so, herself. I found it much easier to talk to a stranger than to my own daughter. In fact, meeting her made me realize what I had never had in a daughter. We just connected immediately. Naturally, she assumed I was so sad because I was losing a daughter, and she rushed to reassure me about what a nice man Mac was. As we went back into the yard and down the walkway, I had a strong premonition that it was the last time I would see her. That she was an angel—not really an angel, but some angelic presence that I would not be blessed with again—so that it seemed important to say a meaningful good-bye. I said that in my experience, it was rare to find a kindred spirit. "Don't be sad," she said. "You'll visit often."

I knew I would not.

"And I'm a good letter writer," she said, taking my hand, as if she, too, knew that I would not be a welcome visitor.

She wrote with a fountain pen on cream-colored stationery. As with Helen Fox, something passed between us— in this case, a very pleasant, reassuring thing—that I did not completely understand, though I knew the bond was exceptional. I think we could have really become friends if Nina had not told Mary Catherine that she and I were not close. I can only assume that's what happened, because pretty abruptly, the letters stopped. They were notes, really, not letters—more a flourish of handwriting, on her part, than real communications—but she never failed to say that Nina was well and happy. Maybe Mac brought his bride chrysanthemums, and they made her very, very happy. Maybe he was as wonderful as everyone said. I'm sure he did not interrogate Nina, in the guise of getting closer to her. All those questions about Nina's childhood . . . who did he think he was? A psychiatrist? She was an ordinary child. Or, all right, she wasn't an ordinary child. She chose to keep her father and me at a distance.

And then Mac died. For a long time, Mary Catherine didn't write, though eventually she did write, to express her sorrow. She said that she felt guilty. That it made her uncomfortable that we'd written to each other behind Nina's back. "What was the impulse that made me want to whisper behind her back, as if she were a child?" she wrote. I knew what it was. It was the message Nina secretly communicated, herself: that she was weak; that there were things she didn't care to confront. She was both weak- and strong-willed: she never minded implying that she was a victim, while actually she schemed to have things on her own terms.

I didn't answer Mary Catherine's question. I didn't write back and beg her to keep contact with me. Somehow, Nina had poisoned her, and I knew things would never be the same. If she wanted to break off contact, so be it. I did not weep, or take a drink, or try to make her feel guilty by pretending that without her letters, I would be bereft.

Though I did save her letters. Every one. As I had Frank's. As was my way. Six or seven months after Mac's death, I bundled them together and returned them to her. The returned letters must have made an impression, because soon afterward she did write, saying that she hoped I hadn't thought she'd been hinting for their return. I responded, saying only that I wanted her to know that I had kept and valued them. Months passed and then, eventually, came a note, making no mention of Nina. I assumed the omission was her way of justifying our continued correspondence. Spring was beautiful in Cambridge, she said. Why do otherwise intelligent people think that mothers want to hear about the weather? Her husband had gotten a new job. She didn't say what his job was. She was keeping things neutral, skating on the surface. At least I lived with some intensity; at least I didn't make pointless remarks. Mary Catherine wrote that as soon as they saved a little more money, they planned to vacation in France.

Nina changes people. She makes them neutral. She makes them put on a false front. Well: I wouldn't do that. If I wanted to have a drink, I had a drink, even if Miss Carrie Nation was present. If I had something to say, I said it.

It was just that I had so little to say. I wasn't going to say, "How was your day, dear?" to a man who'd been screwing his nurse.

I never wrote back. As I see it, I broke off contact with Mary Catherine, not she with me. If someone is not interested in you, let them go, is my philosophy. Before I met Frank, the boy I intended to marry, Richard Crane, married, instead, a woman he hardly knew. We went to the jewelers to pick out my engagement ring and the next thing I knew, there was a tearful scene—don't tell *me* men don't cry, not after the life I've led—and my fiancé was telling me that he'd fallen in love with the saleswoman. If you saw that as a scene in some Woody Allen movie, you might believe it. But *then?*

The clerk called to tell him that the ring had been sized sooner than we'd expected. She was laying a trap. When he returned for the ring, she made eyes at him. He admitted to me that she did. But how did she flirt so effectively that my future changed, without my even being present? You have such a thing happen once in your life, and you'll always look at women in a different way. I tried to tell Nina that she needed to be on guard against other women. All she thought was that I was trying to instill paranoia. I suppose the advice was given too soon, and by the time she might have used it, she'd dismissed it from her mind. Nina was always more male-oriented, to tell the truth. I had to encourage her to make friends with other girls. Even a girl who needed a girl-friend so desperately, like poor Patty Arthur, wouldn't have even had a visit from Nina, if I hadn't insisted.

Richard Crane never delivered the ring to me, and when Frank proposed that same year, I refused to let him buy me an engagement ring. A plain platinum wedding band was fine. He was taken aback that I didn't want a diamond, though secretly he must have been relieved. He was just starting out, and didn't have much money. He probably thought I declined out of consideration for him. I look back, and I think my rejecting the engagement ring signified more than I knew. It also signified a more general reluctance—though my ambivalence made me even more capti-vating to Frank. My mother had become his biggest advocate. She thought he was a gift from heaven: the perfect mate for her daughter—in part, because she'd been so embarrassed about my broken engagement. She was so wor-ried about what people would think. I could have told them what to think about a man so fickle, but everyone avoided the subject. No one asked me what went wrong.

There was a boy who all but asked me. He lived next door, with his mother. He was the person I felt most at ease with, so why didn't I tell him the truth? He said that if I wanted to talk about it, he would keep anything I said secret. But I thought it best not to indulge my unhappiness, and to say only that Richard hadn't been the man I thought. Steven was such a kind person. He gave me such a significant look when he said that he understood. Poor Steven: he'd always had delicate lungs and had never been able to play sports at school. He had a job as a clerk at the drugstore, though he didn't go out on cold winter days. He didn't have to, because his uncle owned the drugstore. Steven died of pneumonia the winter of my broken engagement. It made me so sad that I hadn't told him what had really happened. It was as though I'd deceived him, and then he'd gone to the grave. I had nightmares. I'd be with him somewhere—that didn't make any sense, because we never went anywhere: we only visited on his mother's sun porch, or sometimes, on sunny days, in the backyard. In my dreams, he and I would be dancing, or walking in a field, and I would feel warm and good, because he and I had romantic feelings for each other, but that made no sense, either, since he only liked girls as friends. As we danced, Richard would always appear. I would see him far away, coming toward us, and in order to stop him from approaching, I would make up some lie, do whatever I needed to do to end the dance and say good night. But then Richard would reappear, somewhere along the way: he'd be looking out from behind a tree, or through the crack in some door. I would have to change my route, knowing all the while that I risked getting lost. No matter how lost I was, he would find me: once again I would see him in the distance, once again I'd take another path. It would go on for what seemed like hours—the same dream, the same anxiety, the same repetitive rerouting. I asked Frank what the dream meant, and he went on a tirade against Sigmund Freud! Frank did not want to analyze my dreams. He did not want to hear about any of my aches or pains, either—though of course it's common for doctors not to treat members of their own family.

Poor Steven. He didn't have much of a life. I'd cheated him by not telling him my story. My story was not very different from so many people's, since broken engagements are as common as broken bones. I never told Frank about Steven. I just said that he was some person—some man I danced with in my dreams, but I never gave him a name. I've always regretted omitting his name. I read in the newspaper that Richard Crane died in a fire, and I didn't even finish reading the obituary. Since I never knew the clerk's name, I don't know whether he married her, or someone else. I didn't really care. Good riddance to a bad man.

Eventually, when he was old enough, I told Andrew about my past. That I married his father on the rebound; that I was drawn to him because he was more smitten with me than I with him. He really did want me to have a diamond ring, but after what happened to me, I didn't even enjoy seeing engagement rings on other women's fingers. It is interesting that Nina did not have an engagement ring, either.

Nina always shut me out. She'd mock me by telling me

what my response was going to be before I even made it. Imagine having a child that impertinent and sarcastic. I'd take one drink, and Nina would leave the room. So what was she doing, off in somebody's basement, photographing nude girls? What else could she have been doing, but pimping? I said to Frank: Do you think Nina was excited about naked girls? Do you think Miss Prim and Proper would have been there at all, if her brother hadn't led her astray? I was astonished, myself, but unlike Frank, I realized that no girl would instigate such a thing. Why did Andrew want her so involved in his private life? She wanted him involved in the stories she wrote as a little girl; he wanted her involved in the enactment of his adolescent fantasies. And both of them, always happiest nestled in the same bed at night—though that's what so many children do, drawing near each other for comfort.

So Frank was seeing that woman, too. That woman in whose basement our children were misbehaving. He got what he deserved for that. Maybe worse than he deserved. That was such a terrible time, when he was threatened with that lawsuit for attacking a child. I believed him when he said he harmed no one; that the daughter was lying just to cover her humiliation.

He never hurt our children. He would talk to them. He felt that it was necessary to let them know that there were certain expectations in our house.

One of which he didn't talk about. That was that he could cheat on his wife.

The time finally came when I realized that I simply wasn't valued for my contributions at home, so I thought: Why shouldn't I go out and earn a paycheck? That was part of my thinking. The other part was that if I became a nurse, I could force Frank to get rid of his hussy. We could run our little mom-and-pop doctor's office, with me at the front desk, and Frank in his office behind the examination room with its bay window and its grand mahogany desk. He kept a picture of me and the children on his desk. Most people do, but Frank selected the oddest picture: one of me, cutting the lawn, with Andrew doing something on the front step, playing with something, or repairing something, and Nina bending over, so you couldn't see her face. I replaced it with a photograph I had taken at a department store, of the three of us smiling into the camera. He thanked me and took it to the office, but one time when I'd locked myself out of the house I went there, and he hadn't put it out. But something told me not to ask, and as it turned out, it was good I didn't: it had been displayed on his desk, but apparently fell to the floor when the office was being cleaned. The cracked glass cut the picture. After Frank died, someone sent me the photograph in the mail, and explained what had happened. Frank must have been brokenhearted, so he had taken it to be restored, but then he had forgotten to pick it up. It was so unexpected, receiving the photograph after his death. You hear of postcards from abroad that show up after the sender has died, but getting a photograph left behind in a store for—what? twenty years?—was quite amazing. The restorer must have called and told him to pick it up. Knowing Frank, it was amazing that he dropped it off; going to collect it would have meant running a second errand, and Frank didn't do errands. I suspect they did call, and he just didn't go. ▲

I gave the picture to Andrew, when he visited. He listened

to my story and took the photograph in its envelope without even looking at it, and without comment. He was still sulking, after so many years, about being made to dress and pose for a professional photograph! And Nina: Nina had had to be dragged, kicking and screaming. She was so self-conscious. She always hated to look at pictures of herself. There was no photographer at her wedding. If one of the bridesmaids hadn't had a camera, I would have no keepsake of that day.

Peter O'Malley, who taught the nursing course I took, was a charismatic teacher. He gave the instruction straightforwardly, but he picked his favorites in the classroom and indulged the select few. I was so pleased to be among them. Peter had spent fifteen years in nursing before he turned to teaching. I have always thought that to teach is a noble occupation. Frank, though, looked down on Peter because becoming a nurse was so much easier than becoming a doctor. Anyone I liked, Frank found fault with. He was always jealous, though I gave him no reason for jealousy. I did, however, love my time away from the house; I liked school because it had nothing to do with my family. I got off to a good start and was a dedicated student, but not too far into the course Andrew got sick with bronchitis, and my own bad stomach—my curse; it began to occur soon after Frank and I were married—forced me to miss more classes, until finally, even though I'd done the reading, I fell farther and farther behind. Reluctantly, I decided it was best to drop out and to take the class the following fall.

A gloom descended over me when I quit, though. I put the textbook in a drawer so I wouldn't have to look at it. For a while, I let Frank think I was still attending school. When I did explain, it was obvious that he was secretly gratified. It surprised me, though, to find out that Frank had phoned Peter to find out why I had fallen behind. Peter had never before received such a call from anyone's husband. I'm not sure if Peter would have stayed in touch with me, if he had not called to report on Frank's request, so at least, inadvertently, Frank did me a service. I was humiliated to have been checked up on, but I was happy to hear my teacher's voice again. He was calling to ask if my inability to keep up had anything to do with his teaching. I told him that it did not. It was as I'd said: my son had gotten sick, and then I'd had some bad days, myself. I reassured him that I had enjoyed the classes. He didn't want to get off the phone, I could tell. He persisted in asking if anything else was wrong. I reassured him that it was not, and told him that he could expect to see me the following year. We hung up, but he called back almost immediately and invited me for coffee the next day. He wanted me to come to a restaurant across from the school. He was such a nice, conscientious person. It was obvious that he had some lingering doubt that my dropping out might have been because of some inadequacy of his.

I found him sitting near the back, a folded newspaper on the tabletop, an empty cup of coffee in front of him. He stood and pulled out a chair for me. Whether because of his kindness or my being frazzled at being late, I found myself on the verge of tears. I picked up the menu to use as a sort of curtain between him and me. He suggested that we order lunch. I was flustered. I was supposed to be at the children's school, to see the art show in which Andrew had won second place. The hour for viewing had almost passed. I would have to really hurry, or forget it entirely. So I joined Peter for lunch. We both had toasted cheese sandwiches with tomato. The pointless details the mind retains. . . . He expressed pleasure that I meant to take the course the following year. He kept returning to the subject of my leaving, though, rephrasing his question about why I had dropped out.

Finally, he got to the point. He said that he had found my husband's manner, on the phone, threatening. He had been puzzled that Frank referred to himself in the third person. *The doctor does not admire failure*, Frank had apparently said to Peter. Peter wanted to know whether Frank was mocking him, or mocking himself. I was taken aback—not so much by what Peter had said, but because I was Frank's wife, and I didn't know what to do: try to defend my husband—he did not mock people—or admit to this man who was almost a stranger that I did not always understand everything my husband did. I tried to evade his question. "He's quite adamant about everyone doing their best," I said. Peter looked at me. He did not ask again about Frank. Before we left, though, he said that he wanted me to know that I had a friend, if anything was—he hesitated—*wrong*, he finally said.

I don't remember how we got out of the restaurant. He must have paid. He might even have said that he would call me again. I don't know. I do know that a week passed in which he did not call, so that when I heard from him again I was relieved, and delighted to hear his voice. It was his idea that we see a movie together. I knew that if Frank found out, there would be hell to pay. But still, I understood my own motivations. Frank had nothing to worry about. So I went. We saw *The Misfits*. We were both impressed by how good it was. Stunned, really. You expected Marilyn Monroe to be cast in a particular sort of role, but she was not.

All that spring we went to movies. We went until Peter's mother became ill in Pittsburgh. He told me that she had been suffering for years with emphysema. The day after we saw what I didn't know would be the last movie we were ever to see together, as he intended to fly to Pennsylvania. He took the ticket out of his breast pocket and put it on the table like a child presenting you with something curious he had not yet encountered. He asked me if I would keep his dog while he was away. I thought: What kind of a friend would I be, if I refused to do him that favor, while his mother was so sick? I realized that I had not known much about his life: that his mother lived in Pittsburgh; that he had a pet. I said that I would be pleased to take the dog. That he could drop the dog by the house. I hoped that he and Frank might get along, if they actually met.

But he had anticipated my answer. He already had the dog in the car. I hadn't expected that. I had expected . . . what? Some time to get used to the idea? A few hours, during which I'd mull over a way to tell Frank that my former teacher was coming by, to drop off his dog for a few days? I took a deep breath and decided that taking care of a dog could not be very difficult. I walked to his car with him, and he opened the back door, taking a leash out of his pocket and leaning in to fasten it to the dog's collar.

The dog was a mutt. A nice, placid dog. There was a big bag of dry dog food that Peter transferred from his car to mine. I patted the dog, which seemed docile enough. Rather large, but I'd always been afraid of those high-strung little dogs. Of all things, the dog's name was Molly. I warmed to her immediately, just because she had that name. I tried not to appear flustered, leading the animal on its leash. Fortunately, the dog walked as tentatively as I did. At my car, Molly seemed unwilling to get in, but Peter coaxed her gently, snapping his fingers, and finally Molly jumped onto the seat.

The dog whimpered as I drove away. I felt like a criminal. The poor animal was so distraught. I talked to it, reassured it with explanations it didn't understand. *She*, not *it*. Frank was the one who called the dog *it*, and acted as if I'd taken in a leper. It was almost funny, how much the presence of my friend's dog rattled him. He wanted me to board *it*, but the children adored the dog. Even Frank picked his battles. He was disdainful, really, because of the dog's owner, not because of the dog. He didn't want anyone in my life except himself, and Molly's presence indicated that I had more of a relationship with my ex-teacher than he'd realized. I thought he would go on a rampage. That was my worst fear. But instead, he became amorous. He was in my bedroom night after night. The dog was an aphrodisiac to Frank.

Peter had asked me to keep her for a week. At the end of that time, he called and asked if I could keep her for a few more days: his mother was dying. His voice was strained. The phone call was brief. As we spoke, the children were outside, playing games with the dog. Andrew had spent his own money to get a brush for Molly. Even coldhearted Nina wrapped her arms around Molly's neck. I knew it was going to be a problem returning the dog. Days passed, a week passed, and then a call came from a friend of Peter's. Peter was delayed in Pittsburgh, he said, and had asked him to pick up the dog. I assured him that there was no need to do that. "Well, I'm the co-owner," he said. "I've been in Michigan on business, but I'm back now."

A co-owner? I asked the man to call back, but he was adamant: he needed to pick up the dog that evening. He intended to take the dog when he drove to Pittsburgh, to join Peter. He sounded perturbed, the more I hesitated. Finally, I made myself a silent promise: if the dog did not indicate she knew him, I would find a way, whatever it took, not to release her.

Only Nina was home when the man came. Frank was usually home by six, but that night he was not. Andrew had returned and gone out again, to the library. I didn't have the heart to tell him Molly might not be there when he returned. I had a drink and tried to calm down. What was I going to do if the man seemed strange, and there was no one there to support me? Nina saw me sipping my drink, and went directly to her room. I followed her, wanting to ask her advice, but she would not open her door, and I thought: It would serve her right if something terrible happened. If this man coming for the dog was a dognapper.

He was not. He was a short, slight man, with an acne-scarred face and dyed blond hair. The dog was overjoyed to see him. The man fussed over the dog. Feeling sad, I got some twine and wrapped it around the bag of dog food. I patted the happy dog, which seemed already to have forgotten me. "We'll go back to the apartment and get my stuff and set off tonight, Molly," the man crooned. Nina must have heard the commotion. Why didn't she come down?

Why stay upstairs until they departed, then descend to glare at me with her cold eyes? It would have been better if she had said good-bye, but Nina always had the ability to pretend painful things weren't happening. Whatever anguish she felt she saved for Andrew. She said nothing to me at all when she finally came downstairs, even though I sat in the living room, bereft.

Though I heard from Peter again, he only called to say that his mother had died and that he would be leaving his job at the end of the semester and moving to Michigan. He said this in such a way that I knew he did not want to be questioned. He thanked me profusely for caring for the dog. At the end of the tense call, he said, "I want you to know that wherever I go, you still have a friend."

For months after that, I had nightmares in which the dog was found buried under mounds of trash. I would wake up amid tangled sheets I'd kicked aside, my feet digging for her. It would take a drink to get me back to sleep. The dreams persisted until finally the anxiety they caused me erased almost all fondness I'd had for Molly's owner. What had it all been about? I kept asking myself. His singling me out in the first place. Our shared enthusiasms. Our guilty pleasure in going to movies, goofing off. Our toasted sandwiches, for all that.

The more time passed, the more I began to feel embarrassed. I was so glad Frank never discovered what had gone on. I must have been crazy to risk his discovering the extent of my friendship with another man. I was also grateful that Frank hadn't seen the man who came to reclaim the dog. In time, I decided that Peter and I had been fated to meet. He had come along at a time when I was feeling low, and flattered me by his attention. I had needed someone to acknowledge that I was special, and his attention had done that. In time the nightmares ended, and I allowed myself to think more fondly of him. I thought that perhaps he had been like the brother I never had. It gave me some insight into Nina's closeness to Andrew. It made me more at ease about their private bond.

But about the dog . . . I don't think Andrew or Nina ever forgave me for giving back the dog. It must have signified to them that I would do other things behind their backs, that I couldn't be depended on. Like so many things, Peter and the situation with the dog was a blessing in one way, and a curse in another.

Why do I say that my relationship with Peter was anything like Andrew and Nina's relationship? It was not.

Why think of it at all?

Why think that after all this time, somewhere a bottle will be tossed overboard with a note inside, and that note will miraculously find its way into my hands. What would I even want such a note to say? "Come away with me and my faithful dog and my blond-haired friend, and vanish into . . ." What? Into another version of Nina's fairyland? Her watercolor world where smudges possessed a clarity more real than human figures?

I knew my husband all too well, and my children only when they were truly children. I have frozen them in time before I stopped knowing them. I remember them when they needed me. They didn't really cry as they got older, but they let me know they might have. Nina's cold squint kept tears back; Andrew's puzzled frown did the same. How their faces were transformed when Molly the dog arrived. When she left, it was as if I'd done the most traitorous thing a mother could ever do; it was as if I'd given their childhood away.

he fairy sprinkled fairy dust on the dog's head. She said, "We'll keep it our secret that now you can fly. The ghost and I have magic powers. The important thing is to believe in them even if the other person stops believing. But don't feel bad. I would never do that. I am giving you the last of my fairy dust so all three of us can have special powers. Put your paws forward and keep your back legs close together. Fly. Then pass through other galaxies where the stars are Hershey's kisses. From far away you will appear so small that people will mistake you for a shooting star. The sky is not blue there. It is black but it is not scary. The air you fly through will be as soft as the ghost's skin. You have no reason to be afraid."

WHEN NINA AND I WERE YOUNG, there had been elaborate signals between us. We mimed sentences with a gesture, passing each other in the hallway. We fought, but we always kept our secrets. We were capable of reading each other's minds when it was necessary—as it was, so often—for one of us to answer for the other. If our mother wanted to know why Nina was coming home late from school, I would be able to turn my best guess into an assertion—usually correctly enough that on questioning, Nina wouldn't contradict me. Our mother, unlike our father, had no reason to want to trip us up, though. She wanted everything to go smoothly; she really didn't want to focus on either of us, with the exception of my being useful as her late-night companion. Our father, also, wanted us out of his thoughts, unless he decided it was better to lick the thorn in his side. You could never be sure, though, when something was festering. Sometimes it required no time to pass—he acted the minute the thorn pierced him. Other times, it was as if he decided to stop and take note of what sort of shape he was in. When he did that, a major problem was always found. There was simple punishment for sloppiness, such as towels left over the backs of chairs, or boots stepped out of in the middle of the hallway.

But for things that he thought affected him—meaning, Nina's and my actions—he found it necessary to complicate the punishment, and to make sure he punished himself in the process. Maybe punishment provided its own kind of relief. Maybe digging his feet in distracted him from his more immediate, ongoing problems—such as his terrible relationship with his wife. In any case, he became such a parody of the concerned parent that his meanness built in his pressure cooker of a brain until it led to an explosion. Orgasmic release, even.

Quite the notion. One of Mac's observations years after the fact, not my own.

My sister is a person you have to take on her own terms. If you visit and she doesn't feel like talking, she will simply declare talk off limits and insist that you sit silently and listen to music. I'm sympathetic, of course; she's had to take care of herself since Mac died, and within the confines of her house, she sets her own rules. Sensitive people, like my former fiancée, Serena, realize that Nina isn't standoffish, but shy. "Traumatized" would be a better word. Through the years, some of those people have tried to extend themselves, hoping to bring her out of herself. Serena had more luck than anyone else, so perhaps it is natural that Nina blames me for Serena's departure, which meant the end of their friendship. For a long time Nina has refused to meet anyone new I'm going out with. I think it would be wrong to mislead her, though, and pretend that because she doesn't have a social life, I don't either.

Like so many people in distress, Nina denies that she is.

She has no perspective on what she's doing when she insists that our mother has rejected her, when she's the one who has rejected our mother. Nina insisted on selling our parents' house immediately when our father died, having long ago convinced herself that our mother was senile, which is also her excuse for not visiting her.

"How is your sister?" my mother always asks when I call. "How is the old maid?"

I tell her Nina is involved in a great romance. One I'm not allowed to disclose any details of. It's become my standard response, and since I've said it so often, my mother has come to suspect that there may be some truth in it. When Hound figures it out, I might finally be telling my mother the truth. But as it stands now, I no longer report to Nina on my visits to my mother. If Nina defines our mother as a senile alcoholic who watches daytime TV, I don't point out that she, herself, turns on the TV the moment she rises.

My mother has decided that Mac's death was, in effect, the death of her daughter—a notion close to the truth. Mac was always so hopeful when he talked to Nina about her childhood: he thought that through the power of positive thinking, he could convince her that she was nowhere near as damaged as she thought. When he talked to me privately, he was appalled. He loved my sister, but he knew she was an enormous undertaking. It wasn't just at the track that he gambled.

After the breakup of my relationship with Serena, I saw a porn movie on late-night TV about a woman who decides to look up boys from high school, and I decided that however ludicrous the movie was, the idea, itself, was interesting. As coincidence would have it, not long afterward Josie Bower contacted me. Through the years I had seen some of the people from high school—running into them on the street; calling one or two when I was going to be in their part of the world—but Josie was the only significant person from those days who'd ever gotten in touch with me, even though it had only been by way of mailing an invitation to a high school reunion. I didn't want to go, but it got me thinking about her again, and about the past, which I thought I looked at pretty squarely, as I always try to do. My father looked at things so squarely, everything he saw was framed in negativity; my mother never looked at anything she could avoid confronting. Nina hedged her bets: she had one standard for me—perfection—and another, much lower standard for people she intuited might harm her. Nothing could be done about our father, but she had good radar for avoiding those people otherwise.

The day the announcement arrived, I was a little suprised there was no personal note, but because I'd never been contacted previously, I figured the invitation was pointed, and that Josie would like to see me again. She might even have heard that I'd looked up a few people from high school over the years—girls, I'll admit, though I never had any intention of living my own version of the porn movie. When I got her letter, I felt a lot of conflicting emotions, but I thought—considering what she and I had been through together—that at the very least, it would be interesting to meet again as adults. I can usually be counted on to be my own worst enemy, as Serena would tell anyone who'd listen. If so, it was predictable that I'd follow through with Josie. I subscribe to the Chinese curse of wishing myself an interesting life; considering my mother's and my sister's empty lives, I feel the need to at least try to be involved in something interesting.

I took a day off from work and went to meet Josie when she was traveling. It was her suggestion, but I thought it was a good one. People are different when they're on the road: cut free from the usual routines, they tend to be more receptive—more open to chance, it seems. If it was true of Josie, of course the same held true for me. I didn't have an exact scenario, and I hadn't really tried to imagine one. I was just going to see what it felt like to be with her again. You can't help but experience some degree of discomfort about being with a person you knew when both of you were young; someone who was part of your life when you didn't have the sophistication—to be honest, the defenses—to be the cool person you prayed you'd eventually evolve into. When children set off on their bikes they forget the days of training wheels, but no adult ever forgets the struggles of adolescence: every dumb remark, every embarrassing pimple, every moment of paralysis. That adolescent is always there, hovering, needing to be integrated into the person you've become.

It helped that we met on neutral ground. She sent me a postcard with the name and address of a bar, which I tucked in the inside pocket of my leather jacket. At first Josie and I didn't know what to say to each other, but it didn't take long to relax. She looked much the same and said that I did, too. We sat side by side in the bar making small talk, though I pretty quickly turned to the painful subject I knew it would be pointless to avoid: I brought up the time I was made to visit her in the hospital, and how much I suspected she'd liked seeing me, even though she hadn't acted that way. I was not a secure or presumptuous young boy; if I felt that, it had been because something in the air, like the secret messages that went back and forth between Nina and me, had reverberated strongly. Josie agreed: she had been happy, but at the same time she hadn't wanted to see anyone, she was so self-conscious about the way she looked. Imagine that, she said: she could deal with the physical pain she had after surgery, but her appearance made her acutely embarrassed.

Her mother and my father had been having an affair. I hadn't known it that day, though I soon figured it out, even if I could not immediately put it into words. That day his lover, Josie's mother, had been trying to break away from him, which she physically enacted as I stood in the room. I could remember feeling Josie's surprise and dismay. I ran because I knew that whenever my father had me as his audience he got crazier and crazier. It was as if my presence added gasoline to his fire. I knew that what was happening was somehow disastrous, and I also remember thinking that if I removed myself, there would be some chance he might not go up in flames. That he—that everything—might quiet down. He could never resist boasting, demonstrating his power to me. I now see that he was more insecure than I was. I thought that if I left, Josie might not have to hear it. It wasn't cowardice; it was the first selfless thing I can remember doing.

No: that isn't true. It was my first gallant act toward someone other than my sister.

A long time had passed before Josie and I finally spoke about our troubled childhoods and the way they had, yet hadn't, overlapped. Her eyes filled with pain again; I felt the same impulse to go toward her, and to retreat.

What details would Serena insist on here?

This was happening in a bar in southern Vermont. Josie was there to visit a relative who lived in a nursing home. If she had been Serena, she would have wanted the two of us to go into a closet in the nursing home and have sex, but she was not Serena. She was a girl I'd known in school, now dressed in jeans and a turtleneck, having coffee, perched on a barstool. I had swiveled my stool to face her. I had ordered scotch. I hadn't looked her up after getting the invitation because I had romantic feelings about her, though as I sat there, I calculated—just for the sake of speculation—how many more drinks it would take until the possibility of having sex became a moot point. I thought about having just that many drinks. Or not having that many. Meanwhile, she told me about her marriage, her children. What she said about her husband let me understand she wasn't very happy, though she absolutely adored her children. She told me about their favorite toys, their favorite necklaces and junk food enthusiasms, their kittens—all the trivia that made up their childhoods. She apologized for being an adoring mother. I said I could imagine being the same way, if I were a father. That led me into talking about the breakup of my marriage. I tried not to misrepresent Caitlin, but the truth was, she seemed so completely gone from my life I could barely think of the specific things that had led us to part. I suppose it was somewhat funny that ridiculous details came to mind, none of which I was so stupid as to announce: that she had preferred Ajax to Comet; that she indignantly returned roses to the flower shop if they wilted too soon. It was much easier to tell Josie about my on-and-off, more recent, difficult relationship with Serena.

As I spoke, I realized that everything I talked about sounded like a proposition. Though it was unintended, sentences seemed heavy with sexual innuendo, so that it didn't seem like anything I said about the past did not apply to the two of us in the present. Serena herself would have analyzed the situation and decided that consciously or unconsciously, I did have a scenario for our meeting. How else to account for the air between us being so charged? It had also been called to my attention, by Hound and by others, that I'd gotten spoiled by all the attention that had come my way during Caitlin's attempts to banish my memory of my lost love from high school, and later by Serena's rather tantalizing impulsiveness. Serena was not the sort of person who would even remember to go to the store, let alone prefer one cleaning product to another. In the time we were together, I never saw her clean anything. If she had bought roses that died, she might have held a funeral for them. She was high-strung but very original—a difficult person to outguess, which was something she took secret pride in. Like Josie, though, I cut myself short. Details were nothing but details; they did not explain anything any more than generalizations did.

"Don't digress," Serena would be saying, at this point.

The point being that I realized I was going to have to take the initiative if anything meaningful was to happen between us. Regardless of what my sister would think, that meaningful thing would not have necessarily had anything to do with sex. But I wasn't sure that anything should happen. What I'd intended to do with Josie was to clear the air, since we'd never spoken about that day. Having touched on the subject, though, where, exactly, should I begin? I mulled it over with another drink, and we made small talk. She switched from coffee to wine, but when it came time to order again, she ordered coffee. She had actually been more forthcoming drinking coffee than wine, telling me that her husband was antisocial and wanted only to be with her and their children; he did not have one other friend, she told me, which she saw not as a compliment, but as a way of giving up on life. He had been particularly depressed after his knee was operated on unsuccessfully, and he could no longer take long hikes alone on the weekends.

I still could not decide how to say what I wanted to say about my father's atrocious behavior and about what must have looked like my own cowardice. Abruptly, she looked at her watch and said she should get to her aunt's. I paid the bill and was pleased there was no silly feminist flurry of debate. As I held open the door, she surprised me by saying, "My husband isn't the sort of man who'd be pleased that his wife had a drink with an old friend. I hope you'll come visit us in Connecticut, but if you do, it would be better not to mention that we saw each other today." I felt my cheeks turn hot. Was this my signal to do something, or was she making a simple statement?

Unsure, I extended my hand, though kissing her cheek had been my impulse. "Oh, you know you were the most handsome boy in high school," she said. "Stop making fun."

She leaned forward and kissed me briefly, on the mouth. "Call us," she said. "You know, I was surprised to hear from you. I would have expected Patty Arthur to get the call, not me."

We had mentioned so many names in the time we talked. I had said the name still difficult to speak: *Serena*. She'd called her husband *Harry*. We had mentioned *Mrs. Gless* the history teacher, and *Nona*, her aunt in the rest home. She'd even told me the names of her children's pets. But until that second, I had no idea she, or anyone except my sister, knew anything about my involvement with Patty. That was stupid of me. People always knew things they didn't let on to, except for those people who couldn't resist a last-minute provocation.

"Are you just going to stand there and not react?" she said. "What I was trying to find out was whether you were still in touch. I've talked to her, but I've never mentioned your name."

I wasn't in touch. Patty Arthur had become a sort of fantasy fairy of my past; I was smart enough to know that to get together with someone who had never been quite real— either because she was larger than life, or because for one brief period, she had effectively lifted both of us out of mundane living—was to risk disappointment. "No," I said simply.

"You didn't really come all this way to see me, did you?" she said.

"Yes," I said.

"Are you on your way to see her?"

I shook my head no. She looked down and looked up again. She said: "Then I'm giving myself one more guess. If I'm not second best, I assume you came because I survived, so I'm sort of like a good luck charm."

"I don't believe in good luck charms," I said.

She walked up to me. She put out her hand. I took it. I stood there, confused, holding her hand. People walked around us. I thought that if I hadn't had three drinks, I might better understand what was going on.

"Alice Manzetti was always so smitten with you, but for you there was only Patty Arthur," she said. "Isn't high school painful? It's good we didn't realize that all that crap would follow us all our lives."

"Did Patty tell you about us, or did more people than I realize know?" I asked.

She answered with a question. "What happened?" she said. "I thought for sure you two would be the couple from high school to get married."

"She went to college and fell in love with somebody else."

"And you were so devastated, you just accepted that?"

"I never assumed we'd get married."

"One of her professors. Fifteen years older," Josie said, shaking her head. "I thought *that* was the most shocking thing I'd ever heard of back then." She took a step closer. Her limp was almost imperceptible, but I knew that she knew I noticed. We had said nothing about that. We had said nothing else about her surgery, nothing more about that dreadful day in the hospital. We also had said nothing about the one time we'd had sex, so long ago. I wondered if she might have blocked it out of her mind. For a long time—years—I hadn't thought of it, myself, though now it seemed so momentous, I couldn't think how I'd forgotten.

"Don't get into it again," she said. "Advice from an old friend."

"I didn't look you up to get back in touch with her. I didn't even know you knew."

"Then I don't get it," she said. "You skipped the reunion, then came all the way from Boston to Brattleboro to talk to me about the past without really talking about it?"

"I got caught up in talking about the things we talked about," I said. I added, not quite truthfully: "It was interesting to hear about the kind of life you lead. The girls, your job."

"My hermit husband," she finished.

"I can tell you aren't happy," I said.

"The person who organizes reunions is either ecstatic or desperate. There's no in between."

"Let's have another drink," I said.

We had been walking slowly as we talked. We were standing in front of a store. Behind my shoulder things were cluttered in a shop window: pig push toys; aprons patterned with maple leaves. Someone had assembled a pyramid out of plastic jugs of maple syrup.

"Call Alice," she said. "Alice has carried a torch for you all these years." She closed the distance between us and kissed me a second time on the lips. "Believe me," she said. They were almost her last words, and when she spoke again, there was no confusion between past and present; she was talking about Patty Arthur, not the two of us, standing, both slightly unhinged, on a sidewalk in a town neither of us lived in. "Stay away," she said.

Nothing could have made me more determined, though until that moment I hadn't thought about looking up Patty. Why go through it? Everyone knows what it's like: the romanticized figure has been changed by time, or more shocking still, you've changed.

I let her walk a block and turn a corner. Then I followed. I couldn't let her go without finding out where Patty was. What she'd meant by her warning.

"Men are so predictable," she said. "I came here knowing what you wanted, and sure enough, here it comes," she said. "You want her phone number, don't you?" I hadn't said Patty's name. All I had done was come up behind her, putting my hand on her shoulder. She looked at me. "Andrew, I knew what this was about and I came anyway, didn't I? Maybe you should listen when I tell you that things aren't great in Patty's world, and that in my opinion you'd do well to keep away."

She was so emphatic, I only nodded. I even tried to make light of it, giving her a little chagrined smile and shrugging.

"That day you ran out of the hospital room it was like I was on your heels, getting out of that miserable, overheated room, getting away from your father and my mother. Imagine the two of them, having a fight right in front of me, when I was so sick I couldn't even keep water down. I want you to know that it gave me hope," she said. "I figured if you had the guts to break and run, eventually I could, too. When you did that, you didn't know what a big favor you were doing me." She had been looking at the sidewalk as she spoke. She looked up. Her lips parted. She was about to say something else. Then she turned and began to walk away.

It was the point in the movie where the music comes up. Certainly the point when a different person would have pursued her. *Ecstatic or desperate* rang in my ears. That needed further discussion, even if Patty did not.

But I couldn't do it. I couldn't do it any more than I could get up from the park bench and walk to the clinic the day Serena went for the abortion. And before that, there had been the time I couldn't press the button in the hospital elevator the night Mac died and I stood there leaning my head against the side of the elevator until a custodian got on and asked if I was okay. And before that, I had never been able to bring myself to walk out of my mother's bedroom, as a child, until it was clear she had finished delivering her self-serving re-creations of her past. I seemed never to be able to do the things that most needed doing. Unlike Serena, I could easily let myself off the hook for not dealing well with complexity, but simple things? Continuing to walk after a friend, who all but begged me to follow her?

Nina wants to know why I ever started looking up girls from high school. I'm equally curious about why she doesn't consider getting together again with some of the guys. Because you maintain a real connection with those people, the same way you never really disconnect from your family. You can't renounce the people who defined your adolescence any more than you can banish family members. Because they aren't family, though, with time, the bullshit ends. The cliques dissolve, the girls grow up—they've all had the same hard knocks everybody's had—and what it's come down to is that most of them aren't very happily married. It's not about having sex with them, as Nina nastily insists.

Or actually, she might be a little right. Everyone new you date mirrors who you are, but the high school girls mirror who you were. I know who I am, and Nina might be surprised to know that my view of myself is sometimes even more negative than hers. But the person I was then—that person still exists in the first meeting of their eyes with mine, the first spark of electricity when you touch their hand. Or kiss their cheek. Or brush a strand of hair off their face. There are those things that tell you: once you felt this; once you knew that. They're the rock, and you're the flint. They're the mirror that proves you are not a ghost.

When Josie was out of sight, I walked back to my car. I got inside and put the key in the ignition and turned it on. The needle of the gas tank rose to the half-full mark. The temperature gauge did not rise at all. The speedometer suggested the car could reach a speed of 140 miles an hour. I considered sitting there forever. I considered driving fast, seeing how close to 140 it would really go. I got out and went back to the bar. The bartender tried not to look surprised to see me again. Business was slow: only two other customers. "What'll it be?" he said, trying to look casual. He had decided he didn't want to get into it. Neither did I. Although I thought Josie and I had said almost none of the necessary things, I didn't want to think about that. I certainly did not want to behave like some loser in a bad cartoon, blubbering to the bartender. "Coffee," I said, though it took great effort not to order another scotch.

I got together with Hound the day after I drove home and tried to describe what an odd encounter I'd had with Josie. He and I were also sitting in a bar, on our way to Coolidge Corner, having a beer. He kept fixating on the fact that I'd driven to Vermont to see someone who hadn't even been a girlfriend.

"Come on," I said. "It's something lots of people do, looking up people they knew in high school."

"Yeah, if they happen to be in the area, or if they're real losers with women."

"Reunions are very popular," I said. "You've gone to them yourself. People keep their yearbooks and look through them and get all misty-eyed. They hear some song on the radio and they call information in Arizona, to see if the girl they almost took to the senior prom still lives there. They join AA and call the fat girl and apologize for making her life a living hell. They put ads in the personals column and advertise their nostalgia, asking their former classmates to call."

"So are you in love with her?" he said.

"No."

"Sleep with her?"

"No."

"Plan to see her again?"

He was asking every question I had asked myself while sitting at the bar, having my final coffee.

"I don't think so," I said.

"You are one strange character."

"Come on," I said. "You've never felt the urge to see how somebody turned out?"

"I was glad to get away from that crowd," he said. "I'd had enough of those people for a lifetime."

"What about whoever you dated back then? You're telling me you never once thought about her?"

"Thought, yeah. Drive to Ohio to see Georgia Sheron? No way."

Hound prided himself on being moderate. This, from the

same person who'd been in analysis for twenty years and still couldn't admit that my sister was the unrequited love of his life. Which was none of my business, especially since I thought it was inevitable that they'd get together, they were so perfect for each other. It wasn't even worth teasing him about, he was so adamant about its not being true. His relationship with his wife, Kate, was lousy; she didn't want to admit she'd made a mistake a second time. And Hound doted on her son. It was hard not to dislike her for manipulating him the way she did, but I was hardly in a position to say anything, since I'd once been lured into having a little something with her. Neither did I think I could occasionally try to nudge things along vis-à-vis my sister. After Kate confessed our brief affair to Hound, Hound and I had never again been friends in the same easy way.

"What did you expect?" Serena would say. And she would have been right. She was always right those times she pointed out what a bastard I was, but it was a reproach I found hard to accept. It implied such superiority on her part; it suggested that she did not make the kinds of mistakes I made. Other mistakes—perhaps even worse mistakes—but not those particularly pathetic mistakes.

Here's an easy question: What boy would take pleasure in being his mother's confidant?

She had a hard time, being married to my father. I was the person she singled out to talk to. Even though she didn't understand men, she intended to make it her mission to keep trying. If she couldn't understand my father, then maybe she could understand his son. If she couldn't impress my father with the difficulty she had raising the children, maybe she could explain herself directly to one of them. Even if she'd had a willing partner, I doubt that she was up to the task. Though my sister and I weren't very troublesome, we obviously overwhelmed her. My father was absent from the house as often as possible. Since he was a doctor, it was almost always possible. My mother tuned us out and drank. My father had affairs.

I might not think about those years so much, except that women want to know everything about your past. They don't always take the direct approach by asking for information, the way men do. Instead, they question you relentlessly, until you give them what they want. My mother was that way; she was never direct, but would ask leading questions well enough disguised that you might take them for a statement. They could seem to be simple remarks, so that if the listener got upset, she could pretend that she'd only been making an observation. If you didn't comment on what she was interested in, however, she'd push like an iceberg.

What she was usually looking for was information about my father. Since I could never anticipate what information she might want, I fell into the habit of taking note of everything, however unimportant. It was good training, ultimately: it kept me on my toes; it sharpened my senses. But it also put me at a remove from situations, made me an observer, rather than a participant. I was a quiet child. As I grew older, there were times I thought I wanted to be a doctor just to prove to myself that I could do it differently than my father. Other times, I was determined to go in the opposite direction: to write, or play music, or paint.

My sister was once a very inventive writer. She ignored her gifts and edits other people's work, immersing herself in particulars and settling for making adjustments, rather than creating anything. When we were children she wrote stories about fantasy fairies and their adventures. The scathing way my father characterized what he assumed she wrote about (he always derided "Nina and her foolish fantasy fairy friends") became our perfectly neutral way of speaking about it. Of course, shut up in her room, our mother had no idea what either of us did. She never knew that I stopped taking piano lessons. I doubt that she knew Nina wrote. "What did the fantasy fairies do today?" I'd ask Nina late at night, and snuggle deep under the covers to hear their adventures, which sometimes touched on the ways my sister and I had spent our day and sometimes came from no context I could recognize. For a while I illustrated some of the stories, but as she got older and they became more convoluted, she began criticizing the choices I made about what to illustrate. Looking back, I think she wanted the stories to be entirely her own, without illustrations, but since she didn't know how to tell me, she criticized my drawings.

I'd been so puzzled. Suddenly she didn't want to read the stories to me, when she was the one who had instigated the nightly ritual. I thought it was just mean-spiritedness that she found fault with my drawings, because I knew they were good. Her voice had always been an important part of every story; I had learned, when she spoke softly, to pay special attention and to remember to illustrate that moment, because it was obviously one she found particularly significant. I had put so much effort into listening that I was hurt when she accused me of no longer understanding what was most important. It was as if she'd suddenly decided to say—in spite of everything I did for her—that we were not close, when we were. I was hurt, so I did what I knew to do back then: I covered my hurt with anger; I told her that her stories were less and less interesting. She took the criticism as a challenge. The story she produced was so ugly, so much not the story of the fantasy fairies, so much not a story that could ever be published in a book, that she could see from my expression how well she'd told it, and how pained I was. I felt betrayed. I told her that if she wrote more stories like those, I would never again listen, and that if she did write them, it would be like Pinocchio's nose growing as he lied: she would turn ugly; she'd be no different than our sadistic father. She gave me a look then that I will never forget. She never again came into my room late at night and she also punished me by never writing another story. When finally I was overwhelmed by guilt and suggested we work on creating new ones together, she ignored me entirely.

I suppose it is true that you can be cruelest to those you love the most. One thing that could be said on behalf of my father is that at least I could never disappoint him as deeply as I disappointed my sensitive sister. He didn't want anything from me, including, quite possibly, my existence.

Serena made much of that rift between Nina and me over my illustrations. I don't know how Nina explained it to her, but I'm sure that whatever she said made a martyr of her. Leave it to my sister to take some simple situation and blow it out of proportion. Because of their talk, Serena saw my opting out of certain complexities that arose in our lives as pas-

sive aggression. In Serena's opinion I overreacted to the possibility of being overwhelmed every time something difficult
entered my life. She was thinking selfishly, of course. When
she got pregnant by accident, she wanted to have the child
and I didn't. "Andrew's having another Michelangelo period,
thinking he has to paint every cherub in the sky, lying on his
back," she said sardonically. I assured her that I had never in
my life felt like Michelangelo. "Then an indentured *servant*. A
lackey! Poor put-upon you, being asked to deal with anything
difficult." It began on the platform outside the Harvard stop
on the Red Line, and continued through the change to the
Green Line at Park. Inside the train, she whispered; changing
cars, surrounded by the noise of the trains, mixed with music
from whatever scruffy musician was playing on the platform,
she raised her voice and berated me. Serena reminded me of a
pot come to a boil, subsiding when salt was added, but finally
and inevitably bubbling over.

No. Serena was nothing like a pot of water. She was flesh
and blood.

Hound was smitten with her. He agreed with me that
when she became pregnant, it was not the right time to have
a child, but he had a better way of communicating with her
because he had a woman's ability to persuade. Tactfulness was
not something instilled in me by my parents. When someone
is drunk, what you hear are declarations. People who've had
one too many drinks don't phrase things delicately. Egoma-
niacs don't speak tentatively. So Hound was better able to
communicate with Serena, acting as my stand-in. You would
have thought the sacrifice she was making was entirely for his
benefit, not that she granted my point at all.

Hound—like the rest of us, he is all grown up: important to remember that he is Henry now. Hound accompanied her to the clinic. She wanted it that way. I was a little jealous, but mostly I felt relieved. I suppose we all pick friends who are capable of carrying on where we leave off. He carried on very well that day. I sat on a park bench one block away, feeding pigeons. Of course a continuous parade of children passed by, and even the birds seemed to make eye contact. I looked at my watch and looked at my watch, though I had no idea how long such a thing took. I'd bought myself a sandwich and a cup of coffee, but I couldn't manage more than two bites, and then I began tearing up bread to feed the birds. In that same park, I saw a boy kill a pigeon with a pellet gun. He took aim as he saw me coming. He looked at me, and I looked at him, and he shot the bird. I kept walking. I worried he might shoot me in the back as I went by, but I made it a point— boys learn this early on—not to flinch. I never looked back, and nothing more came of it, except that I've thought about what happened over the years. Not the day of the abortion so much as that bleak moment in the park with that stranger. The coldhearted deliberateness of what he did. The meanness.

When I was a child, my mother would call me into her room. She'd do this as if she were making a request, though actually it was a command. Inside the room, nothing terrible happened. Nothing bizarre, nothing that couldn't have been done with the door open, during the day instead of in the middle of the night, except that ours was not the sort of house where people left their doors open, and having taken so many naps, my mother was more alert at night than she was in the daytime. Doors were almost always closed, and privacy was tremendously important. Of course, that was because, except for my sister and me, no one wanted to be with anyone else. My mother wanted to drink and to watch TV, and my father wanted to take sleeping pills and sleep, undisturbed, in his own room, where an all-night jazz station played much of the night.

One time my mother agreed to take a friend's dog for a week. I have no idea why, or even whose dog it was, since as far as I knew my mother's friends were exclusively people she talked to on the telephone, but anyway: the dog came. A nice, brown mongrel. The dog always wanted to be with someone, but our mother's door and our father's door were kept closed, so every time the dog began whimpering, either my sister or I would bring it into one of our rooms, although we had been forbidden to do so. One of us always had the dog, and the person who did would walk it. One night, when I assumed my sister had the dog and she assumed I did, it was sleeping somewhere in the house when we went to bed. It awoke in the middle of the night and began running from door to door, whimpering. Eventually, since no one else seemed to hear it, I got up and put a coat over my pajamas, put on my slippers, and walked the dog and brought it back to my room. My sister had heard it too, though, and when I got back from the walk, she was sitting on my bed, wanting to take the dog into her room for the night. She had gotten it into her head that I was always taking the dog away from her. Since I wasn't, I told her to go ahead and take it. But then it seemed she did not want to do that, because she knew that the dog would have to be given back soon, so she was practicing not caring about it. That was why she had pretended, earlier, to be asleep when it whimpered. I actually had been asleep, and she might have saved me from awakening if she'd just gotten the dog, but in her mind, what she'd done had been completely logical. Then and now, that is the way my sister thinks: whatever she decides is objectively true. I'm sure I was out of sorts with her. That's how our fight began. She felt that I was—as she put it—"everyone's favorite," by which she meant our mother's and the dog's, since even my sister could not make a case for my being my father's favorite. His favorite person was himself. I asked her for evidence, and she told me she knew I went into our mother's room at night. She must have come looking for me and found me gone— otherwise, since my mother and I whispered so quietly, I don't see how she could have known.

Her reason for bringing it up was not what I thought, however. She didn't want to know what I did there, she only wanted to ask me to use my special position to do her, or us, a favor. "You can make her let us keep the dog," she said. I asked how she thought I could do that, since it had an owner. She declared that the dog did not have an owner. That it had come from the pound. The proof was that it had not been brought to our house by its so-called owner, but that our mother—who rarely went out—had driven to get it, which my sister was sure she had gotten at the pound, inventing the story of the vacationing owner in order to see how the dog fit into our house. If it didn't, she could just take it back. My sister told me to wait and went to her room and returned with a flyer from the ASPCA, which had come in the mail addressed to our parents. There was a picture of a boxer looking soulfully at the camera on the front, and information inside about adopting pets. For the first time, this made me grant the possibility that what she said was true. But even if she was right, what could I say? The dog was curled beside the bed, where we sat talking quietly. I *did* like the dog. My sister's suggestion was that I point out to our mother how good it was, and how happy we were with it. Then, if she wasn't evil—a favorite word of my sister's at the time—she would understand that we should keep it.

I waited to be summoned into our mother's room. Sometimes weeks would pass without my being called in. I worried that this was one of those times. I also worried that I'd blow it, somehow, and reveal that we knew where the dog had come from. I had come to agree with my sister: it was no accident they got the brochure, and then a dog appeared. Finally, I knocked on our mother's door. She did not respond. I was reluctant enough, doing it, because I knew a closed door meant Privacy, but still: I might not have much more time. I went into the bathroom, next to her bedroom, and ran the water and flushed the toilet. I thought that might awaken her if she was asleep. Then I knocked again. Still nothing. I whispered, "Mom?"

Our father opened the door. He was wearing pajama bottoms, and his hair was matted. His eyes were red. "What?" he said.

It wasn't exactly the Wolf impersonating Grandma, but I was still so surprised I couldn't think what to say. I hadn't heard him come home. I had no idea he was even in the house. I could not remember ever having seen him go into her room. I could hear some musician quietly playing a saxophone down the hallway. "I said, *What do you want?*" he said.

"The dog," I managed. Behind him, I could see my mother stretched out on the bed. Her eyes were closed, and she never moved. Still, I said: "We want to keep the dog." I knew she wouldn't hear, and I knew he wouldn't care. There was something about saying it, though. Something about saying what I'd come to say. To say nothing of the fact that I could report to Nina that I had made the statement.

"You can't," he said, and closed the door.

I stood there, half expecting that my mother would get up and say something. After all, I had never before knocked on her door. But time passed. There was no sound. I didn't dare knock again. Instead, I went to my sister's room and reported on what had happened. The dog was sleeping on her bed. It beat its tail a few times, but seemed too sleepy to rouse itself.

"*He* was there?" she said.

I nodded. I said: "She never looked up."

"She was dead," my sister whispered, cupping her hands over her mouth after she spoke. "He killed her."

I knew he hadn't. I knew it. But my sister had set her jaw, certain she was right.

"He said we can't keep the dog," I said. "I tried."

I felt terrible. My eyes had filled with tears. Not because she was dead—she *wasn't* dead—but because I'd failed.

I had left Nina's door ajar when I tiptoed in to tell her. The dog began to bark mightily. My sister and I jumped, in unison. Our father had pushed the door farther open and was standing there in his pajama bottoms, his hair a mess, looking at us. The dog jumped from the bed and raced toward him and he caught it with his foot and threw it so that it flipped backward. The dog yelped, scrambled to its feet, and dove under the bed. It all happened so fast, we were stunned.

"What are you doing in here?" our father said.

I was almost paralyzed with fear. "I'm telling her we can't keep the dog," I said.

He hated our being together, and always had. I could remember him carrying her, when she was still a baby, out of my room, where I had quieted her down, and forcing her to sleep in her own room, terrified.

"Then tell her and go to your room," he said.

I looked at my sister, who had begun to cry. "We can't," I said.

"You can't *what?*" our father said.

"Keep it," I said.

"A complete sentence, please," our father said.

I dropped my eyes. Finally, joining Nina in tears—and I hated to cry; I really hated it—I said: "We can't keep the dog."

"Yes! I want to keep her! She's my best friend!" my sister shrieked. Since her days of screaming protest were long over, she always went mute in my father's presence. My sister never screamed. Our father was taken aback, I could see. He cocked his head. "You don't want a dog that belongs to your mother's boyfriend," he said.

Telepathically, I heard Nina questioning me: *Boyfriend?*

"Do you know your mother's boyfriend?" he said. "No? You never met him? The man who was supposedly Mom's teacher?"

We stared at him, wide-eyed. Neither of us spoke.

"Come into Mom's room, and she'll tell you about her boyfriend," he said.

My sister drew back. Our father took a step forward.

"All this about her boyfriend's dog," he said, shaking his head sorrowfully. "Come on. Come tell Mom that you want to keep her boyfriend's dog and we'll see if she thinks you can."

"No," I said.

"No? You won't? But you knocked on the door at two o'clock in the morning, it was so important to you. Unless you're one of your mother's boyfriends, too."

I dropped my eyes. I could feel my sister's terror. It was his tone of voice that upset her; she was too young to understand what he was implying.

"Maybe you *can* keep the dog," he said. "You can make a direct appeal to Mom and see if you can keep her boyfriend's dog. In fact, maybe your sister would like to speak to Mom, since the dog is her best friend."

"Leave her alone," I said.

"You think that's what I should do?" he said. "Would that be because her brother is more capable of raising her than her own father? Or her dutiful mother, who provides both her children with such happy moments, but who particularly dotes on her son? Leave her alone," he said again, as if he could not comprehend the thought. He raised a finger, pretending to have just received inspiration. "All right, I'll leave her alone," he said. "Then *you* come see Mom."

I got up. Either the mattress springs creaked, or the dog whimpered. I wasn't sure which. I crossed the room. My father stepped aside and waited for me to go through the doorway—looking at me and daring me to react. He followed behind me. I could hear my sister sobbing. This was definitely one of the worst nights of my life. On what seemed like an interminable walk down the hallway, I began to integrate my sister's fear. Going toward my mother's room, I wondered if Nina might have been right, after all: if she might be dead. If that might be what he was taking me to see.

He turned on the overhead light, which seemed unnaturally bright. It was one of his favorite things to do at night. He liked to follow the sudden brightness by a comment: "Just checking." That night, he said nothing. My mother did not react to the light. She had rolled onto her side, the covers tangled beneath her. The sharp smell of vomit filled the room. She had thrown up on the rug at the side of the bed. She was not moving, but looking at her, I felt sure she wasn't dead.

"Make your appeal," my father said.

"What?"

"*Ask her*," he said.

I thought that if I did what he wanted, eventually, sometime, sometime before I died, myself, this might be over. "Mom?" I said. "Can we keep the dog?"

Of course there was no response.

"Maybe you need to shake her," he said.

I didn't think I needed to shake her. But if I didn't, this might never end. I put my hand on her arm and gripped it lightly. Her skin was clammy. I had no idea what time it was. There seemed to be some light coming up, out the window.

"Mom," I said again, with no prompting. "Can we keep the dog?"

Nothing. I waited for what he'd do next.

"I believe Mom has passed out from drinking too much," he said. "That's the thing about women: they like alcohol, but they can't handle it. In part, it has to do with body weight. Women weighing less than men, and so forth."

I said nothing.

"It's disappointing, isn't it?" he said. "But you can take advantage of women when they're in this state. There is that."

He was speaking as if we were old friends, having a casual conversation. I was sure that, like me, he could hear my sister crying.

"By 'taking advantage' I mean having sex, of course," he said.

I knew what he'd meant. I said nothing.

"But since Mom doesn't seem able to rouse herself, maybe if you wrote her a note about the dog and put it on her pillow. Or down there," he said, gesturing toward the acrid vomit. "Maybe there, because she'll be sure to find it, when she's cleaning up. My suggestion would be to put it in writing, that you both very much want to keep the dog."

I wished I had never seen the dog. It wasn't the dog's fault, but still.

I went to her desk, sat down, and wrote one sentence, certain that he had something more elaborate in mind, but with not much idea about what he might want me to write. I was surprised he didn't ask to look at it. He just nodded and gestured, again, to the floor. He did it with extreme graciousness, like a well-tipped maître d' showing a rich patron to a table. I bent and placed it a few inches away from the mess.

"Well, that's about the best you can do in a circumstance like this, don't you think?" he said.

I nodded.

"And now, being such a compassionate person, I'm sure you'll want to go console your sister. But compassion can only go so far, don't you think? The limits of compassion are so frustrating, but so real. You'll have to be kind but firm. She'll have to realize you can't keep the dog, because Mom has no negotiating power. How can Mom negotiate, when she's not even conscious?" He looked at his watch. "Look how late it's gotten!" he said, looking from his wrist to the window. There was a slight pink brightening of the sky.

I did intend to console Nina, but once out of the room I found myself inexplicably angry at her. I was angry with all of them, and thought—as I did on a daily basis—of adulthood as an ideal condition, in which I could do what I wanted when I wanted. That night I did not knock on my sister's door. Fortunately, she'd become silent, so there was no longer a clear reason to go to her. Years later she would say she had had "heart attacks" and passed out, she was sometimes so terrified. Her husband, who was a doctor, said they were anxiety attacks; he doubted that she had passed out, but thought, instead, that she had shut down her senses. That she had passed into a state something like hibernation. Fat lot of good that did her: at our house, every day was always the day we awoke in the cave and stumbled out, confused, into the light.

Part of the reason he acted the way he did, I think, was because he was secretly happy that I'd discovered him in our mother's bedroom. His presence there became an occasion to assert that he had the upper hand in the relationship—yet if he *had* had sex with her when she'd passed out, could he have thought that was anything worth bragging about? What was the impulse, in my family, to say or do such ugly things? Wouldn't any decent person keep quiet about their baser motives? If he felt powerful in that pathetic situation, I now realize how powerless he must have felt to begin with.

From the time I was six I fixed my sister's and my breakfast. She told Mac about that the first time they dated. In fact, he joked that she talked so much about me, he suspected he didn't have a chance. One of the things I've come to understand is that she doesn't take me for granted, but Nina has hardened into someone who will not, or cannot, express gratitude. She didn't even overtly delight in Mac; her fixity was something so extreme, though, that few people could have tolerated her devotion. He knew that, and knew, as well, that at some point it might become a problem. But he also told me that he'd never had a happy relationship with a woman until he met Nina.

He'd dated a woman before her, whose name couldn't be mentioned in Nina's presence. (I'd been taken by Mac to have drinks with her. It was a mystery to me why he still wanted to associate with her, except that Jan was extremely sexy.) She had taken money from his wallet and denied doing it, and worse than that, she had stashed drugs in the apartment and sworn, when he found them, that they weren't hers. She had thrown one of his textbooks out the window on a rainy night. She was spoiled, and petulant, and childish—the exact opposite of Nina who, if she felt any such impulses, kept them in check. But Mac had a very unrealistic idea about lovers who'd parted ways remaining friends. Not long after Mac moved in with Nina, he and Jan decided to have a last day of drinking beer and betting at the dog track, indulging in their vice one last time. It was a very un-Mac thing to do, and I wondered if his confiding in me about their gambling was some kind of test of me, as well as a secret it pleased him to keep hidden from my sister. And I suppose the truth is that I blamed Jan for it, not Mac.

After their outing the three of us met up for drinks, and she acted pretty bizarrely: it was clear that she'd not only lost money that day, but that she was also losing Mac. Jan had insisted upon meeting the new woman he said he'd fallen in love with, and, because he couldn't think how to say no, he'd told her Nina would join them for drinks, and instead, he had produced me. A meeting between Nina and any of Mac's former girlfriends would never have worked, but he admitted to me later that Jan had been so adamant about it, he hadn't known what to do. I wondered, when he first introduced me to her, whether he might have wanted us to become a threesome who met occasionally behind Nina's back. Jan blew it, if that had been the case. Sensing that she was losing him, she'd come on to me right in front of him. She was trouble, and what that told me was that because he'd been involved with her, Mac had to have more problems than were apparent.

"Armchair shrink?" Serena would say. "Have everyone figured out but yourself?"

Serena could be so maddening; I would be the first to admit that I didn't have myself figured out. That I don't. Serena would want me to take that admission as an occasion to reimmerse myself in my childhood. Sometimes, with her in mind, I do. I see myself as a boy. I see myself doing something. I see Nina, like a shadow protruding into the light. But while I can easily envision her face, I never envision my own. Whatever is happening mystifies me because I don't really feel part of the scene.

My sister and I had a routine of going to our father's room, where every morning the door that had been so resolutely closed the night before stood open, and assessing the condition of the bed. We would look at the unmade—or the made—bed without comment. Then we would go to the kitchen sink and check to see if there were breakfast dishes. It was as if, over and over, we stalked an animal, understanding the directions it moved in by studying the pattern of the footprints, knowing what kind of animal it was because we recognized its droppings.

The worst problem I had with Serena was that she was obsessed with my childhood. When something really interested her, she wouldn't let go. Her orientation toward the world was psychological. In spite of her deriding me for being too analytical, she believed anything any psychiatrist said, and she consulted them as often as possible. Still, as a form of addiction, Serena's beliefs were hugely superior, in my mind, to liquor and drugs. I was even willing to go with her a few times, to see what she found so profound about the experience. Of course, the psychiatrist's orientation was also psychological, so being there with her was a little like being a twig in a brushfire.

That's too histrionic: I was not wood devoured by flames. The experience was more like freezing than burning. Feeling the cold chill of recognition. Would that be an honest enough admission for Serena?

I've had trouble living with women. My wife Caitlin was beautiful, and in many cases she used her beauty as a buffer against the world. Beauty would draw things to her; not only people, but possibilities. But it was always as if the world was courting her, and she was empowered by saying no to those things people who weren't beautiful wanted: no to this fascinating job; no to that friendship. In retrospect, I think she chose to marry me because I said no to her first. I even told her why, when I realized things were getting serious. That was back in the days when I thought I could tell a woman the truth, and not have it boomerang.

I told her that I still had not gotten over a girl I knew in high school. I wanted to get over her, but so far, in spite of distance and age and perspective, I had not. It was as if I'd slapped her. Her first question was whether the girl had been especially beautiful. The question forced me to conjure up an image, but to my surprise, no one image appeared, since I'd meant it more generally. I'd said girl, but I'd thought of it as girls. Rochelle Rogan, perhaps, with her pouting lips and arched eyebrows, or Josie, "the Dead Girl"—who, as fate would have it, remained very much alive. Patty Arthur? Of course Patty. I saw her breasts so vividly, it was as if I could touch them. But for years, I had forced Patty to the back of my mind. The Patty I remembered was casual and unadorned and wore no more makeup than my sister. She had beautiful eyes, yet she was not a girl you would call beautiful. I told Caitlin that she had not been particularly attractive. It was the wrong answer, because then Caitlin had a million questions to find out what it had been.

As I described what it was like the first time I walked into Patty Arthur's bedroom, she got impatient and urged me to talk about the person, not the place. But the room had *been* Patty Arthur. You couldn't distinguish between them, the way people are so fond of saying that you cannot distinguish between love and architecture, viewing the Taj Mahal. The fact that Patty had been my first girlfriend was certainly significant, but the idea of the exotic, coupled with sex, made a powerful impression, so that one was always a letdown without the other. But when a person is no longer a teenager, what's exotic? Faraway places? Incense (as Caitlin—as so many of my girlfriends—seem to think)? Private dancers?

What I yearned for, after Patty Arthur, was being taken by surprise, so that familiarity never became a foundation for anything with me, but the thing that precluded the possibility of a relationship's deepening. When I confessed this to Caitlin—the last woman I ever did say it to   she thought I was talking about excitement in our sex life. She thought I meant that I wanted to see her in skimpy outfits, or to be seduced in secluded places. Which, being a man, I can't say I minded—but I really wanted that rush that happens when something transforms you instantly: a variation of that strange moment when I exited the present, then was catapulted into someone else's world, where I felt simultaneously comfortable and uncomfortable. The uncomfortable part was important, too. It made me trust the moment, because I knew I wasn't idealizing. It sort of validates the metamorphosis, as if you've paid a price for it. This gets abstract, the more I try to put it into words. I wanted to do what quantum physicists do all the time: close a door on an empty box and open it on Schrödinger's cat. I was one person when I walked into Patty Arthur's room and another when I left. Transformations do not happen only in fairy tales.

A few tense days after our talk, Caitlin determined to surprise me. My life became a chaos of unexpected moments. They didn't do much for me because it wasn't newness I was looking for. They made her someone she was not, and they underscored for me how difficult, if not impossible, it was to become totally immersed in experiences that were someone else's idea. After months of silly posturing, Caitlin came to the conclusion that youth would always be the missing factor. She was up against the impossible: meaning that only in youth could one truly be open to transformation. She had even been jealous of my sister because my sister had known me when I was young. Caitlin was irrational, and after my confession she became more so, bringing up Patty constantly, even going so far as to consult a Ouija board, to see how deep the bond still was between me and a person I had never seen as an adult.

When Caitlin redecorated the house, I didn't know if it was her last desperate thought, or her final retaliation: the furniture gone, new furniture brought in—all done behind my back, so that when I walked through the front door I stood there, disoriented, convinced that I had somehow entered another person's house. The memory of that awful moment makes my sister's house doubly attractive to me: the way it stays the same through the years. Though I wish for her sake that she would make changes—bring in a comfortable footstool, even put some flowers in a vase. Instead, she's chosen to keep everything as it was, as if the whole house is a roped-off crime scene.

Perhaps it is, though the crime happened elsewhere, in the darkness, on a highway.

Jan called me when Mac died. She remembered my name and found it in the phone book and called the same day his obituary was in the paper, hardly able to speak for crying. My first thought was that she was so upset, she might call Nina next. Because of that, I decided I needed to see her one more time. I asked her to come to my apartment, even though her tears were so excessive that I just knew she wasn't so much crying for Mac, as she was crying out to me. Mac's death had provided her with a second chance to try to get together with her second choice.

At the time of Mac's death, Hound's boss, Gary, was crashing at my apartment for a couple of weeks, because Kate couldn't stand the man. Gary's wife had thrown him out, and he was a basket case. The two of us were basket cases: I knew I would never have another friend like Mac, and I was worried Nina might have to be hospitalized, she was so despondent.

I was in the shower when Jan arrived. Gary opened the door. I came out in my bathrobe, ready to lie to her and tell her how much she had meant to Mac, while also letting her know I wasn't available, to find Gary and Jan deep in conversation. She was saying that when Mac died, she had lost her soul mate; he was telling her that nothing he promised about changing his ways would make his wife take him back. I had only been in the shower for five minutes. How had they gotten into it so quickly? Jan's mascara was streaked under her eyes like a clown's. Gary jumped up and got her a tissue. I could tell that he was confused: what should his role be? He was obviously attracted to her, so he wanted to stay, but at the same time, he suspected he should go.

To my surprise, I began to feel competitive. I'd invited her over to tell her how important she had been in Mac's life, but also to gently disabuse her of any notion that she and Mac might have gotten back together. Instead, before I had said much more than hello, she already seemed to be connecting with his replacement. I decided that she and I should have a one-night stand. "Will you excuse us?" I said to Gary, giving him his cue, and he said that oh, he had just been about to go out, so sorry. He got his jacket and left quickly, after shaking Jan's hand and saying how nice it was to meet her. The door closed, and I smiled at her. I expected her to rush into my arms, to say something about the awful thing that had happened to Mac. Instead, she said: "Would you mind if I went with your friend? We were in the middle of a serious conversation when you more or less told him to beat it." She got up and started toward the door before I could answer. I blocked her. I said that yes, I would mind. That she and I had something to discuss. She dropped her arms to her side. "Yes?" she said, patronizingly. She was looking at me coldly. She had called just a short time before, convulsed with misery, and now she was acting as if I were some petty annoyance. I no longer felt the slightest desire for her—not even out of competition with Gary: freeloading, self-pitying Gary, who wasn't even my friend, but Hound's. She cocked her head. "What, exactly, are you stopping me for?" she said. It reminded me too much of Serena's confrontations. It even reminded me of my long-ago fight with Nina, little Nina, and our pointless fight about her fantasy fairies. I stepped aside.

I called Hound and told him his boss had just gotten together with Mac's old girlfriend, no doubt to commemorate his death. "I didn't know he had an old girlfriend," Hound said. He was tired of telling me how grateful he was that I was putting up his friend. He said nothing. Finally, he asked how I was doing. Okay, I said. He asked how Nina was. Okay, I lied. He asked if I needed distraction; if I wanted to go to a movie. I said that I didn't. I felt suddenly foolish about calling him. I dressed and went out and began to walk, thinking about Mac, thinking about what a weird, unpleasant woman Jan was. I walked a long distance, and finally found myself in the park where I'd once fed pigeons as I waited for the return of my best friend and the woman I almost married.

There were few pigeons in the park. A bum was sleeping on one of the benches. He made me angry—he was repulsive: ugly, dirty. I moved quickly away. As I did, I was surprised to be crying. The possibility of crazy Jan's calling Nina seemed more and more real. I hurried to Nina's, convinced that the most important thing I could do would be to intercept the inevitable phone call another woman who disliked me was about to make to my sister. The walk took longer than I thought. It was late, and Nina was asleep. I had to knock many times before I heard her moving. I stood there, shaking, as she asked sleepily, with a catch in her throat, who was at the door. When I said my name, she undid the chain and let me in, not even bothering to ask what I was doing there. I had already come by that morning, and that afternoon. She said nothing—just did a zombie walk back to bed, disheveled, having fallen asleep in her underwear. She pulled the covers over her without saying a word. I stood at the side of the bed, feeling the seepage of cold air from the narrow crack Nina always left at the bottom of the window, looking out to where, in the moonlight, I could see the limb of a tree swaying in the wind. I moved closer to the glass. There were a few stars in the sky, but on the ground, there was nothing worth noticing. In the distance, lights cast an eerie, pinkish glow. Everything my eye went to seemed profoundly empty. I realized that I was hoping for some movement: a squirrel; a bird. But they were all asleep. Suddenly exhausted, now more puzzled than angry about my encounter with Mac's former girlfriend, I took off my shoes and lay on my back on the rug beside Nina's bed. I was so tired that the only thing that kept me from sleep was that I was listening for the phone.

Which did not ring all night.

I never heard from Jan again. Gary said she had spoken bitterly to him about my convincing Mac that she should not remain one of his friends, which was nothing Mac and I had ever discussed. Gary warned me that she really had it in for me—that she had called me "God's gift to women." He had not gone back to her apartment with her. Instead, they had walked around and finally had a drink before parting.

By then, it was clear to him that whatever they did would only have allowed her to act out some weird agenda between herself and Mac, or between herself and me. At the end of the week his wife had taken him back. I never heard from him again, either.

No armchair explanation of all of that, Serena. Just something else that happened the week Mac died.

The day I gave Serena the engagement ring, we went to my sister's. Unlike Caitlin, Serena was pretty but not beautiful. I had never said a thing to her about wishing for another metamorphosis, because by the time we got together I'd given up on that kind of desire. By then I had learned that desires, too, could be done away with—they didn't need to be dignified any more than ideas, or old jokes. I loved Serena. I suppose she was somewhat exotic, being English. And without setting her mind to it, as Caitlin had, she had a taste for kinky sex. Though she blames me totally for the pregnancies, you have to wonder about a person who used no birth control herself. In summer I would wear long-sleeved shirts to cover the spots where the ropes Serena laughingly bound me with chafed my wrists. I once explained the reddened wrists to Hound as we were driving along. We'd never talked about the abortion, let alone our sex lives. It was just that he'd said, "How'd you do that?"—so casual, so disinterested—that I'd decided what the hell, and answered honestly.

The people around me have always been interested in my sex life—whether because they don't have one, or because theirs is unsuccessful, or because they sense a slightly masochistic streak in me, I don't know. I suppose I was something of a masochist, since I never really took on my father, which was one of the biggest mistakes of my life. In my experience, if you don't face down your aggressor immediately, others will take up where the first person left off. While I think that it's a simplification to say that victims invite victimhood, I do believe that when someone is victimized it seems to make it open season for other people to have at them in the same way. Somehow the malice gets into the air. My father always thought of me as his rival. We don't need Freud to explain what it meant that our father called our mother Mom—she told me, proudly, that he did, even when we children weren't in the room. Years later, it occurs to me that he might have felt so bad about his behavior that it was easier for him to assume everyone, including his son, would act the same way. His idea of a bonding experience was to show me pornography. That he was so obsessed with my being a man, as he put it, only makes me think that he, himself, had serious problems.

A psychological insight Serena would approve of. Perhaps a bit facile, though.

When Alice Manzetti called, I was missing Serena. Though I didn't really want to see her, I found myself inviting her to come to Boston. All the other times, I'd been willing to travel, but I couldn't bring myself to fly to Syracuse. I didn't even think about her visit until the last minute, and then I took her to a restaurant in the neighborhood I sometimes went to when I was tired and just wanted something quick to eat. Of all coincidences, she came on Serena's birthday. I was wallowing in what it felt like to be a bastard. As for the restaurant, I didn't much enjoy being there, myself.

Inside, I ran into a colleague from work. Since nobody at work knew anything about my life, I imagine the sighting seemed significant to him. He was a new guy named Phil Ross, who'd come from a software company in Silicon Valley that had gone belly-up. He was with his girlfriend: a small woman with high cheekbones and good definition in her arms, wearing turquoise jewelry. Mac's old girlfriend Jan had worn turquoise jewelry. Maybe that was why I disliked Ross's girlfriend on first sight, even though she smiled at me.

I barely knew the Alice I introduced; she'd taken a cab to the restaurant, and I'd met her outside, on the sidewalk, for no more than a quick hug and a few glib remarks about the difficulty of travel. As I introduced her, I imagined I saw her through the other woman's eyes: a little heavy; out of shape beneath the blazer and skirt; the coat over her arm an unattractive muddy red. I thought of Serena's camel hair coat—the one we'd draped over the covers in a chilly bed-and-breakfast in Maine, when she was telling me for the millionth time that she would eventually leave me, because she was certain I could never be loyal to any woman. I wondered if Alice liked her coat anywhere near as much as Serena and I had liked hers. Amid all the fighting and frustration, Serena's coat had been such a comfort. I remembered stroking it as I absorbed Serena's wrath. She had found out I'd had a one-night stand with a waitress. I wondered, in the restaurant with Alice, whether Serena still had the coat. Whether Serena might be wearing it in London, as I sat in a restaurant she and I had avoided.

"It's good to see you," I said.

"It *is*," she said. She still had that cheerleader's way of punching last words. She put her folded coat next to her in the booth. There was a greasy, sharp smell in the air that made me wish we had gone to the Italian place next door, though it was always too crowded and noisy. Phil Ross and his girlfriend were probably avoiding the restaurant, themselves, so they could hear each other.

"So you said on the phone that you were coming for the show at the MFA?" I said. Across the restaurant, Phil and the girlfriend were deep in conversation. They looked like California people: blond; bright-eyed; spines straight, as if the overheated restaurant couldn't wilt them. I couldn't imagine what they were doing there.

"Not really," she said. "Really, I came to see you."

I tried to look pleasantly surprised. "I'm flattered," I said. "Have you kept in touch with many people from high school?"

"No," she said. "A couple of the girls."

"And one of the guys," I said, smiling. I wanted our meeting to be over. I wanted to be by myself. "What do you most remember about me?" I said.

"How nice you were to your sister," she said.

"You're kidding."

"No. You were obviously so *close*. My brother was in Catholic school, and I used to wish he could go to our school, and that he'd act the way you did. Like I was a real person, I mean. Even after all this time, we barely tolerate each other. How is Nina?"

"She lives in Cambridge," I said. "Actually, I wouldn't say

that I've been much help to her in having a happier life. She was married to a really great guy, but he died in a car crash. A long time ago," I added.

"Oh, that's *awful*," she said. "But it must be an enormous help that you're so close by."

"We don't see that much of each other," I said. Why did I lie? Probably because I didn't want to have anything that resembled a heart-to-heart with Alice. It was a strange feeling, sitting across from someone I had no real memories of, knowing that person often thought of me.

"What does Nina do?" she asked. "She was so creative when she was a kid."

"She edits books and fact-checks for magazines. She got some insurance money when her husband died, and it stopped her from focusing on a career. The freelance editing seemed like a blessing, at first. It came along at the right time, but she sort of got trapped there, and she's never done anything else."

"Good for her," Alice said.

"Excuse me?"

"Good for her for doing what she wants. So many people in our generation seem to feel they have to do something extraordinary. Like whatever they do is never enough. It's made for a bunch of unsatisfied overachievers, if you ask me."

Our waitress was not an overachiever. When she finally took our drink order, she was distracted by a noisy group of people coming into the restaurant and had to ask twice what we wanted. One of the women in the group wore a hat with a tassel, which reminded me of a hat Nina had worn when she was a child. As we got older, both of us refused to wear hats.

Wearing boots was the most humiliating thing either of us could imagine. But since no one saw us off in the morning, we could leave behind whatever we didn't want to wear. The woman settled herself into a booth. She had a bright smile, and for a second I thought I might know her, but when I saw her face in profile, I realized I was mistaken. I had the crazy urge to get to know her. To get up, go up to her, take her by the arm, and steer both of us out of the restaurant.

"This is a nice place," Alice said, sliding back in the booth. "Not all chichi."

It was not nice. It was smoke-filled and dreary. I resisted looking in the direction of the noisy group, who had by now settled into two booths near the front.

"So tell me about yourself," I said. "Obviously you're in touch with Josie."

"We lost track of each other but got reconnected because of my mother. My mother looked her up a couple of years ago. She doesn't have any friends of her own, so she started looking up mine. Isn't that funny? Sad, I mean, but funny, too. She thinks high school was the most meaningful experience of my life, and that I was surrounded by wonderful friends. I hated every minute of it. I didn't have any school feeling at all. You know, my mother *made* me become a cheerleader."

I understood I should chime in and complain about high school. Instead, I said: "I guess you know I saw Josie recently, in Vermont."

Alice nodded. She said: "She gave me your number."

The waitress brought our drinks and set my scotch down in front of Alice and her ginger ale in front of me. We switched glasses. Alice was waiting for me to say something. I took a sip of my drink. I looked over my shoulder. The woman in the booth was not looking at me. Her long blond hair curled at her shoulders. The hat sat in front of her, on a place mat. "Josie looked good," I said.

"Oh, Josie takes care of herself," she said. "I was going to aerobics class for a while, but I twisted my ankle. In the summer, it's always easier to exercise." She reached in her handbag. "Mind if I smoke?" she said.

"Doesn't bother me."

"You were always so . . . well, things *didn't* bother you, did they?" She struck a match and lit her cigarette. She waved out the match, dropping it in an ashtray. "If Nina lives in Cambridge, maybe she'd like to join us," she said.

The idea startled me. How would I begin to explain how reclusive my sister was? Suddenly—because Alice insisted on seeing our relationship as being so ideal—I felt I might be held responsible in some way for Nina's behavior.

"Not a good idea?" she said, picking up my hesitation.

"She'd like to see you, I'm sure," I said. "But she doesn't go out much. I'll give you her number. You can call. I'm sure she'll ask you over."

"Is this, like, agoraphobia?"

"No. No. She meets me and a friend of mine for dinner every now and then."

"So maybe she'd like to come out."

"No. I know she wouldn't do it."

Alice took a puff of her cigarette. She said, "She's still depressed because of her husband?"

Depressed? Was that what my sister was? Reclusive and

private was easier to think. She hadn't been much different as a girl. Also, Nina did things I didn't think a depressed person would do. She was the one who'd insisted on selling our parents' house without involving a realtor when our mother went into the rest home, and she'd shown everyone through the house herself, taken care of everything until we brought in a lawyer for the closing. Nina went to specialty stores to find the best ingredients to cook with; she laughed at jokes; she baby-sat the neighbors' boy and was always full of stories about the cute things Justin had done. But Alice's question had confused me. Nina might be agoraphobic. She might be—I knew she was—depressed.

"You never married?" she said.

I hadn't been expecting the question. I had been lost in thought: avoiding thinking about Nina, avoiding thinking about the woman in the booth.

"I've been divorced for years," I said.

"You struck out, huh? I guess we didn't invent that rite of passage, though sometimes it seems that way, doesn't it?"

This did not seem like a meeting with someone who carried the torch for me, as Josie had put it. It was more like Alice wanted to use the torch to repel me. "What about the reunion?" I said, changing the subject. "How was that?"

"I went hoping to see you," she said.

"Really?"

"Yeah," she said. "Really. I more or less came in saying that, right?" She tilted her head back and blew smoke at the ceiling. "I heard you called Nancy Dimmitt and her husband hung up on you," she said. She snorted. "Is he like—was he the only one who put his foot down? I mean, from the way

Nancy tells it, it seems like her husband has amazing radar, or something, if you call and say you and his wife were high school pals and he says, 'That was a long time ago, and it's going to stay a long time ago' and hangs up."

"The way some jerk acted on the phone seems to have delighted you, Alice. Were you wishing I'd gotten your husband, so his paranoia could have kept you from being here?"

"Listen," she said, "for what it's worth, I think you might not be as bad as you seem. But the way you act only makes other people feel bad. First I hear about how great Josie looks. Then you refuse to let me get together with your sister, like I'm not worthy of her company. Then you pretend you want me to tell you about a reunion you didn't care enough about to go to, condescending to me because I'm just some dull, unimportant person. Not pretty, like Josie. Not important, like your sister."

Across the restaurant, Phil Ross was helping his girlfriend into a black leather coat. I looked away, hoping they wouldn't look in our direction.

"I needed a cheap dinner and somebody to fuck," she said. "Is that what you think?"

She was a lot crazier than Nancy's husband. A lot crazier. I was glad that the waitress hadn't come to take our order. I considered seriously just getting up and walking away.

"As a matter of fact, I am here," she said quietly, "because my niece is a freshman at Northeastern, and as I told you on the phone, she and I are going to the MFA to have lunch to celebrate her birthday. I wanted to see you, but I didn't make this trip exclusively for that purpose." She rummaged in her purse. She withdrew a museum ticket, then slipped it back into her bag. "But you'd never believe that, would you? You're so conceited, of course you wouldn't. You remember how girls used to be called cockteases if they flirted with boys when they didn't have any intention of going all the way? I don't know exactly what the male equivalent is, but it occurs to me that that's what you've become: go to Brattleboro to look up somebody you know will be easy, because she's upset about her dying relative. Then don't think twice about asking for the phone number of the next vulnerable person, poor Patty Arthur."

"Go right ahead," I said. "As long as you're not going to shoot me at the end of this rant."

She narrowed her eyes. She said: "I might have my problems. I might have a not-so-great marriage. I might have a mother going around trying to pass herself off as cheerful, when she cries herself to sleep. But I'll tell you one thing: *I got over being the cheerleader.* And in the guise of being Mr. Nice Guy, you're nothing but an exploiter. You know what? I'm not going to give you the letter Patty sent you in care of me. I visited Patty just a couple of days ago, it so happens. You know what I did? I brought the letter here, because I was going to give it to you, but when I saw you coming down the sidewalk, I ripped it up and put it in the trash outside. Just like high school again, isn't it? The girls, all abuzz about you."

I could hardly believe how angry she was. It was an anger that preceded even seeing me, though. I was sure of it. As I started to get up to walk away, she moved faster. She snatched up her coat and stalked out of the restaurant. I sat back down.

As she pushed open the restaurant door, she must have

been crying. The blonde stared after her. When the door closed, the blonde did not—she quite deliberately did not— look back in my direction. Across the table from her, a man with a stubble of beard dropped her hat onto his beer bottle and swirled it around. She reached out and took his hand.

I sat there until the waitress came to the table. Then I ordered a hamburger and a Coke. I found what had just happened so astonishing that I considered calling Nina immediately to tell her what she'd missed. If I'd had a tape recorder, I could have played the tape for Serena's old shrink, who thought my responses were often curiously passive, and asked his considered opinion about what, exactly, I might have said or done. That evening on the radio, I had heard a report about air rage, like road rage in the sky. Alice seemed to have restaurant rage. I sat sideways, leaning my back against the wall, and made myself as comfortable as I could in the booth with its sharp, cracked leather seats.

Not looking again at the blonde in the booth seemed the most important thing. It was still possible she might stand—at the very least, lock eyes with me again—when I got up to go, but until I did I resolved not to look in her direction.

I did not think about Patty until—no eyes having followed me out of the restaurant—I saw the trash receptacle Alice had referred to. Then sadness overwhelmed me, as if something really unlikely and inappropriate was in there—as if the destroyed note was cremains, rather than ripped paper. I never thought of dipping in my hand.

From my apartment, I called Hound. Kate said that he was working late. I called his office, but got no answer. I spoke to Kate a second time and asked her to tell him to call me when he got home.

"You sound like hell," she said. "What's wrong?"

I said that nothing was wrong. I was just tired.

"Girl problems," she said, making an educated guess.

Yes—though it was not something I could talk to Kate about. It was understood that we would never again talk about ourselves. Our pillow talk had come to an end.

My mother lost a child between my birth and the birth of my sister. She said it made my father sad, because it seemed for a while that she could not have another child, and my father— according to her—very much wanted a daughter. I was incapable, then as now, of imagining my father caring about a family. I would watch my father for signs that he cared. I hung around him more, after my mother told me that, and asked questions I thought were harmless and cute, like how many years he thought it would be before I, too, shaved. No matter the topic, or the time I approached him, he was never in the mood for talking. He clearly cared more about the newspaper, and the look of satisfaction on his face as he smoked his pipe was not an expression I ever saw, those few times he bothered to say good night to my sister or me.

At odd hours of the day, my mother did what might be thought of as motherly things. She did the wash and ironed—often in the middle of the night, the ironing board set up in her bedroom, where a small pink plastic TV sat on top of her bureau. She sometimes even baked bread, though we never enjoyed it as much as we might have if our father had allowed butter in the house. Jams or jellies weren't allowed, either. They were special treats, included in tiny jars in our Christmas stockings. I'm sure my sister now loves teatime because it's an excuse to eat things with jelly. When I think of my childhood, I realize that I focus on the things we had to do without. We were to be quiet at all times. We were to pick up after ourselves. We were to prepare our own breakfasts, if our mother did not appear. As an adult, I throw my clothes all over the apartment because it's a way of rejecting my training. I also eat jelly on many things, including ice cream. These observations—first made by Caitlin, later noticed by Serena—I was able to explain and even to laugh about, though both women continued to be more annoyed than amused. They had their own eccentricities, but somehow theirs were nobler because they couldn't be traced back to their childhoods.

My mother was a childish person. Not that she had the gayness or the sometimes pleasing self-centeredness of a child. Instead, she had the self-absorption of an alcoholic and the moroseness of someone who has decided that nothing she can do is viable. At night she was more childish than she was during the day. She would giggle, showing me old photographs of herself as a girl. She would flit from topic to topic. But this gives the mistaken impression that she was animated. She wasn't. She was fidgety, but she moved slowly—to compensate for the disorientating effects of the alcohol, I assume— and dipped into her bureau drawer for a photo album, or went to her night table drawer for a pack of letters like an old person making a great effort to retrieve things. She couldn't sleep and she knew all her stories herself, so in inviting me in, what she was doing was reinvigorating her nighttime playthings by presenting them to someone new.

She had a letter my father had written her when she was in the hospital, after miscarrying his supposedly longed-for daughter. Since his handwriting was almost indecipherable, she had to help me. Finally, after I had read it three or four times—she always wanted me to read it aloud—I knew it well enough to pretend to read it perfectly. The parts my mother liked best were my father's assertion that the child she had already provided him with had made him so happy that any other happiness would be mere excess, and that she, herself, was the love of his life. It was so puzzling to me that I asked if he had once been very different. It was the wrong thing to ask. Whatever did I mean? she wanted to know. A doctor's life was one in which the patients came first, but there was never a night he did not come into her bedroom and pray with her for the health and happiness of the family.

Oh, really? Was that the prayer that went: "This is not *this*"? The prayer that ended with his smashing his fist through a windowpane?

There was a picture over my mother's bureau of a small boy seen from behind, wearing pajamas and kneeling in prayer, as a collie sat beside him, facing the bed. Both the boy and the dog had halos over their heads. As she talked, my eyes went to the picture, but I quickly looked away. Ultimately, though, that was a clue to my mother. That she conflated things, imagining one thing to be another. In her imagination, a little boy or—for all I knew—the dog in the picture became her husband, kneeling. It was funny, on some level—extremely funny—but at the time I had no desire to laugh. It explained why she thought certain things she'd seen in magazines were things my sister had done, like the time she rummaged through my sister's room, intent upon finding the ice skates my sister had worn to the rink, demanding as she looked—futilely—to know where my sister had found the money for such an expensive purchase.

I thought the issue of *Life* magazine about the Olympics in the bathroom was what my mother remembered, but no: she remembered seeing my sister leaving the house with her white skates slung over her shoulder. In looking so often at the photo albums, and at other memorabilia, she fooled herself into thinking that she and my father were still having a life, taking vacations, eating in restaurants. Did our mother ever say anything nice to him about us those times we'd done something well, the way she reported on us immediately if we did something wrong? They rarely spoke to each other, rarely were in the same room at the same time, but since my mother watched soap operas in the afternoon, perhaps she thought they had an exciting, though turbulent relationship. Maybe she woke up in the morning thinking herself the betrayed mistress pregnant with the lawyer's child, and that her husband was not a doctor, but a kleptomaniac lawyer. Maybe our family was always about to be joined by bastard brothers and prostitute half sisters, and maybe a mad arsonist was planning to burn down our house. Who could imagine what her reality consisted of? I hoped that it consisted of more than self-congratulatory nostalgia based on one note her husband had written her—which, truth be told, he may not have written. Would a person really write such a note on sheets ripped off a prescription pad? She involved me because she needed a witness, though the longer I listened, the more silent I became: no help at all.

No, I was help: with my silence, I soothed her.

My sister and I, as teenagers, were not the timid children we had been. We conspired with each other, putting aside our differences in order to fool our mother, to do whatever we wanted behind her back. Most of the things we did were no worse than sharing cigarettes or looking at forbidden magazines. The magazines were right there, at the bottom of a box of plumbing supplies under the bathroom sink. It was my father's stash; he had shown them to me not long before he took me to see one of his patients masturbating.

Nina was as interested as I was in the airbrushed center-folds of *Playboy*. We laughed at everything—even the jokes that made puns we didn't understand. It was because of our giggling that we got caught. My mother found us, by doing the unthinkable: opening the door of the bathroom, without knocking. Once inside, she didn't know what to do, and decided—as she could be relied on to decide things you would never expect—that our looking at what she called pornography meant that it was time for her to explain why the photographs were so misleading. Not only reprehensible, and degrading to women, but misleading. Which led her to the medicine cabinet, from which tumbled pills and jars of Vaseline, and things that had no part in what she intended to talk to us about, such as a flashlight and a toothbrush still in the package. Her discussion with us about the evils of pornography—"lecture" is a better word, since my sister sat as silently as I did—was bizarre. My mother stood over us, holding the things that had fallen into her hand, all of which she believed pertained to the reality behind the magazine's centerfold. The Vaseline, she informed us, was a lubricant because sex was not always comfortable. The pills were for menstrual cramps: although women seemed to have been created as sex objects, actually God had punished them—not the men who had sex with them—with discomfort. She ran out of steam as she looked at the toothbrush. She held the narrow box aloft, but words failed her.

"Are you rehearsing for your career as a nurse?" Nina said, dripping sarcasm.

The look on my mother's face was one of astonishment.

"No, I'm a *concerned parent*, unlike your father, whose years of education don't seem to have lifted his mind from the gutter," she said. She picked up the *Playboy* and threw it in the wastebasket. "How dare you speak to me that way," she said.

Nina was unpredictable: she could be taciturn, then scream; she disdained our mother, then decided to mock her to her face.

Which really wasn't that different from what Mac decided, years later. An old girlfriend? Meet her for a farewell gambling episode and drink, but don't invite Nina along. A quandary about whether to drop out of medical school? Work it out privately. "You know," Mac once said to me, "your sister's always braced for some disaster. Well, she's going to have to adjust her expectations, because she's not going to hear the bad news from me."

Wrong, Mac. Wrong, wrong, wrong.

✦

I went around, jiggling the piece of paper with Patty Arthur's number on it as if it were pocket change. Alice had been right; it had not been difficult to find out where she was. But why call? Why, this many years later, when she had thrown me over for a college professor and I hadn't cared, because I'd been dating a Swedish girl who didn't consider an evening complete without sex? I'd probably persevered because I wanted to prove to Alice that I hadn't been affected by what she'd said—I suppose it seemed like a way of getting even with her, in absentia—and also because I couldn't get Josie out of my mind. I thought Patty might be the antidote. I thought about calling Josie and telling her that her friend Alice had a chip on her shoulder a mile high and giving her my version of our unpleasant meeting, but somehow, I expected she'd call me when she heard. I thought so for weeks, and then I realized that either Alice had said nothing, or that Josie didn't want to get involved. I thought about her on the street in Vermont. About extending my hand, her kiss. She had warned me emphatically, while providing no evidence, that I should stay away from Patty. Since she misread Alice's feelings for me, though, wasn't there every chance she'd misunderstood Patty's?

I returned to the restaurant twice, hoping to see the blonde woman again. Neither time did I find her.

At work, my client list was expanding. I was commended for a program I'd completed that had been sent to an engineering company in Buffalo. Around that time, I began dating a woman named Shaundra Hodges, who had a teenage daughter in boarding school. Shaundra had a parrot who said, "Nice legs" and several obscenities her ex-husband had taught it. There was a framed photograph of the snub-nosed daughter, with the parrot sitting on her shoulder. There was also a snapshot, leaning against the photograph, of her ex-husband: a private detective named Mickey Brenner. The parrot did not appear in that snapshot. A gun did. A gun that was actually a cigarette lighter. Mickey Brenner's head was dipped toward the flame, so that only a bit of a profile, lips dangling a cigarette, could be seen. I didn't think I knew her well enough to ask why she had it there, leaning up against the picture of their daughter. "Mickey, my ex," was her only comment as I stood looking at it. Shaundra worked for an insurance company in Somerville and lived only a few blocks from her office. She thought Somerville was as beautiful as a wildlife refuge, compared to the Bronx, where she had first worked when she moved to New York after splitting with Mickey.

His name stays in my mind, because we never had sex without Mickey being present. Not actually present, but invoked with expletives that would have made the parrot blanch. I told my sister about it—about how Shaundra would become more and more furious at her ex-husband the closer she came to orgasm, cursing him, calling him terrible things.

My sister was horrified. She thought I should have no more to do with the woman, and refused to meet her. She was usually curious enough to meet the women I went out with, but she wanted nothing to do with foulmouthed Shaundra. Nina was aghast that I thought so little of myself that I didn't care if there was a third presence in the room when we had sex. She thought that I picked the wrong women because I knew things wouldn't work out, and that I picked excessive people because I could focus on their shortcomings and never blame myself when the relationship ended. Still, some part of her liked to hear my stories: they convinced her that dating was a minefield of weirdnesses impossible to maneuver without risking harm. It made her feel superior to me, in a way she shouldn't have, just because she'd put herself on a hill high above the battle. From where she was, she would have seen nothing if I hadn't brought back stories. I had been doing that since we were adolescents: showing her magazines, involving her in my discoveries.

When she told Mac about our father's unexpected appearance in a friend's basement, it was the first time I heard the story from her perspective. The way she saw it, she had been the center of attention, taking photographs of girls scantily dressed that she and I had a vague notion of selling to some magazine. I was only the offstage presence, directing the action from behind a closed door. This was not exactly the case, because the girls ran constantly to the door, like penitents to the window of the confessional, to get advice about what to do. It was easier for them to approach someone not part of the scene—easier, and also mysterious and exciting. My sister was both in the scene and apart from it, the eye behind the camera. The girls were lesbians. Lucy Roderick had told me so. She had asked me to watch her make out with her cousin Dianne, who had had an abortion when she was fifteen, vowing never to be with a man again. Now that might be the fulfillment of a conventional male fantasy, but then I was a teenager, and such a thing seemed both titillating and terrifying. It was Lucy who had told me—having learned it from her mother—that our mother did, indeed, have a boyfriend: a man she went shopping and to matinees with. I was surprised to hear this, in part because it was impossible to imagine my mother at a matinee.

Not wanting to be a pawn for Lucy Roderick, I set down my own conditions: that I not be the only person watching; that my sister also be present. After all, Lucy insisted that they weren't embarrassed to be lesbians. The plan was to take pictures to sell to a magazine, the four of us splitting the profits. I brought enough grass to make everybody happy. I'd started buying it from a friend's brother. It made my night-time visits to my mother's room easier, when I had to look at the same things, reread the same notes, react to the same stories I'd heard before. Grass gave me a nice, bemused distance from all that, and since her eyes were redder than mine, since she was more out of it than I was, she never noticed.

The same could not be said about my father, though. Leaving my mother's room one night, I passed the bathroom, where he was peeing into the toilet in the dark. He followed me to my room and stood in the doorway. I had gotten into bed quickly, and was trying to pretend to be asleep.

"What were you doing?" he said, knowing perfectly well I was awake.

"I was going to use the bathroom," I said.

"You were? It's empty now," he said.

"Okay," I said, not moving. "Thanks."

"So you should get up," he said.

Why didn't he ask her what I was doing, coming from her room? Why torture me?

I pushed back the covers. I tried to appear sleepier than I was.

As I passed him, head down, he put a hand on my shoulder. He turned on the overhead light with his other hand and looked into my face. What could he have seen, except my bloodshot eyes? He put the light out. I was shaking, sure that he knew. I went into the bathroom and closed the door. I even went to the toilet, which I did not need to use. The seat was still up. I was about to put it down and sit on it for a few seconds before flushing when I heard my father's voice. "Is that where you keep it?" he said from the other side of the door.

"Keep what?" I managed. I kept it in his workroom, in the back of a Brillo box thick with dust. I looked over my shoulder, realizing I hadn't locked the door.

He opened the door and walked in. "Marijuana," he said. "Or am I to believe that you keep it in your mother's room?"

I stared at him. He was not going to like any answer I gave him.

"You think you're smart, don't you?" he said.

Yes or no. Neither answer would do.

"You probably think that because your mother drinks, it's all right to smoke marijuana," he said. "Actually, marijuana itself is not so bad. It's useful with glaucoma patients. For relief of nausea, with some illnesses. There's even the suggestion that it should be legalized."

Nothing to say. Nothing at all.

"Your mother tells me that you and your sister enjoy *Playboy*," he said. "Isn't that an unusual magazine to be looking at with your sister? You know, I had wanted to keep my magazines hidden from Mom."

"We were looking at the cartoons," I said.

"Is that right? Is that what the doctor should believe?" He went right on, not waiting for an answer. He said: "Your mother drinking, you smoking marijuana—it has a smell, you know, that clings to you just like cigarette smoke. A doctor, with two people abusing substances in his own house. What does your sister do, if I may ask? I would presume that she does exactly what her brother does, since he is the only person who exists in her world."

I looked at the floor.

"I'm glad you're not continuing to lie to me. I do take note of that," he said. Then he said: "How many times have you smoked marijuana?"

"A few times," I said. I was only lying by half a dozen times.

"*A few times*," he repeated slowly. "The doctor's son has smoked marijuana *a few times*. His wife drinks approximately one third of a bottle of scotch and one bottle of wine a day. His daughter . . . but we don't know about her. She may even be the Miss Goody Two-Shoes she appears to be, though somehow I doubt that. I think she has a secret, and that's why she's so condescending toward her parents. Ready to become an informant any day now. Ready to go to the authorities, as they're called, about *the doctor's family*."

I looked at him.

"Could you check that out for me?" he said.

My expression must have told him I had no idea what he was talking about.

"Your sister. Could you check and make sure that she isn't going to become an informer?"

I nodded, hoping he didn't mean right that moment. I knew that he did, though.

"I'll come along, if that's all right with you."

"Listen," I said truthfully. "Nina doesn't know anything about this."

"She doesn't? Can you honestly tell me that you and Nina have never once remarked on your mother's drinking?"

"We have," I said, "but she doesn't know I smoke marijuana. I never gave her any. She doesn't know," I said emphatically.

"I see. Well, that's good that you didn't feel the need to share this experience with your sister. Perhaps if she develops glaucoma, that might be another matter, but right now, you haven't felt the need. That's good. It shows that you have some common sense."

He was not going to end with a compliment. He was just warming up.

"So what do you say? You wake her up, she corroborates that she's never smoked marijuana—I mean, doubting her would be like doubting the pope, wouldn't it, she's such an honest girl. So she says, no, she hasn't, and then half the problem is solved. Then all we have to find out is whether she's going to turn us in."

"She wouldn't," I said. "You know she wouldn't."

"I know that? Do I? Do I know my children? For example, do I know from their teacher that they sign each other's report cards—or you do, or she does, how exactly they're signed I don't know—and did I know, until tonight, that my son smoked marijuana? No, I didn't. I truly didn't. So when it comes to knowing what my children are doing, I think the prudent thing to do is to *ask*, don't you?"

"You just want to upset her. I'm the one you're mad at," I said.

"Such a good brother, always wanting to protect his sister from any unpleasantness. That must be why you tolerate your mother alone, instead of inviting Nina into the room."

Naturally he knew about that. Naturally.

"I get so few answers when I ask questions. It doesn't help me to *know* you," he said.

"It's me who has the stuff. Not Nina," I said.

"Yes, I understand. But my worry is that she might be planning to turn us in, don't you see?" He was exaggerating, crouched like a coach with his hands on his knees, pretending to be very wary of Nina. He rolled his eyes toward her room. Okay: I would wake her up, and whatever happened would happen, and then eventually we could all go to sleep. He had a way of drawing things out when he got angry in the middle of the night.

Nina's room was usually lit with a Tinkerbell night-light, but the bulb must have burned out. Walking slowly in the darkness, I waited for him to flip on the overhead light. For a long time, she had not come into my room, and for a longer time, I had not entered hers. Our morning routine of going to our father's bedroom had also been suspended. There was no point in constantly checking, since we'd found the bed neatly made for months. I crossed the room carefully, groping my way in the dark, and went to her bed, where the dog had once slept. Suddenly, the overhead light went on. A textbook was on top of the blanket, open to the page she'd been reading. The bedspread had slipped halfway to the floor. She was sleeping so deeply that she shifted, but did not respond to the light. "Nina," I said quietly, putting my hand on her back.

"Look at how well he finds his way in the dark," our father said. "What an unerring sense of direction he has." He spoke as Nina, startled, jumped to a sitting position. "What?" Nina said. She squinted at me. At our father. It didn't take her long to register what was happening.

"Dad wants to talk about something," I said.

She struggled up on one elbow. Her eyes darted past me, looking at him. She said nothing else.

"Your brother and I were discussing what an honest girl you are," he said.

Out of the corner of her eye, she was looking at me. There was nothing I could do.

"My question for you is: Have you ever smoked marijuana?"

She didn't know I had because I'd never told her, though she might have suspected. With him staring at us, I could think of nothing to do.

"No," she said.

"But you know what it is," he said.

"Yes," she said slowly. She had a way of looking straight ahead, while she watched me in her peripheral vision. She hated what he was doing even more than I did.

"And are you aware of your brother's smoking marijuana?"

"I told him I did, Nina," I said.

She looked at me, surprised. She looked from me to him without answering.

"What do you have to say about that information?" he said.

She said nothing.

"And your mother," he said. "Your brother has also told me that you've discussed her drinking."

Again, she didn't answer.

"What conclusion have you reached about how to help her?" he said.

"We haven't," I said.

"I'm not speaking to you," he said. "Nina?"

"I don't know," she said.

"That is so often the conclusion people come to, even after much discussion," he said with mock sadness. He nodded his head from side to side. "Yes. Even after much discussion," he repeated.

"I have to go to school tomorrow," she said.

"I realize that. Waking you in the middle of the night with accusations about your brother and your mother. Not very nice, is it, when you, yourself, have done nothing?"

I saw her shoulders sag. Mentioning school only ensured that he would go on longer, she realized now. She knew that I knew she had made a mistake.

"Here's something that's been on my mind, though, that your brother wants to get to the bottom of before we all call it a night. I've been thinking that our family is not one that I would particularly want to come under scrutiny, given that I am a doctor who gives advice to other people in the community when his wife and his son seem to be out of control, as well as *breaking the law*. Your brother . . . well: you ask her the question," he said to me.

"Tell him you wouldn't inform on anybody. That's what he wants to hear," I said.

"What?" she said.

"He wants to know that you wouldn't go to the police," I said. The ridiculousness of the notion came through in my voice.

"I wouldn't," she said.

"Ahh. This verifies my suspicion that my daughter can be very closemouthed. Just what your brother feels is the case, and I'm sure that brings him much consolation," he said. "But tell me this: If someone was hit by a car outside the house, you would call the police, wouldn't you?"

She looked at me. I knew if I showed any expression, he would get even crazier.

"Come, come. This is not a problem to be solved by your beloved brother. The police—an ambulance. You would call someone, I presume?"

"Yes," Nina said.

"You would," he said. "Well, that's good. You would do the right thing if someone was hit by a car, but you would do the wrong thing—according to the authorities, at least—by not reporting your brother for smoking marijuana. You wouldn't ever report your brother for anything, would you, Nina? You would always be—the word is, *complicitous.*"

We both looked at him.

"And on the issue of your mother. You and your brother will have further discussions," he said.

We said nothing.

"I'm trying to understand here, but I'm not quite sure I do understand," he said. "Nina, I asked whether you and your brother would have further *discussions.*"

"No," she said.

"You won't? You'll *stop* discussing it?"

"Yes," she said.

"And about your brother's marijuana use . . . will you be discussing that?"

"Yes," she said, narrowing her eyes. She had every right to be pissed.

"I see," he said. "Well, perhaps I'll leave you to that now. I'm feeling so much better, myself, knowing that our private problems will remain within this house, some of them not even being discussed any longer. Thank you, Nina."

He left. We both waited a long time before moving. Finally, she spoke. "What was that about?" she whispered.

"He smelled grass," I said. "We passed each other in the hallway."

"Why don't you be more careful about getting up if he's walking around?"

"I know," I said. "I'm sorry."

"*You smoke grass?*" she said.

"Big deal," I said. "Half the people I know smoke grass."

"Don't *ever* let him catch you again," she hissed. "He's crazy. You know that."

I went back to my bedroom, relieved that he hadn't carried on more than he had. To my surprise, though, my father was sitting on the foot of my bed, waiting for me. My heart sank.

"If I were a more conventional father, I would have read you the riot act and cut off every privilege you had," he said, "but I was sitting here thinking: *Television?* I'm going to be like those parents I have no respect for who think they're so smart, forbidding their children to watch *television?* What am I supposed to say next: 'No more breakfast cereal for you'? It's ridiculous, isn't it? The withholding of, say, breakfast cereal.

You'll see, when you have a son of your own. Meanwhile, get rid of any marijuana that's in this house—in *the doctor's house*—and stay out of your sister's bedroom, and out of your mother's bedroom, too. The next time she asks you in, tell her I said you were forbidden to go." He got up. I knew something bad was coming. What he said had been too rational. Too self-reflective, even for a man who loved to parody self-reflection. "I'm tired," he said. "It's unpredictable, taking barbiturates. Some nights they wake me up instead of putting me under. Then—you'll get to know what this is like, too—you realize every hour or so you need to get up and piss again."

He got up and walked halfway out of the room, then stopped. "Drugs can confuse a person," he said. "They release people's inhibitions. Terrible things can happen in those circumstances. For example, if you take drugs, you can wake up next to someone you might be horrified to realize you'd had sex with the night before."

I said nothing.

"But you're like every other kid. You think you know it all, and I'm some simpleton. Even though I'm a doctor, to you I'm just someone who really knows nothing, isn't that right?"

I knew I couldn't refuse to answer one more question. "I know drugs are bad," I said.

"Yes, but they're also tempting, aren't they? Would you think that I might know the slightest thing about temptation? Or do you conveniently assume that everything will go along just the way it is, with the doctor being a good doctor and cautioning everyone to always resist temptation?"

It was unanswerable. I was glad I'd responded to his previous question.

"Years from now—or tomorrow, for all I know. If, in spite of everything I've said tonight, tomorrow you find yourself in bed, let's say, with an inappropriate person—would you blame yourself, or would you feel relieved of any responsibility, because it was just the marijuana?"

His words trailed off as he walked away. I lay there, waiting for the grand finale. Considering the way he'd acted other times he was displeased, I knew the worst was yet to come.

I felt that way until the afternoon of the picture taking, not long afterward, when all the fury he hadn't expressed that night came roaring out like an angry genie asked for one too many things. He was furious to have been found out, sneaking into a friend's mother's house. Whether my sister and I asked questions aloud or implicitly, he did not like questions, and of course the looks on our faces formed questions the second our eyes met his. Our father liked to be the questioner, not the questioned. Like us, he was practiced in not giving answers, but unlike us, he would become infuriated—as he was when he chased me through the house, tackling me and calling me "another one of your mother's faggots," pounding my back, dragging me back to the basement, and humiliating me in front of Nina and the girls. "You bastard," I finally said, when I thought the girls couldn't take another second, and I doubted I could. It surprised him. At first he seemed almost gratified, but when he had a notion in his head, he didn't easily discard it. He played with notions like a cat pawing a dying mouse. Examining from a different angle; taking a nibble, followed by a long period of rest before chomping down. His new cause célèbre was that I was a faggot, and proof of this, to him, was that I wouldn't approach the miserable, huddled girls—the lesbians, he might have been amused to know.

It wasn't an orgy he'd stumbled into, just sexually curious kids thinking they were more sophisticated than they were. The only idea that seemed to appease him was that I accost one of them sexually. Nina was staring into the middle distance. Lucy Roderick gagged, she was so terrified.

"Now look at this. Look at the unhappiness the doctor has caused, by being where he wasn't expected to be," he said. "He stumbles on his faggot son and a bunch of little whores, and it's the doctor who has made everyone—all these nice young people—cry. That is such a shame. Such a terrible shame," he said. "I'm overcome with regret. But I'll make you an offer, kids. You don't say you saw me, I won't say I saw you."

Nina and I told Mac that story and Mac looked at us as if we were telling him about life on another planet, a planet where all atmospheric gases were lethal. Of all things, the story had come up as we were having Thanksgiving dinner their first year at the carriage house. Mac was in the first year of his residency and he was always tired, and Nina and I delighted in reviving him, whatever it took. We were both good storytellers, filling in just enough details the other might have omitted, giving a buildup to the punch line. "You never even thought of telling your mother?" he said. "Not a teacher, not a friend's parents, or some relative? Didn't you have any relatives?" We both loved Mac for his practicality. We loved him because we saw that he was naive, to think there was always a way for people to get help. "She was that bad a mother, that you couldn't have told her a story like that and gotten sympathy?" Mac said. We said that we were sure she didn't want to hear about his infidelities. "But who did you feel *protected* you?" Mac had wanted to know.

"We protected each other," Nina said.

"And how did you get out of there? How did you get out of the basement? What happened with the girls?"

"Nobody ever said anything," I said. "Can you believe that? As he might have said himself: The *doctor* got off scot-free."

"Dianne saw me one time and spit on me," Nina said. "She walked up and spit in my face."

It was the first I'd ever heard of it.

"But he just drove you home, Andrew? Didn't your mother notice your injuries?" Mac persisted.

It was strange that she sometimes examined my fingernails, but paid little or no attention to any injuries. "She didn't notice," I said. "As for how we got out of there, he pointed and we ran. Right to his car, and I had to sit up front and get a driving lesson. All the way home, he gave me instructions about how to drive a car. I'm not kidding. He took it as an occasion to explain how to steer, and signal, and brake, like we'd been out for a driving lesson, and nothing else had happened."

He was not the only person who confounded me.

Serena once wrote me a nasty note on the bottom of a sympathy card—a Hallmark card, with a cross and lilies on the front. She sent it to me after the abortion, though she was living with me. It came in the mail. She watched me open it.

The checkout girl's good-bye note—the checkout girl with whom I'd had the one-night stand—was written on top of *The New York Times* that I had delivered to my door. Leaving early in the morning, so quietly that I didn't hear her, she had written: "Read all about it! Amber the One-Night Stand Leaves the Mercurial Andrew!"

A smiling Lyndon and Lady Bird Johnson postcard—he in tall Texas hat; she in sunflower yellow suit—had been mailed to me months after I broke up with Sue McCamber. "I'm giving *you* the bird!" she had written.

Mac could not believe how confrontational people had been with me. It was as if my father's evil curse remained after his death, Mac had said. Mac was one of the few men I ever admired. If he'd lived, I have the feeling he might eventually have stopped registering sympathetic surprise and come to understand my experiences better than I did. Serena, like Mac, could never get enough information about my childhood, but unlike Mac, she acted as if childhood was a colorful piñata, and once smashed, treasures of useful information would pour out.

Patty Arthur had gone out of my life like a shooting star when she was eighteen: on to that vast cosmos of men represented by her college professor. Though I hadn't liked being thrown over, I'd been surprised to realize how relieved I suddenly felt, as if a whole murky, secret part of my past was departing with her. Seeing her again would mean I was risking bringing it back: a scientist, lifting the vial of smallpox.

I was nothing like a scientist. I was a self-involved poseur invoking scientists, as if by analogy I could pretend to some sort of risky yet humanitarian concern.

So what should it have been like—my long-awaited, inevitable reunion with Patty? The conclusion of a fairy tale? The surprise visit in a good movie, the inevitable visit in a bad one? All the years I lived in Cambridge, Patty had been as near as Provincetown.

She drove in from the Cape in her truck. She'd even told me on the phone that she came in every couple of months. Her voice sounded the same: no-nonsense, yet enticing. She told me that her husband bartended and took people out on whale watches. He was a bass player who only had anything resembling steady work as a musician in the summer. Patty's youngest brother lived with them. He was, as she put it, pursuing spiritual awareness. The husband's brother also lived there: a former model, too old to get jobs, thrown out by his stockbroker lover, down on his luck, working part-time waiting tables at the restaurant where Patty's husband tended bar. The brothers and Patty and her husband had a ramshackle house they could have sold for a lot of money, but things had become so expensive on the Cape they couldn't have split up and bought anything else. The down payment had come from Patty's brother, who had been a third grade history teacher before he stopped working and began his study of Buddhism.

All this came out before we got together. It was almost as if she'd decided to filibuster, since she didn't want to hear what I had to say. I half thought she might cancel: the day she was to see me was overcast. Rain was predicted. She was nervous about visiting, I could tell. About the time she said she'd get to my apartment, I looked out the window for her truck. I saw a bag lady hurrying along, pushing a shopping cart piled high with junk.

Half an hour later than she said she'd be, Patty knocked on the door. I opened it. She didn't seem to have done anything special to dress for the occasion. She wore a denim skirt and a dark blue turtleneck flecked with lint. If she'd brought a raincoat, she had left it in the car. Her hair was pulled back in a ponytail. She was thin: her nose was more aquiline, her lips narrower. There were lines in her forehead. As a girl, she'd had bangs. Without them, her high forehead made her look slightly cadaverous. Her hair was streaked with gray.

This was Patty Arthur? I embraced her as an excuse not to look at her any longer. It was simply too painful.

"I'm glad you wanted to see me, Andy," she said, as if she knew I had doubts. I had never before been called Andy, by her or by anyone else. "But it's pointless—you know? Everything's different. I mean, thank God everything's different, but it is."

She sat in a chair and looked around the room. She made no comment.

"You were a big part of my life," I said.

"*Pizza* was a big part of our life back then. Remember how important pizza was?"

She could still make me smile. "Let me get you something," I said. "Coffee? Coke? Beer?"

"Morocco!" she said suddenly. "Remember all that bullshit about how I was going to live in Morocco? We were going to run away together, remember? So I'm in P'town, and you're in la-di-da Cambridge. It doesn't seem like either of us got very far."

I didn't think I'd had plans to go to Morocco, but maybe I had. I had once planned to be a doctor. A musician. A painter. She'd wanted to be an architect.

"Tell me what made you track me down," she said.

"Curiosity about what happened to an old friend," I said.

"I don't quite believe that," she said. "At least back then, you were never exactly Mr. Sociability. We were such a good fit because we were both scared to death." She slipped off her shoes. "I wouldn't have guessed you'd look up friends from the past, because it didn't seem like you had a lot of curiosity. It seemed like you were careful not to ask questions, because you didn't want to know the answers."

"I was pretty curious. You don't think so?"

"Sex, you mean? I lured you into that."

"I didn't mind," I said.

"So what's the deal?" she said, sinking back into a chair. "Are you debriefing the girls now? Alice was so excited she found out how to get in touch with you, and then she said you were so full of yourself she didn't even give you my note. I haven't noticed, so far, that you seem particularly full of yourself. It is a little odd, though, that you're such a good host, now that the roles are reversed: Andrew offering Patty coffee." She took a deep breath and exhaled. "I don't want coffee," she said.

"What was in the note?" I asked. I was sitting across from her.

"Stuff about my fucked-up life. What else?" She shrugged. "I don't know what I hoped: that you'd call, or that you'd read it and not call."

"I called without reading it," I said.

"Yeah. I know. So now you get Snow White, on her day off from the dwarfs. Really: I live with Sleepy and Grumpy and Comet and Blitzen, or whatever the fuck they're called. It would be funny, except it's not funny." She slipped into her shoes again. "I should go if I'm in this black a mood. Really, I should," she said. "You catch me on a bad day. Month. Year." She gave the first faint smile she'd given since she came in. "You had drinks with Josie at a bar, I hear," she said. She added: "Josie-the-writer."

"She didn't mention anything about writing."

I got up and took her jacket from the coatrack. "Let's go get some coffee," I said.

"Yeah," she said, standing up slowly and slipping into the jacket. "She's going to write everything about everybody. She didn't tell you that? Even the score, or whatever she thinks she's doing. Lady Lazarus, doing another encore even though Sylvia Plath is dead."

"We could go to a bar," I said. "Would that be better?"

"It's *noon*," she said.

"I believe I can find a bar that will serve drinks at noon."

"You're funny," she said. "Why did you call me?"

"I called Hank Montgomery, too. He's joining us at the coffee place. It was going to be a surprise."

"He *is*?"

"No," I said. "Just thought I'd see how you'd react." I reached back and took her hand as we walked down the steps, sidestepping a little puddle from a dropped cup of Starbucks coffee. Her hand was small, and fit perfectly inside mine. It gave me a jolt, the sensation was so familiar.

"You're still handsome," she said. "It would never have worked. I could never have kept your interest. If I hadn't fucked you, you wouldn't have been interested then, either."

"Don't dismiss your baking abilities. You did pretty well as Betty Crocker."

"You remember the cake?" She smiled again. "Yeah, well, I would never have been enough for you."

"I didn't notice you trying, running off with your professor."

"We didn't run off," she said. "He taught there."

A boy passed by, walking a whippet. He carried a red shovel and a plastic bag. He was wearing wraparound sunglasses and listening to music through headphones, jutting his chin in and out, silently mouthing the words. The Nikes on his feet were wider than the dog's body.

"That's where I parked," she said, pointing to a parking garage as we turned the corner. "Expensive habit, Cambridge."

I squeezed her hand. "You never thought about calling me?" I said. Now that we were walking, I felt better. I hadn't realized until I began to relax how guarded I'd been when she first walked in.

"Sure I did. I just thought I'd wait until I was at a better place in my life."

"I'm glad you came," I said, moving closer. "Is there anything I can do?"

"My mother helps out," she said. "She's pretty bummed, herself, since she actually believed it was just a few quick steps from not puking up my food to living *la vida loca* in Morocco. My poor mother: I wrecked her life. Being an unwed mother made her into a scaredy-cat good girl for the rest of her life." She pointed with her free hand. "I go to that place and get liquid minerals for my brother. He enjoys remedies from the natural food store when he's not buying drugs from a guy in Medford. Colloidal trace minerals, I believe they're called."

"Do you take drugs with him?" I asked, though I didn't want to know.

"I smoke a little pot," she said. "What did you think—I was a junkie?"

I steered her through a shortcut. Beneath the jacket she was thin. I could remember her small breasts. The way she'd once squirted whipped cream on them, placing candied cherries atop the cream. That seemed very, very sweet now—in all senses. Harmless and sweet, though maybe just a little over the top.

"My brother's his own MTV show on speed," she said. "He entertains us, since we can't afford cable."

"Patty," I said, "you still have that wonderfully unique way of expressing yourself."

"Yeah, you're handsome and I'm funny," she said. "How come we're not a sitcom?"

I held open the door of an old-fashioned coffee shop where the coffee of the day was Maxwell House, and where you could sit in a wooden booth.

"Be right back," she said, heading toward the rest room before we were even seated. "Order me some apple juice, please," she called back. "My stomach couldn't take coffee."

I watched her walk downstairs, still surprised at the gray in her hair. I thought of her split-level house. Of her bedroom. Her bed. Of the cone of piercingly sweet incense she liked to burn. I wondered, now, whether her parents knew—they must have known—and just didn't say anything. They might have been ahead of their time. That, or cowards.

I ordered apple juice and coffee. "How's your sister?" the waitress said. "I haven't seen her in a while."

"She's fine," I said. It was probably the first question I'd answered so far that day. I had trouble getting comfortable as I waited. After what seemed like a long time, I got up and went downstairs, guessing that she might be crying. There was one rest room, with two plaques side by side, of a German shepherd in a tuxedo and a poodle in a ballet outfit. The door was open. I walked back upstairs, mystified. "Left through the kitchen," a young man struggling with a big container of dirty dishes said, as he passed me. "Yeah," he said, acknowledging my surprise. "Every so often they march right through the kitchen, like the front door they came in through doesn't exist anymore."

I dropped a five-dollar bill on the table and ran out, nearly toppling the juice. I suddenly remembered sitting in another coffee place, with Sue McCamber. "I don't want to be here with you," she had suddenly said. Which was one more sentence than I'd heard from Patty.

It was bright enough outside to make me squint. All signs of the storm had passed. Patty had told me where she'd parked her truck. I hurried across the street, trying to guess whether I had any chance of catching her. Josie, Alice, Patty—they were all in worlds of their own. Josie with her mixed signals. Alice, who'd acted like some weekend hunter, ready to shoot the first thing she encountered and call it a day. But this was nuts, what Patty had done. She must have realized I'd be angry. She couldn't have assumed I'd just figure that was that, and drink my coffee.

I could have used some caffeine on my way to the garage.

When I got there, out of breath, I asked the man in the booth if any trucks had gone out recently. "You mean like a real pickup truck?" he said.

She roared up then, as if on cue. I stared, knowing—just knowing—she'd drive through the bar the second she saw me. I saw the splintered wood; the shock on the attendant's face. I heard the alarm go off. I felt my heart racing. But she didn't do it. She held money out the window, pretending to look straight through me. I ran around in front of the truck, pulled open the door on the passenger side, and jumped in. I was panting, and as angry as I'd been in a long while. She took the money the cashier had handed back and stuffed it in her jacket pocket. She still would not look at me. Her jacket was red plaid. Her hair cascaded over her shoulders. There was a worn spot in the elbow of the jacket. A glove protruded from one pocket.

"As bad as I look, as out of control as I feel, you want to do it that much?" she said.

I hadn't considered sex. Even thinking briefly of her breasts had not really been thinking of sex. I had not been waiting for her in the coffee shop, thinking we'd go back to my apartment and undress. But the minute she said it, yes. Yes: I did want to have sex that much.

"So," she said, shrugging. "Your place or mine?"

"My place might have the advantage of not having three other men present, including your husband."

"Right," she said.

The car behind us waiting to exit honked. Patty stepped on the gas, barely stopping in time to let a boy on a skateboard shoot past.

"You're going to have to tell me how to get there," she said. "All these goddamn one-way streets."

"Go right," I said. "Right," I said once more. I had her park on a block where we'd get a ticket, but they wouldn't tow the car. She backed into a space between a Lexus and a battered Subaru. Since she seemed to be parking with her eyes closed, I was amazed she didn't hit either car. I watched as she took the keys out of the ignition and dropped them in her pocket. The jacket elbow was torn, rather than worn. It might even have been a recent tear. I locked my door, then went around and locked hers. "You can't leave your truck unlocked around here," I said.

I grabbed her hand and we walked in silence to the building. Everything about it suddenly looked wrong. Someone had put a frying pan with burnt meat in it outside one of the doors, I saw, as we took the stairs. The guy who lived across the hall from me had yet to bring in his *Boston Globe*. Things were definitely going in slower motion now—for Patty, as well as for me. I could feel the calm between us, as if we'd walked back through a storm, after all, and now we were safe. My heart had almost stopped racing. "Nice," she said, tiredly, as the key opened the door. She acted as if she had not been in the apartment before. I took her jacket and hung it up.

"Are you still offering coffee?" she said.

"I don't suppose you feel like explaining what just happened?" I said.

"What's to explain?" she asked. "Here we are. All roads lead to Rome. If not Morocco."

A tear rolled down her cheek. I handed her my handkerchief. "I don't fucking believe it. A guy who carries a handkerchief," she said. "It's probably French roast coffee, too." She dabbed her eyes and handed the handkerchief back, as if returning it would stop her tears.

"Okay," I said. "I'm making coffee. Which isn't French roast."

"Jamaican blue mountain," she said sourly. "Fucking decaf Sumatra."

She curled up silently in the chair. I went into the kitchen and opened the refrigerator and took out the bag of coffee. I noticed that my hand was shaking.

Back in the living room, she had slid from the chair to the rug. She was lying there with her hands crossed over her chest like a mummy, tears rolling down her cheeks.

"Jesus," I said. "Patty. What is it?"

"I'm a mess," she said. "I don't know why you called me." She rolled onto her side.

In the apartment below, a Dionne Warwick revival had begun. Better that than the Beach Boys festival the neighbor had entertained me with previously. Eyes squeezed shut, Patty undid the side zipper on her skirt, raised her hips, and bumped awkwardly out of her clothing. Underneath was a short white half slip, which she shrugged down around her hips and tossed off. Then she amazed me by reaching one-handed for her purse and unzipping a pouch from which she withdrew a prophylactic. All at once I remembered her former stockpile, kept in an arabesque box: her rather large collection, which she said her mother had provided her with, so that what happened to her would not happen to Patty. I took the packet without saying anything. In my entire life, no woman had ever done what Patty did.

"You know why my parents cleared out when you came over to my house?" she said suddenly. "Because they wanted to prove that they trusted me." She was smirking. "Because you were such an upstanding fellow, being born into such a good family. My parents thought they were lowlifes, and there you were: the doctor's son."

The doctor might have been there himself, the words came out so sarcastically. I grabbed her wrist, then realized she had not meant to upset me. I loosened my grip, expecting her to get up and run out of the apartment. That, too—the inevitability—increased my desire. Instead of rising, she frowned and looked at her hand. Her fingernails were a little dirty. There was a bruise, or a smudge of dirt, on one knuckle. "What?" she said, hiding her hand. "What's the matter with you?" In silent reply, I slid my hand up her arm, stopping at her elbow. Then I lay on top of her. We never left the living room. We were momentarily distracted by a fire truck shrieking by, but except for that, we had sex—rough sex—without speaking. Nothing about it was familiar. The lyrics of the songs the neighbor was blaring were familiar, but I could locate nothing of Patty in the person whose body I touched. It was her smell—something about the softness of her skin—the silkiness that emitted a slight scent of jasmine, mixed with a more familiar odor of sweat and soap—that made me bury my head in her shoulder. Her enticing aroma was almost overwhelmed by the smell of freshly dripped coffee, which by now seemed like the most ludicrous substance in the world.

Dazed at how quickly everything had happened, as if once into it, both of us were ready to devour each other, I got up and went into the kitchen and poured two mugs of coffee. I carried them into the living room where she lay. "Glad you didn't feel like apple juice," I said. I put the mug of coffee on the floor beside her. She curled toward it, like a camper edging in on a campfire.

I went into the bedroom and pulled the blanket off the bed. I carried it into the living room, where she remained at the foot of the chair, the coffee steaming, untouched. "You just slept with a pregnant woman," she said, grabbing an edge of the blanket and pulling it over her. "Yeah," she said. "Off on the next adventure."

It took awhile for what she said to register. She'd managed to stun me, though it didn't quite make sense. "If you're pregnant," I said, "I assume you just decided we should practice safe sex?"

She frowned, and I could tell my words caused some inner twinge of pain. For a few seconds, she said nothing. Then she said: "I don't like to shower in other people's places. It's a phobia of mine. The same way I can't stand height."

Height. I had recently taken the twenty-year-old receptionist to the top of a skyscraper for Irish coffee. My fingers had brushed the back of her neck. I had asked where the sweater she was wearing came from; she had me pull up the label to read it, allowing me to peer at the pale skin of her long, lovely neck. *Made in Ireland.*

Height. Nina, dressed as a scarecrow for Halloween, having me walk behind her in case she faltered on the stilts she'd practiced on for weeks. My earnest, childish version of Prince Philip.

Height. I had spread my arms as wide as they would go. *This much, Serena. This is how much I love you.* What I had really been demonstrating—unbeknownst to me—was the size of the love that got away. Love became a remarkable fish, back in the water, off for a swim.

Patty never touched the coffee. She was either very quiet, or she had fallen asleep. Eventually, I sipped mine, looking around the apartment. I had furnished it long ago with things from my parents' house, though I'd bought the cherry bookcase, and been given some freebies, as well as a chopping block I'd found curbside that I propped on an iron log holder and used as a coffee table. Most often, I sat in Hound's old leather chair that Kate made him get rid of because he always fell asleep the moment he sat in it. The end tables had been left in the apartment by the previous tenant. There was an Oriental rug, bleached by sunlight, that Serena and I had bought together on a whim, at a country auction we'd stumbled into at a fair. A Gabbeh, it was called. Little pieces of color were scattered against the blue background like software icons, waiting to be clicked on.

Patty turned onto her side and said, almost too quietly for me to hear her, that she should go. I leaned forward and kissed her back, moving my lips up her spine, then waited silently while she grabbed her clothes and walked off to the bathroom. I insisted on walking out with her and I also took the parking ticket off her windshield, folding it and putting it in my pocket without comment. "A guy like you could be very useful if I move back to the city," she said.

"Call me about being useful," I said. "I'm more than willing."

"Useful," she echoed. "That's a good way to think of the afternoon."

Then she closed the door and rolled down the window. "If you don't hear from me," she said, touching my shoulder lightly, "you can know it's because they cut off the phone."

"Call collect from a pay phone," I said.

"Hey—I just might. I might see if you'll disappear with me," she said.

Disappeared, I thought, as I walked back to the apartment, had recently become a euphemism for dead.

In the time I was gone, the light had changed and the rug was even paler. I went into the bedroom and closed the blinds. Sitting back on the bed and covering my face with my arm, I felt too confused to sleep, so I was surprised when I woke up hours later and it was dark. I went into the living room and put on a light. It was a table lamp that had sat on my mother's dresser. The same light under which she'd held photographs, examined notes, taken my hand in hers, in the guise of inspecting my fingernails, because as I grew, she was wary about how to touch me. Nina made things easy on her by always being elsewhere, by slipping through the cracks. Those times she could not physically escape, her disdain transported her, and our mother was left to confront a chrysalis. *The doctor's son*, I heard Patty saying. I understood that she had been mocking her mother for being naive, and even that she might have been angry at her mother, though when she first said the words, they'd seemed like a slap in my own face. Downstairs, Huey Lewis and the News was playing. Time was moving right along.

I looked at the phone. I looked at my watch. There was no way she could already be back in P'town. Even if she was, what was I going to do? Call and get her husband?

It would be convenient to think that I escaped that moment of perplexity by moving straight into a new relationship, but that wasn't the way it happened. The woman I saw later that night was someone I'd seen once before, briefly, for a quick drink after work. Nina would have been gratified to know that she was not a woman I'd pined for for years, that she wasn't married, and that I had turned her down a few days before when she'd called and asked me out. She had come in as a consultant to the company where I worked; we'd joked at the Xerox machine, she'd given me her card in the bar, ostensibly so I could get in touch with her if I had additional thoughts about the problem she'd been called in to solve. Somehow, I knew that if I didn't call her, she would call me. I also had the feeling that the date probably held the possibility of no more than that: an extra ticket to a preview at the MFA.

It must have meant something that, fumbling for my key to let Patty and me back into the apartment, I had pulled her card out of my pants pocket with my keys. I remembered that Lauren—her name was Lauren—had said she was about to turn thirty. I had a frozen Sara Lee chocolate cake in the freezer and thought I'd see if she might want to come over on the spur of the moment. If she didn't stand on formality, and if it wasn't a matter of pride, she might be happy I called, if she wasn't otherwise occupied.

"Steve?" she said.

"No. It's Andrew. From the other night. But I have the distinct impression you expected to hear from someone else."

"Well, yeah," she said. "What can I say?"

"But if he hasn't called," I said, "I was wondering if you'd like to come over and have a piece of cake."

"Really?" she said. "It's eleven o'clock at night."

I looked at my watch. It was just after nine. The clock on the stove corroborated it. I said: "I think your watch is fast."

"I don't think so," she said hazily.

"Well, in any case," I said, "chocolate cake." I hoped it was still good; it had been in the freezer since Hound put it there months ago.

"I have to go," she said. "See you in the morning."

I was slow; it had taken me too long to realize that something was wrong with her. "Lauren?" I said. "You don't sound good. Are you sick?"

She was crying, but the sound came from far off. "I took medicine," she said. She hung up. Jesus Christ: I had called somebody when they were OD'ing. "Lauren?" I said, much louder. "Lauren, can you hear me?"

I called her name several times before I realized I should hang up and call 911. I felt terrible hanging up on her, but I needed a dial tone. The truth is, I didn't really think: I just hung up the phone, then picked it up again in my instantly sweaty hand. I had forgotten her last name and had to fumble for the card on the table; she might be dying, and I knew only that she was named Lauren. All the card said was *Lauren*, in big italic letters. There was a phone number, a fax number, and e-mail. There was no street address. Great: *Lauren*, who thought a first name was enough, like Oprah, or Cher. I explained the situation calmly to the 911 operator, told her I'd just happened to call a person whose last name I didn't know. "Don't worry, I'm on a search," the operator said. "Conover?" she said. I heard her repeat the name to someone else with more certainty. There was already someone else on the line. "Sir, where are you calling from?" the operator said. I gave her my address in Cambridge. I could still see the frying pan in the hallway, the dirty pan Patty and I had walked past, after which she'd said, "Nice" and walked into my apartment. This sort of flashing on a pointless detail made me crazy: it was my version of an anxiety attack—that something inconsequential would intrude, and the image would paralyze me temporarily, prohibiting me from speaking a word. I took two deep breaths in and out and a word came to me. It was a single word: "Overdose?" "I understand," the operator said, but someone else—a man's voice—was talking to her at the same time. "They're on their way," she said. I saw the white puddle of Patty's slip, her legs, kicking free of it. Nina, in shock, trembling so hard she might have been kicking. Should I think of this as being in the right place at the right time, or the wrong place at the wrong time? I was afraid both things were the same. That the flip side of one was always the other. She was a woman I'd hardly even flirted with—just a glass of wine in some greenhouse of a bar, an impulse to see her again at nine o'clock, it was *still* just after nine o'clock. I couldn't bear it, the way women could make time stand still.

Someone was coming to my apartment. Why, I didn't know. It was just the way things were when something was taking its course. Instead of an evening getting to know someone, a cop would probably appear at the door and get to know me. But what did I have to do with any of it? I hadn't even envisioned what our evening would be like. We might not have gotten along. She was a person I hardly knew. There was no story I had to tell; because of what she'd done, the story would be all hers—when she was able to recount it.

So I didn't wait around. I could imagine some cop coming over . . . why should I be obliged to talk to him, why should I have to erase any suspicion some stranger might have just because he wore a uniform, or enumerate facts while he filled out what would surely be form after form? It wasn't my problem. I hadn't done anything wrong, and furthermore, I had done the right thing. She would be getting help. I needed to quell my panic as I threw on my coat and hurried out without locking the door. I told myself that they didn't know what I looked like, so even if they drove up, even if they saw me running—and I was winded because, after all, it was the second time I'd gone running in one day—they'd have no reason to stop me. Everybody ran, all the time. When they weren't sculling, when they weren't rollerblading, when they weren't biking.

I turned the corner and went one street over, to be safe. I heard no sirens, but still, I kept up the pace. I could have been running a race, the way I flew to Nina's. I was almost there before I realized where I'd intended to go.

I am going back to fairyland and no one can come with me. Fairyland is beautiful. The whole kingdom is like a big jeweled pillow and everything sparkles. Even the air is pink but before you arrive you have to pass through a long hallway with the doors shut that is like a tunnel and not even ghosts are allowed to go with you. You must take care when you walk alone in case there is a strong wind. Even fairies are sometimes blown about though people might be surprised to know the strongest part of a fairy is its wings. They keep the fairy up no matter how much the wind blows. They also work even if they get bruised. The remedy for hurt fairy wings is as follows. Wet them with tears and roll in sunbeams to dry them. Good-bye.